UNNATURAL DISASTERS

UNNATURAL DISASTERS

JEFF HIRSCH

CLARION BOOKS
HOUGHTON MIFFLIN HARCOURT
BOSTON NEW YORK

Clarion Books
3 Park Avenue
New York, New York 10016
Copyright © 2019 by Jeff Hirsch

Clarion Books is an imprint of Houghton Mifflin Harcourt Publishing Company.

hmhco.com

The text was set in Minion Pro.

Library of Congress Cataloging-in-Publication Data is available.
ISBN 978-0-544-99916-9

Printed in the United States of America

DOC 10 9 8 7 6 5 4 3 2 1
4500739470

FOR REBA, WITH LOVE

ALL HAIL THE PENGUIN KING

ONE

THE FUNNY THING about Luke and I being at prom the night of the sixteenth was that we'd never even talked about going until a few weeks before.

We were at the Beth watching *Cannibal Creek Massacre* for the hundred millionth time. It was the capper to this weeklong horror fest I'd talked my boss into putting on instead of the subtitled weepies and black-and-white American classics he usually played. I'd chosen some seriously brutal shit. Adolf Bonhoffer's *Needles Beneath My Skin.* Cho Sun Pak's *Scream, My Beloved.* Aguilar's *Black Suitcase*, of course. I'll be the first to admit that it was not exactly a rip-roaring success. The only person besides Luke to buy a ticket was Mr. Stahlberg, a Beth diehard ever since his wife passed away the previous spring. I was supposed to be working the concession stand, but Mr. Stahlberg always smuggled in his own snacks, so I took a seat with Luke down front.

It had just gotten to my favorite part (Michael St. Vincent getting that arrow through his throat), but I couldn't seem to enjoy it. I was stuck on how, when the two of us had walked into school that morning, the hallways had been draped, entrance to exit, with a candy-colored spew of prom-aganda.

I elbowed Luke in the side. "I mean, how is prom even still a thing? We're halfway through the twenty-first century and people are still getting all torqued up about prom? Seriously?"

Luke shushed me.

"What?"

He pointed up at the screen. I turned around. Mr. Stahlberg was eight rows back and fast asleep. I scrunched down in my seat and pressed on, sotto voce.

"All I'm saying is these people are telling themselves they're going to have this deep, meaningful experience, when the truth is any marrow prom *ever* had in its bones was sucked dry over a hundred years ago. The only reason people go now is because it's *a thing you do*. Their parents did it, their grandparents did it . . ."

Luke opened his mouth, but I knew what he was going to say.

"And don't come at me with rites of passage and shared rituals. Calling this low-rent gropefest a ritual is an insult to good rituals."

Luke slid down until we were cheek to cheek. His breath was fruity and sweet from the Mike and Ikes I'd embezzled from the concession stand.

"So?" he asked. "What would you prefer?"

"Old-school bacchanalia. Everybody gets naked in the light of the full moon and they drink wine and dance until they completely lose their minds."

"Please. You *hate* parties. Remember Connor Albright's birthday? We weren't there ten minutes before you said we had to leave because his taste in music was giving you chlamydia."

"I'm not talking about a *party*. I'm talking about a transformative, communal *experience*. One that's so intense you actually, like, leave your body and become one with God."

"This also might be a good time for me to remind you that you're an atheist."

I grabbed the box of Mike and Ikes. "Well, maybe I wouldn't have to be if we lived back before communing with God meant going to some megachurch nightmare like your mom and dad do. Seriously, Luke, it's got its own McDonald's franchise!"

He snatched his candy back. "Hey, that McDonald's is the best part of my Sunday. Oh! I love this scene."

One of the camp counselors grabbed a flashlight and headed out into a rainstorm alone. Instantly, the theater filled with the whispery chanting of the unseen cannibal tribe. I dug my fingers into Luke's bicep, resisting the urge to shut my eyes. See, the thing everybody gets wrong about people who love horror is the idea that we don't get scared. Not true. Movies I'd seen a thousand times still scared the hell out of me. In fact, sometimes it was even *better* when I knew what was coming. Sure, the jump scares might not have worked anymore, but jump scares weren't horror. Seeing an awful thing coming from a thousand miles away and being utterly powerless to stop it? *That* was horror.

We watched the rest of the movie straight through, huddled together, the crowns of our knees kissing. By the time sweet, virginal Alice ended up running through the jungle — clothes torn and covered in the blood of her fellow campers — I was breathless and lightheaded and my heart was going *buh-duh-bump buh-duh-bump buh-duh-bump buh-duh-bump*. And then, BAM! Just when you think Alice is about to reach the rescue helicopter, the cannibal king explodes out of the jungle and drags her, screaming, back into the trees. The camera stays on the shaking branches as they go still, like nothing happened, like Alice was never even there. As the credits rolled, the fist that had been squeezing my heart released, leaving me a boneless puddle in my seat.

Most people would leave then, but Luke and I always stayed. We figured that since all those gaffers and best boys worked so hard, the least we could do was read their names. When the screen went to black and the lights came up, Luke yawned and stretched, then turned to me, eyebrows raised, ready to go.

"At the original Bacchanalia in Rome," I said, "they used to go so insane for Bacchus that they'd tear live bulls apart with their bare hands and drink their blood."

"So you're saying you'd be okay with prom if it involved the slaughtering of livestock?"

"Wouldn't you?"

Luke smiled, which made his eyes go all twinkly. He kissed me; then we rolled out of our seats and headed up the aisle. Mr. Stahlberg was slumped over, snoring gently. I nudged his shoulder.

"Hey. Mr. Stahlberg. Movie's over."

His snowy brows twitched and then his eyes slowly opened. He looked like a little kid for a second, fresh from a nap. He sat up and rubbed at his stubbly face.

"I take it that movie was your doing, Lucy?"

"Pretty, awesome, right?"

"It was *terrible*."

"How do *you* know? You slept through the whole thing!"

"I saw enough." He wagged his finger at me. "Amanda would

have given you a piece of her mind if she'd been here. She would have instructed you on the classics."

I was pretty sure he was right, given that instructing me on the classics was exactly what Amanda Stahlberg had done the last time I'd seen her, roughly six months before a bout of skin cancer finally caught up to her. She was horrified when I admitted that I found Jane Austen kind of boring. Amanda was a retired English professor, so when she got going on books, it was like God calling down from on high. When she was done with me I went to the library and checked out every Austen they had.

I took Mr. Stahlberg's hand. "I would've liked that."

"Yes," he said. "So would I."

I helped him up and the three of us went to the lobby. Luke and Mr. Stahlberg chatted while I changed and did closing — shutting down the projector, taking out the trash, putting the day's skimpy take in the safe. By the time I was done it was nearly eight o'clock. The three of us stepped out of the air-conditioned chill of the theater and onto the sidewalk, where we were struck by a wall of steamy heat. Sundown had taken the edge off our hundred-degree day, our third that spring, but it still had a little punch to it.

"I hear the highways are melting again in Arizona," Mr. Stahlberg said. "Imagine that. Black rivers flowing through Phoenix. They'll need kayaks instead of cars. Kayaks with hulls of steel."

Luke said, "There'll be wildfires in California again."

"If there's anything left to burn."

Mr. Stahlberg fanned himself, distressingly red-faced and sweaty after only thirty seconds outside. Luke asked him where he'd parked and he explained that his car had died earlier that day, forcing him to walk. He protested when I said we'd give him a ride home, but all I had to do was curl my arm around his and he gave in. Luke's car was in a lot a few blocks away, so we joined the Friday night shoppers as they strolled along Main Street sipping at tall, icy concoctions from Bethany Square.

"So," I said. "Tell us about your prom night, Mr. Stahlberg."

He threw his head back and laughed. "I haven't thought about prom in years. The spring of 1984! Wonderful night. I was dating a poet named Sophie at the time and we went with her cousin Jim and this magnificently stupid girl he was dating. We must have smoked a metric *ton* of pot beforehand. My God, we laughed until we couldn't breathe. Let's see, I was in a blue tuxedo and Sophie was wearing black leather . . ."

———

Luke still had some time before his curfew after we dropped off Mr. Stahlberg, so we headed up to Bethany Ridge. The welcome center parking lot was deserted. We took a spot with a good view of the lights from town and sat on the hood of his car. It was cooler at the top of the mountain. Pine-scented breezes blew across my bare arms, raising tiny goose bumps. Luke's phone pinged. He laughed as the blue/gray light of the screen washed over him.

"What?"

"Carter got ahold of Mom's phone again," he said. "He's become *really* invested in keeping me updated on Greg's adventures. Greg's the pet goldfish."

"Goldfish have adventures?"

"They involve swimming in circles and pooping, apparently."

Luke tap-tap-tapped to his little brother. I flopped onto my back and looked up at the stars. Insects were chitter-chattering around us, a sound that immediately morphed into *Cannibal Creek*'s whispery theme. I entertained myself by turning every snapped twig and fallen branch out in the woods into the tread of a blood-thirsty murderer, every gust of wind into the breath of some nightmarish elder god brought back to life to spread madness and ruin across the countryside. I could see it all so clearly that I got the dull edge of a thrill, a pitter-pat in my chest, a squirt of adrenaline. I swear, if someone had put a camera in my hand right then, I could've put Aquilar herself to shame.

After a while Luke leaned back, phone face-down on his chest. I drew his arm around me and snuggled in close. He smelled like soap and boy.

"I had this dream last night that we were in Antarctica surrounded by a horde of penguins."

"There are penguins left in Antarctica?"

"There were in my dream," I said. "They were all squawking and flapping their little penguin arms."

"Sounds scary."

"They were just excited because earlier that day they'd made you their king."

"Were you the queen?"

"No, you had a penguin queen. Her name was Emily. I was jealous at first but then I realized you two were actually really good together."

Luke kissed the top of my head. "That's very mature of you. So does this mean Antarctica is on the list now?"

I turned on my side and slipped my hand in between the buttons of his shirt.

"Well, you *are* their king."

Luke kissed me again, and the next thing I knew it was nearly an hour later and we'd gone from the hood of the car to the back seat and were all jumbled up in a knot of tingling limbs and bare, sweaty skin. The air was humid, the windows steamed white. I reached between the front seats to pull a pen and our trip journal out of the glove box. I'd read somewhere that most people traveled to Antarctica by sailing from Tierra del Fuego, so I flipped pages until I got to South America, then wrote *Antarctica* at the bottom in bright green ink. Beside it I drew a penguin army hoisting Luke into the air, along with a speech bubble that read *ALL HAIL THE PENGUIN KING!* I sat there awhile staring at the words, tracing their peaks and contours, giddy. In less than six months, everyone we knew would be conquering freshman dorms while we'd be conquering the world.

Luke nibbled at my shoulder. I put the notebook away. I didn't really have a curfew, but Luke's parents were fanatical about his (as they were about many, many things), so it wouldn't be long before we'd have to head back down the mountain. He traced a lazy fingertip down my arm, raising even more goose bumps.

"Hey. Weaver."

"Hmm."

He leaned in close, and his warm candy breath filled my ear. "You wanna go to prom with me?"

I laughed. "Damn, Vaughn, I thought you'd never ask."

TWO

THE DAY OF PROM was a typical Saturday. Dad and I were hanging out in the living room while my Aunt Carol tore through our house with a vacuum and a mop, cleaning with a vengeance that was frightening to behold. She'd already done her and my Aunt Bernadette's house earlier that morning, but now that she was into her second trimester, her nesting instinct was too much for one household to contain.

I had a few hours before Luke got there, so I hunkered down on the couch with a bag of sour cream and onion potato chips and my laptop, intending to cross a few items off my Things to Do Before Luke and I Flee Bethany list. Currently occupying the number one spot? Find Dad a soulmate. Why did *I* have to do this, you ask? Because in the history of dads there was no dad quite as filled with the spirit of dadness as good ol' Roger Weaver. Case in point: At that very moment, was he taking advantage of his God-given weekend by relaxing with a good book? Maybe watching a favorite movie? No! He was doing what he did every weekend: speed-drinking coffee while hunched over his computer trying to sort through his clients' accounting conundrums, the ones he hadn't gotten to during the actual workweek. Later on he'd probably mow the lawn, hit the grocery store, and re-tar the driveway.

Sure, he had his Scrabble nights with Carol and Bernie and his movie nights with me and Luke, but what was going to happen when Luke and I left in the fall and Carol and Bernie had their baby? I had nightmare visions of him standing in the kitchen after work, suit rumpled, his face gray in the light of the microwave as he made himself one of those single-serving cups of mac and cheese. After his sad little dinner he'd pad up through an empty house and lie in bed, staring into the dark, surrounded by a silence so enormous it was like an ocean he'd fallen into. If nothing changed, he'd descend deeper and deeper and deeper until the pressure of all that quiet crushed him like a soda can.

We knew he'd never do it himself, so Luke and I had started a secret account for him on a dating site. For his profile pic I'd chosen one that Bernie had taken a couple of years earlier when we'd all spent the Fourth of July weekend at Rehoboth Beach. He was windblown and grinning, wearing this pale blue shirt that really made his eyes pop. He looked smart and kind and a little goofy. Dad to a T. All that was left was to complete his profile!

"Hey, Dad. What would you say is your favorite food?"

"My favorite food? Why?"

"It's, uh, for a report. For school."

He stopped typing and looked over the edge of the screen. "Your school wants you to do a report on my favorite food?"

We were on dangerous ground. He was clearly suspicious. I figured my best play was sheer audacity. I scooped a chip out of the bag and popped it into my mouth.

"Yeah, and not just that. They also want to know" — I checked my screen — "your favorite books and TV shows. Also, what you do on a typical Friday night."

"Well, thank God your teachers aren't wasting your time on trigonometry or physics."

"Ha. Yeah, pretty sure they have worse senioritis than we do. So? Favorite food?"

"I dunno," he said, returning to his spreadsheets. "Pizza?"

Pizza? It had the benefit of being true, but there was no way something as pedestrian as pizza was going to attract the kind of woman Dad deserved. Pizza was going to get us a newly divorced real estate agent who lived in a sad little condo and watched soft-focus romantic comedies in her spare time. Dad needed someone earthy, but worldly, too. An artist, maybe, or an importer-exporter with a slightly shady past. But if I wanted to reel in someone like that, I had to find the right bait. It took nearly an hour of hunting around on foodie websites before I found what I was looking for — tarantulas fried in garlic. That was it! Using it as my inspiration, I fabricated a tale about the year Dad spent backpacking through Southeast Asia after college and how he'd become a huge fan of the dish after trying it at a back-alley food stall in Thailand.

I was really getting into it when the sound of Carol's vacuuming abruptly cut out.

"Oh, those poor people," she sighed.

I turned to find her standing in the doorway, absently rubbing her belly as she stared past me at the TV mounted above the fireplace. A newsfeed Dad had left running as background noise was showing an armada of rickety fishing boats pitching and rolling through rough seas. There were hundreds of them. Each boat was packed with so many people they were literally hanging off the sides. I grabbed the remote and cranked the volume. Jessica Ramos's brisk voice filled the living room.

"... after years of political instability, the Libyan government has officially collapsed, sending swarms of refugees into the Mediterranean, hoping to find safety in Europe. Greek president Alexander Agalatos has vowed that he will not allow a single refugee to, quote, 'contaminate European soil.'"

Jessica turned to a different camera.

"Here in Washington, President Hargrove plans what she's calling an all-hands-on-deck meeting at the White House later tonight. On the agenda will be the US response to this latest refugee crisis."

"'The US response'?" Carol mocked, as the report continued. "Please, Jessie. We're going to do what we always do, join up with a bunch of European fascists and push the poor bastards back where they came from. I swear, if I could have any superpower, it'd be to teleport every single person on those boats right into the middle of downtown Washington, DC. Let those shit weasels try and ignore them when they're standing on their own doorsteps."

That's right — *shit weasels.* The further along Carol got in her pregnancy, the clearer it became that she was *not* to be messed with.

"And as the refugees flee," Jessica continued onscreen, "the al-Asiri Empire is moving to take advantage of this latest power vacuum in the region. New drone footage shows fighters streaming out of their bases in Egypt and into undefended Libyan territory."

"And this," Carol sputtered. "*This* —"

Dad didn't even look up from his work. "Lucy, turn it off, would ya? It's making your Aunt Carol upset."

"I'm not *upset*, Roger."

"Fine. Turn this off; it's making a grown man afraid of his little sister."

I hit the remote and the screen went blank, reflecting Carol back at us. She was rigid as a steel rod, arms crossed over her chest, hands balled into fists. Dad and I exchanged a look.

"You know what we should do," he said in a familiar *just theorizing* drawl. "We should get Bernie to hook up with some of the guys from her old unit and hijack a ship. A big one!"

I saw where he was going and fell into my role as straight man. "What? Like an aircraft carrier or something?"

"Exactly. They sail it over to the Mediterranean, pick those people up, and drop 'em off right in front of the White House. What do ya think, Carol?"

"Don't make *jokes*, Roger."

"I'm not making jokes, I'm — hey, where are you going?"

She'd turned away from us and was stomping up the stairs. "I'm going to go scrub the bathroom. Tell me when Luke gets here."

"Carol!"

But she was already gone.

We weren't trying to be jerks. Honestly. Carol's doctor had advised that she reduce her stress, and we knew what news like that did to her. When President Hargrove closed the southern border after Mexico's government was nearly brought down by years of drought, Bernie would find Carol up at all hours of the night glued to the newsfeeds, electric with rage. When the protests started, she nearly drove herself into the ground trying to attend every single one.

"So, when's that no-good boyfriend of yours getting here?"

Dad had closed his laptop and was digging into the bag of potato chips he'd swiped from beside me. He loved playing the "father suspicious of his daughter's boyfriend" role, even though he and Luke had been buds since day one.

I shook the last few minutes out of my head. "Uh . . . not sure. A couple hours, I think?"

"And you have the whole prom experience all planned out?"

Prom. The word made me cringe. We'd spent the last two years avoiding the shambling horde of suburban ogres we went to school with. So why were we getting all spiffed up to act out some bullshit rite of passage with them now?

"I don't know. Honestly, it's possible we'll ditch the whole thing and grab burgers at the Yankee Clipper. Maybe see a movie. We're mostly going as a joke."

"A joke? But Lucy—"

My phone dinged with a text from Luke.

Have acquired live bull. Will be there in an hour and a half

I smiled. If I was going to do this ridiculous and entirely pointless thing, at least I'd be doing it with him. I texted back a smiley face wearing a top hat, then shut my laptop too. Dad's soulmate would have to wait. Mine was on his way.

I launched myself off the couch and called back to Dad as I headed up the stairs.

"While I'm getting ready, do me a favor and start assembling a comprehensive list of turn-ons and turn-offs."

"Your school wants to know *that*?"

"We'll go over your answers when we get back!"

Upstairs, I brushed the sour cream and onion out of my teeth, then swept into my room and shut the door. I'd already showered and done all the highly invasive grooming society demanded, so all that was left was the dress. I threw open my closet door. Fancy dresses weren't usually my thing, but I had to admit, when I saw this one, the misgivings I had about prom were temporarily wiped away. Bernie had actually found it, which was funny, because if there was anyone who knew less about fancy dresses than me, it was Bernie. She and Carol and I had spent three straight weekends trolling every vintage and secondhand store in a hundred-mile radius. We were almost ready to give up when Bernie reached into a water-damaged cardboard box sitting in a corner of this small-town Goodwill, and there it was. She lofted it over her head like Excalibur and marched it to me, her face aglow with triumph.

"Behold! The dress of destiny!"

It was a 1940s-esque strapless number in a dusky red that hugged every curve I had like it was holding on for dear life. It was going to make dancing nearly impossible, but honestly, who cared? The second I tried it on it was like the rules of body dysmorphia were temporarily suspended.

I wiggled into the thing, then accessorized with a massive diamond necklace and a matching ring the size of a golf ball — imitation, of course, also from Goodwill — and then did my hair up in ringlets, topped with a black brocade fascinator. My makeup was smoky and dramatic. I looked like some kind of femme fatale vampire witch.

The doorbell gonged.

"Lucy!" Dad called up the stairs. "Luke's here!"

I checked the clock. How had all that time passed? This was it. Prom. Ridiculous or not, there was no turning back. I took a deep breath (no easy feat in the dress of destiny) and pulled myself away from the mirror. Carol had joined Dad downstairs. The two of them were crowded around the front door, blocking Luke from view. They parted as I came down the stairs.

The first thing you noticed about Luke was how there seemed to be an overabundance of him. Even though he'd never set foot on a farm in his life, he had this kind of classic farmboy physique — six feet tall with impossibly broad shoulders and muscly arms and legs. His jaw was the jutting square of a comic-book superhero and his lips (O sweet, sweet lips, whose praises I swore to sing until my dying day) were pillowy soft and a red so deep that he used to get beat up when he was little because the other boys accused him of wearing lipstick. His hair was a tangle of jet-black that resisted even the most determined efforts to restrain it, and his eyes were a clear, emerald green, rimmed by lashes so long and thick he was the envy of half the girls in our school.

He was hot in jeans and a T-shirt, but that night he was wearing a coal-black tuxedo with narrow, shiny lapels and a razor-thin tie the color of rubies. His tie clip was a silver pair of miniature dice showing snake eyes. He'd found it, and the matching set of cufflinks, after weeks of hunting through all the same secondhand stores I had. That was how he'd found the tux, too. It was two sizes too big for him, but after our friend Tilly put her considerable sewing skills to the task, it was perfectly fitted, from his shoulders down to his impeccably shined shoes. I reminded myself to buy Tilly something for her trouble. Possibly a vacation home.

With that tux and his black hair and his dimpled chin and his green eyes and his bashful smile he was . . . man, I didn't even know. No. I did. He was the penguin king. That's what he was. He was the goddamn penguin king.

I reached the bottom of the stairs. No one made a sound. Luke's eyes were locked on me and his lips were parted slightly, like he wanted to speak but couldn't find the words. Eventually, he let out a breathy, awed, *"Whoa."*

Dad and Carol laughed. I blushed. A jumpy, Pop Rocks feeling started in the pit of my stomach.

"You . . . you look amazing," he said. "I uh, I got you this."

He pulled a clear plastic box from behind his back. Inside was a small rose, jet-black, nestled in baby's breath.

Dad spoke up from behind me. "Classy move, Mr. Vaughn."

Luke beamed, then pulled the corsage out of the box, fumbling nervously as he pinned it in place. The black was perfect against the red of my dress. We ended up side by side with his arm around my waist, facing Dad and Carol, who seemed to be putting every scrap of their energy into not blubbering uncontrollably.

"Okay, guys," I cautioned. "Let's try to keep it together before someone passes out."

"I'm fine," Carol said through emotion-strained vocal cords.

"Yep, me too," Dad squeaked. "Just taking it all in. Taking in my little girl."

We were saved from a full-on existential meltdown by the squeal of car tires in the driveway.

"Hey! Look! Bernie's here for picture time!" They didn't move. Ugh. "Luke, would you by any chance like to go outside and have my Aunt Bernie take some pictures that will immortalize this moment forever?"

"You know it!"

We shoved Dad and Carol out the door, just in time to see Bernie sprinting awkwardly across the front yard, hauling what looked like several tons of camera equipment. After she'd finished her tour in North Korea, she'd stayed in the Marine Corps to do PR — making commercials, taking pictures, things like that — which made her our family's official chronicler.

"It's about time!" Carol groused as she crossed the lawn to meet her. "Where were you?"

Bernie skidded to a halt and gave Carol a peck on the cheek. "Sorry, babe. I was on the phone with Mom."

"Is everything okay? Is she —"

"She's fine," Bernie said quickly, then wheeled on me and Luke. "You guys look amazing! Let's take some pictures!"

She moved us into pose after pose. At first we had all the grace of a couple of department-store mannequins, but after a while we relaxed. Our smiles came more easily and we flowed from pose to pose, laughing. We made goofy faces. Luke did a handstand. The world got all swimmy. Maybe it was the near hundred-degree heat or maybe it was the weird, disorienting sense that we were all smack dab in the middle of a Moment, one we were expected to remember and treasure for years and years. It was a feeling I would have mocked ten minutes earlier, but right then, as I was in it, it felt true. And then the pictures were over and Luke and I got separated. I didn't even notice it happening. One second I was with him and the next I was stumbling toward the sidewalk, drunk with a kind of pre-emptive nostalgia, Bernie's hand on my arm. She was saying something in a low, earnest voice. It sounded incredibly meaningful, but if you put a hundred million dollars in my hand right now, I couldn't tell you what it was.

Dad and Luke were at the edge of the yard, drenched in end-of-day sunlight. My guys. My two favorite guys. They were standing close and talking intently, but all I could hear were a few manly rumbles. Dad pulled him into a hug. Carol came into focus beside me, beaming.

"How ya doin', Goose?" she asked, using my little kid nickname. It had started out as Lucy Goosey and eventually just became Goose.

I mumbled something about being good, but my ability to talk was hampered by a sudden, weirdly intense surge of love for her, which wasn't surprising since I was also feeling the same surge of love for Bernie and my soon-to-be-born cousin and Luke and Dad and our house and the lawn and America. Before I knew it I was gliding toward the driveway, the grass a mint-green blur beneath my feet. *(I love you, grass!)* There was a click as a car door opened.

"Your chariot, madam."

I looked up at our "limo" for the first time. Luke had parked it at the very top of the driveway, so it had been blocked by the house for the entire picture-taking session. When I finally saw it, all I could do was laugh.

At some point during the day he'd gotten hold of many, many cans of spray paint and had turned his broke-ass powder-blue Nissan flat black, from hood to trunk. Not only that, but he had affixed a homemade grille and hood ornament made out of . . . well, I don't even know what, but they were painted a gleaming silver and looked convincingly like chrome. It was ridiculous and amazing and perfect. *(I love you, car!)*

Luke stood by the open passenger-side door. I grabbed his arm and pulled him close.

"You are one hell of a man, Luke Vaughn," I breathed into the nape of his neck in a way I knew got him all hot and bothered. "And you are going to get soooooo lucky tonight."

Luke guided me into my seat and shut the door behind me. He waved to Dad, then dropped in behind the wheel and retrieved his sunglasses from the dash. Silver-framed aviators. The lenses gleamed. Luke turned the engine on, sending a delicious little hum up my calves. Luke's Dad had offered to get him an autonomous car, but Luke had said zombie cars weren't for him. I was glad. He liked to drive and I liked when he did it.

On the other side of the windshield, Carol and Bernadette and Dad huddled together, grinning and waving. I waved back. They looked so far away. Like they were on another planet. Luke took my hand and pulled out of the driveway. I twisted around in my seat, watching Dad and Carol and Bernie get smaller and smaller until we turned a corner and they disappeared. Then I faced front, grinning as we sped away.

THREE

THE NORTHAMPTON WAS NESTLED deep in the woods about an hour north of Bethany. With its spires and fountains and cobblestone driveway it seemed more like a castle than a hotel. I half expected to see horse-drawn carriages and princesses in gowns accompanied by talking forest creatures.

Red-jacketed attendants waved us to an enormous lot behind the main building. Luke parked, and then we were swept away in a stream of tuxedoed and begowned bodies headed for the front door. We passed through the lobby and beneath a grand archway that led into the main hall. There we found a continent-size dance floor packed to capacity with our fellow Bethany High seniors.

The committee in charge of such things had really gone all out on that year's theme — Casino Night! Obviously I'd have preferred a moonlit Italian hillside, perfect for bloody worship of a pre-Christian god, but I had to admit they'd done it up right. Glitter-trimmed dice and dollar signs were plastered all around, and one half of the room was filled with gaming tables where you could bet phony money on blackjack and roulette and craps. I was about to suggest we put our skills to the test when Luke's phone went off. He slipped it out of his pocket and glanced at the screen. His lips pressed into a tight line.

"Who is it?"

"Carter. I'll call him back later. We should —"

He started to put the phone away but I stopped his hand. "No. Take it. I'll be over at the baccarat tables doubling our money. Come find me when you're done."

I gave him a peck on the cheek and he jogged out toward the lobby, pressing the phone to his ear.

"Hey, buddy," I heard him say. "Is everything all right?"

I decided to skip the gambling tables and wander the hall. All of our friends had the good sense to stay away, so I people-watched and eavesdropped. The conversations weren't particularly varied. They mostly revolved around one of two phrases: *"Do you remember when . . . ?"* or *"What are you doing in the fall?"* The *"Do you remember when . . . ?"* conversations were largely about parties and games I hadn't gone to. The *"What are you doing in the fall?"* ones involved things that would throw any self-respecting parent into a grand mal seizure of pride. Bryan Markey was headed to Yale, while his girlfriend — whose name I could never remember but who was wearing a super cute, flapper-style dress — was going to Harvard. They played up the Ivy League rivalry like they were contractually obligated to do it, which, who knows, maybe they were. Betty Oyama was going to Cambodia with her church for a year to build homes for people who'd lost theirs in the last monsoon, before starting up at NYU to study international relations. Ken Angelo was joining the Marines, which was terrifying since the only thing I knew about him was a rumor that during sophomore year he'd gotten hammered and set his own testicles on fire. Semper Fi!

The DJ put on something that kicked off a prom-wide fit of squealing. A flood of bodies moved toward the dance floor and within seconds everyone was linked hand to hand, revolving in complicated patterns they all seemed to know by heart. I retreated to the dimmest corner I could find and watched. That was when the sheer strangeness of my being there hit me. I knew most everyone's names, had heard things about them, but I didn't *know* them, know them. Not really. We'd been in classes together, a few had scowled at me from the other end of a lunch table or whispered about me while huddled around lockers between classes, but that was all. No surprise there, I guess. I'd come into freshman year as a serious contender for Least Popular Student in History. And while most of the outright hostility had faded into the background eventually, lines had been drawn. I was on one side and everybody else — except for Luke and our small group of weirdo friends — was on the other. I wasn't mad about it or anything. I mean, I had been *super* mad, but that was a long time ago. As I looked at everyone that night — all sparkly in their fancy clothes, ready to fling themselves out into the world — this weird kind of benevolence came over me, even toward the ones who'd been the cruelest in those first couple of years. I'd read somewhere that our bodies were constantly in the process of remaking themselves. Old skin cells died and fell away and new ones were born. Same with the cells that made up our bones and blood and hair. So maybe after all those years we had literally become different people, and whatever our previous selves had said or done didn't matter anymore. We were moving on. We were free.

The song changed. The dancers scattered and reformed. I was seriously considering joining them when I caught a whiff of smoke coming from a nook farther down the wall from me. I squinted into the dark, but all I could make out was a silhouette in the light coming through a propped-open exit door. A lone girl blew out a match, then exhaled a cloud of smoke into the hallway behind her. There was a warm and spicy smell. Cloves. Who the hell would be gutsy enough, and stubbornly old-school enough, to be smoking an honest-to-God, lit-with-a-match clove cigarette in the middle of prom? A name sounded in my head like the peal of a bell.

Jenna Pearl.

No way, I thought. Could it really be her? I'd heard she was finishing out her senior year doing some kind of weird study abroad thing, in Mongolia or someplace. Had she come back for *this?* I left my corner and moved toward the open door, slowly enough that I could easily abort if it turned out I was stalking some stranger. With every step I took, the scent of cloves got stronger.

Jenna and I had met on the first day of sixth grade and had immediately become best friends. We were two moody, painfully serious girls, the only ones not taking our theater class for the easy A. We eventually hounded Mr. Cronin — our poor, long-suffering teacher — until he let us mount what had to be the bloodiest ever middle school production of Sondheim's *Sweeney Todd*. It was stunningly inappropriate. When we weren't planning our next theatrical provocation (an even bloodier version of Shakespeare's *Macbeth*), we were lying on Jenna's bedroom floor watching gruesome horror movies and occasionally slipping outside to smoke the clove cigarettes we stole from her mom's purse.

To say we diverged after middle school would be a wee bit of an understatement. Obviously, I was pretty consumed with my own shit at the time, but the really big thing was that, toward the end of eighth grade, it was discovered that Jenna was a genius. And I don't mean in the way people said it when someone remembered to, like, bring Pringles on a road trip. *(Pringles! Dude! You're a genius!)* I mean like a real, tested genius. When Bethany High found out she was headed their way, they set up what could only be described as quarantine procedures. Job number one was to get her as far away as possible from the shambling hordes of mouth-breathers so she wouldn't be infected by our dumbassedness. She was moved straight into the most advanced classes the school had to offer. High-end computer programming. College-level math. Latin. Classes the rest of us didn't even know existed. On top of that, they pushed her into special outside tutoring, plus a dozen clubs and academic teams, all designed to make the name Jenna Pearl sweeter to the ears of Ivy League college admissions officers than the names of their own children.

Needless to say, Jenna's ascent up academic Mount Olympus put a cramp in our hanging-out-and-watching-horror-movies time. She went her way. I went mine. It happens. But standing there in that old hotel, the air positively choked with nostalgia, what we used to mean to each other made my heart ache. It ached a little more when I got close enough to see her clearly in the light from the hall. She hadn't changed a bit. If anything, she was more Jenna than ever. She'd always been a little goth, but it looked like she'd really taken that ball and run with it.

Her heart-shaped face was vampire pale, with slashes of black around her mouth and eyes. Her hair was long and straight and dyed a shade of midnight so deep it was nearly black. She was wearing a dress, but instead of everyone else's jewel-toned runway approximations, she'd put together this truly stunning evil-queen-just-crawled-out-of-the-grave number. It was tattered black-and-gray lace, and she wore it with this super-tight, brocaded corset. The heels of her knee-high patent-leather boots gave her at least two inches on me.

"Well, Jenna Pearl, as I live and breathe."

She flinched, holding her clove out into the hallway, expecting a teacher, I guess. Her eyes narrowed as I stepped into the spill of light.

"*Weaver?*"

"In the flesh," I said. "Long time no see, huh?"

"Uh, yeah. Wow. Long time." She took a furtive sip of the clove. "So, how, uh, how are you?"

"Good. Great. I heard you were in Mongolia."

"Bhutan."

"Ah. Right. Bhutan. Cool."

And just like that we hit a wall. Jenna puffed at her clove. I watched the dance floor. I considered cutting my losses and going to find Luke, but then Jenna held out the pack in her hand.

"Want one?"

I moved into the nook beside her and slid one out. When she leaned forward and lit another match, the flame illuminated tiny silver skulls that had been braided into her hair.

"Thanks," I said, breathing a cloud of bluish-gray smoke back into the hallway. "So, who'd you come with?"

Jenna lifted her chin, nodding across the room at Grant Miller, the school's star basketball player and, next to Luke, the most beautiful human being I had ever seen in real life. Word was the NBA was courting him heavily, along with several modeling agencies.

"Seriously?"

She nodded. "If there's one thing I've learned it's that all the jocks are secretly hot for the freaks. You're with Luke Vaughn, right?"

I said I was, and then we plunged into silence again. I checked the main door. No sign of Luke. I fiddled with the clove.

"Oh, hey," I said. "Did you see the new Alejandra Aguilar?"

She seemed surprised. "You're into Aguilar?"

"Got into her stuff freshman year. Her. Bonhoffer. Cho Sun Pak. Mary Neville. Figured you might be too."

Jenna laughed. "Yeah. *Mr. Maxwell* wasn't bad," she agreed. "I mean, it was no *Black Suitcase,* but . . ."

I got a little thrill hearing her say that. *Black Suitcase* was my favorite. Bar none. I could still remember seeing it for the first time, halfway to a heart attack as Esperanza Belén finally went into the gardener's shed and opened that suitcase. I didn't sleep a wink that night; all I could do was lie in bed staring at the ceiling, shivering with terror and gloriously happy.

"I've been watching a lot of Ukrainian movies lately," Jenna said. "Stanislas Chekhov?"

"Didn't the Russians throw him in jail?"

She tossed her spent clove into the hallway and lit another one. "They did, but I got ahold of this bootleg of *The Bamboo Forest.* Literally nothing happens in the entire movie, but it's the most horrifying thing I've ever seen in my life. Real existential-dread-type stuff."

"Oh man, I love existential dread."

"It's the best kind of dread. No question."

I turned toward her, blocking out the rest of the room. "I'm surprised you even have time for movies anymore. Did I hear it's Yale for you in the fall?"

The skulls jingled as Jenna shook her head. "Oxford. But I told them I want to defer until next year. Think I'm gonna start my own company instead."

"Doing what?"

Jenna hesitated.

"I'd never understand in a million years, would I?"

"It's a biotech thing," she said. "Doesn't matter. Figure I'll make a few hundred million off it, then invest in something that's actually important."

I nodded soberly, like I'd been considering the same thing.

"What about you?" she asked. "NYU?"

"Nope."

"One of the SUNYs?"

"Uh-uh."

"You defer a year too?"

"Didn't apply."

"You didn't apply *anywhere?*"

"Nope."

I took a warm drag off the clove. Jenna just stared. I have to admit I enjoyed shocking her.

"So what are you doing instead?"

"Me and Luke are hitting the road."

"Hitting the road? To do what?"

"See as much of the world as we can. Neither of us were feeling college, and we figured this was our chance."

"So where are you going?"

"Everywhere. Well, pretty much everywhere. Dad made me promise not to go anywhere *too* dangerous. Right now the plan is fifteen countries and all forty-nine states. And Antarctica. We've got a little money saved up. Figure we'll do odd jobs and stuff when we run out."

"And Luke's folks aren't giving him trouble about it? Aren't they kind of . . ."

She trailed off, not wanting to say *crazy*, I guess.

"Yeah, well, it's possible they haven't been fully briefed on our plans."

"Damn! A world tour. That's gutsy, Weaver."

"Or incredibly stupid. We'll see which way it shakes out. In the end we're planning on settling in Colorado near the mountains. Build ourselves a house."

"Jenna Pearl!"

We both turned. The crowd parted and Grant appeared, striding toward us, smiling his million-watt smile. Luke was trailing along behind him, looking distracted and pale, tie askew, his phone clenched in one hand.

Jenna stubbed out her clove on the linoleum. "All righty, then. This whole prom thing has been fun. Priceless memories have been made." Grant glided into place beside her. "You got us a hotel room, right?"

"I most certainly did."

"Well, then, let's get to the main event!"

She kicked open the door behind her. Grant, likely thanking whatever god he prayed to for his good fortune, dutifully went through. Jenna paused in the doorway. The light caught her green eyes, which seemed even brighter surrounded by all that black. She smiled and said,

"It was really good to see you, Weaver."

"You too."

"You should call me. Maybe before we all move on we could . . ."

"Yeah. Definitely," I said, knowing I wouldn't, knowing that some people belonged to the past and some belonged to the future and that was just the way it was.

The door shut behind Jenna and Grant, leaving me and Luke in the clove-scented dark. There was a cheer as the DJ put on this slow, Latin-flavored song everyone had been obsessed with back when we were freshmen. I turned to say something to Luke about it and found him glowering at the floor, jaw tense, the phone still in his fist. I dropped my clove and ground it out.

"Come on, your highness. It's time to dance."

I seized Luke's arm and joined the crowd on the dance floor. Once we got out to the center, I pulled him in close. He'd put the phone away, but he was as stiff as a board. His muscles were tied up in knots.

"Is everything okay?" I asked. "Is Carter —"

"He's fine."

It was a little too quick. I leaned slightly out of his embrace. He was staring out over my shoulder, grinding his teeth.

"Mom and Dad have a visitor tonight?"

He nodded.

"Pastor Todd?"

"Dad wanted to clean up before he got there so he —"

"Moved Carter's Legos."

"Yeah."

Carter had been building this truly amazing Lego city for over a year. He didn't use any instructions or a plan; he pulled the whole thing right out of his head. Next to Greg the goldfish, it was his favorite thing in the universe.

"He lost it," Luke went on. "Just lost it. Screaming. Hitting himself. And then Todd showed up and started praying and trying to touch him."

"Fucking asshole," I said, imagining my hands wrapping around Pastor Todd's beefy neck. "What'd Carter do?"

"Squirmed away. Ran upstairs."

"Do we need to leave and —"

"No. It's okay. He's in his tent with Greg. He'll be fine."

I rested my cheek on Luke's chest and we swayed gently to the music. One of the first times I'd met Carter, Luke's dad had just taken away one of his toy cars for God knew what reason (most likely reason? God) and Carter had responded by stuffing himself in one of the kitchen cabinets and wailing. Mr. Vaughn tried to talk him down, but ended up getting mad and stomping off. Their mom was no help either. All she knew how to do was pray, which she did with ever-increasing fervor until she might as well have been on a different planet. When they gave up, Luke and I sat on the kitchen floor next to the cabinet. I was all but useless, since Carter's howls nearly incapacitated me. Luke, though, he should have been sainted that day. He didn't bother trying to talk about what happened; he simply grabbed his guitar and started singing. Halfway through "Lovely Rita" Carter emerged, shirtless and barefoot, in yellow shorts. He asked if he could have some Teddy Grahams and juice, and that was it. All better.

I stopped dancing and stepped away from Luke. The rest of prom twirled around us.

"We should take him," I said.

"What?"

"When we get back from our trip, when we're settled, he should move in with us. Would your parents let him?"

"I don't —" Luke stopped himself. He looked up at the streamers hanging from the ceiling.

"They would," I said. "Wouldn't they? No more fits for them to deal with. No more interruptions of their holy rolling. What do you think?"

"I — it wouldn't be easy. Seriously. Carter is awesome, but sometimes he . . . You'd have to be really sure."

I saw it all in a flash, so clear and perfect it was like I'd opened a window in time and was peering straight through. The three of us, tucked into a little house at the foot of a mountain, near a stream. We'd have a garden and a dog and a whole room that was reserved for Carter's Legos. We'd find him a school, a good one — one that really knew how to help him. Luke and I would get jobs, maybe not great jobs or anything, but good enough that we could buy food and clothes and towels and all the other little things you needed to build a life. Usually when I looked toward the future everything seemed hazy and out of focus, but right then all the edges were sharp and the colors were so vivid it hurt.

I nodded up at Luke. He pulled me in close. His heart thrummed in my ear.

"Okay," he whispered. "We'll do it."

The DJ queued up another slow song, but I was too excited to stand there swaying in place, so I decided it was time to hit the casino tables in earnest. We made the rounds from the roulette wheels to the poker tables. In the space of an hour we earned reams of play money and exchanged them for carnival prizes — lollipop rings and stuffed horses and oversize Class of 2049 sunglasses. Luke wore his proudly, even when it was time to strip off his jacket and do some serious fling-yourself-around-the-floor dancing. His special extended curfew (ten forty-five!) came and went, but we decided consequences be damned. We sweated and danced and gambled with play money for shiny junk and then we did it all again. At one point Dad texted to say he and Carol and Bernie were bringing their Scrabble night to a close, and I said: don't wait up for us because we are at PROM, BABY!

By the time they were ready to announce prom king and queen, we were a breathless mess. My hair was a rat's nest and Luke had stripped down to his untucked, half-unbuttoned dress shirt, accessorized with the neon-green sunglasses. Everyone gathered at the foot of the stage while Principal Tusso made his way to the mic at the DJ's station. Someone's cell phone rang. I thought it was Luke's at first, his parents calling to hassle him about the blown curfew, but the ringtone was some deeply annoying piece of classical music, all blaring horns and clanging cymbals. *Ba-da-bump, ba-da-bump, ba-da-bump-BA-BA*. It was coming from behind me.

I turned around and squinted into the dimness. Near the back of the crowd I found a tall, skinny kid in a still-perfectly-done-up tuxedo. Jacket buttoned. Tie straight. Shoes shiny. The part in his shellacked-looking hair was ruler straight, and his glasses gleamed. *Karras*, I thought. *Jay Karras*. I rolled my eyes a little. I saw him around school, but we didn't exactly travel in the same circles. He was the epitome of the high school golden boy. The kind of relentlessly energetic achievement-bot who maintained straight As in all AP classes while somehow finding time to be senior class treasurer and captain of the debate team. He didn't walk through school so much as float through it, gliding far above the heads of us lesser mortals on his way to the Ivy Leagues.

His phone rang again. *Ba-da-bump, ba-da-bump, ba-da-bump-BA-BA.* An exceedingly pretty girl in a green dress standing next to him started to say something, but he held up one finger in this very corporate-executive-taking-an-emergency-call-from-his-stockbroker kind of way and slipped past her to answer. He opened his mouth, probably to say, "Hey, I'm at prom; I'll call back later," but then whoever was on the other end said something that shut him up. Jay lowered his head and pressed his palm flat against his opposite ear to block out the noise. He seemed confused at first, and then, as he listened, his face went sort of pale and he became very, very still.

"What's going on?"

Luke had noticed me watching and was leaning down by my ear.

"I dunno," I said. "I think something's —"

Another phone rang across the dance floor. Mikey Everett's. He answered it, but didn't get two words out before he was instantly silenced, just like Jay. Then someone else's phone rang. Text messages pinged and buzzed along with the calls. In seconds, the dimly lit hall was filled with tiny islands of brightness as everyone leaned over screens, texting and swiping. The air in the room was heavy, and Tusso was saying something into the mic, but I couldn't make out what it was. The seed of unease I'd felt when Jay Karras took that first call was growing into panic. I'd been here before. We all had. Something was happening. Something bad.

My phone was in my purse, left on a table at the other side of the hall, near the roulette wheel. Was Dad or Carol or Bernie trying to get in touch with me? I wanted Luke to come with me to get it, but then his phone rang too, and he answered it.

As he talked, I turned back to Jay Karras. By then people were starting to move toward the exits, but he was just standing there in his perfect tux with his head down, his shoulders slumped, and his glasses dangling from his fingertips. His date tugged at his sleeve a couple of times, and then she gave up and headed for the door without him. I guess he must have sensed that someone was staring at him because he turned toward me and our eyes met. It was like two ends of a circuit snapping into place and I knew, all at once, what was going on inside of him. He was terrified. And then, so was I.

Banks of fluorescent lights blazed overhead, and then Luke's hand was on my arm and we were joining the stream of people leaving the Northampton. My panic morphed into a kind of gray numbness. All I could do was stagger through the hall and across the parking lot. The world came at me in bright flashes of prom dresses and distant trees, gravel and headlights. Voices were muffled and strange like I was underwater. The next thing I knew, my door slammed shut and we were pulling out of the lot and onto the highway. Luke didn't say anything and neither did I. The road hummed beneath us. My purse was sitting by my feet. Luke must have grabbed it on the way out. I could have taken out my phone and checked to see what was going on, but my head was too foggy and thick. I couldn't seem to make my hand move toward it.

Luke's car came to a stop in front of my house. I didn't have a single memory of the drive. For some reason my elbow was aching.

"Sorry, Luce. Everybody's freaking out. I have to —"

Luke was ramrod straight in the driver's seat, clasping the steering wheel so hard his knuckles were red.

"Yeah. No. Sure. You should go."

I fumbled with the door handle, but Luke's hand found my knee, stopping me before I could leave.

"Whatever's happening," he said, "we're going to be fine."

His voice was strong, but his hand was shaking. I forced myself to nod. He leaned over and kissed me, and then I opened the door and stepped onto the pavement. A second later he was speeding off. I stood there on the sidewalk. All the houses on the block were dark except for the flickering glow of TV screens. Shadows hunched around them like cavemen in front of camp-fires. I looked up into a clear sky crammed with stars. The moon hung low over our neighbors' roofs and the rounded mountains of Bethany Ridge beyond them. Trees rustled in a warm breeze. I was floating. Disconnected.

Dad and Carol and Bernie leapt up as I walked in. Dad swiped the remote from the coffee table and shut off the TV so fast it was like they were the little kids and I'd caught them watching an R-rated movie.

"Lucy! What are you doing home? The prom can't be over yet; they —"

"Everybody left," I said. "Luke needed to check on Carter."

In the back of my head my own voice asked what was going on, but I couldn't seem to get the words out. Nobody else said anything either. Instead, Carol jumped forward.

"Lucy! What happened to your elbow?"

I looked. A stream of blood was coursing down the length of my forearm, breaking off into tributaries as it went over the back of my hand and along my fingers. I had no idea how it had happened. Had I fallen on the way to the car?

"Oh. I don't — I tripped, maybe. It's fine."

"It's not fine. You're bleeding."

Carol sat me down on the couch, then hurried toward the bathroom in the front hall. Two half-empty glasses of white wine were on the coffee table next to the Scrabble board. The tiles marked out a little maze. They'd played words like *bridegroom* and *wayfarer* and *reliquary*.

Carol came back with the first-aid kit and fussed with my elbow, while Dad and Bernie stood there awkwardly. I sucked a breath through clenched teeth as she dug out scraps of gravel and then dabbed at the wound with disinfectant. While she worked I stared at the scuffed corner of the table. My thumb went to a ridge of scar on my chin.

I was eight when I got cast in my first play. I went racing into the house after school, so excited to tell Mom and Dad about it that I didn't see a pair of shoes left by the door. I tripped over them and went flying chin-first into the coffee table. You'd have thought a small animal had been slaughtered in our living room, there was so much blood. Mom came running downstairs and took me to the emergency room. I squealed the whole way, right up to the second a pretty young doctor came in and set up shop in front of me, organizing her tray of instruments. She snapped on a pair of gloves and raised a gleaming steel needle into the light.

"Now," she said. "Who's gonna be a brave girl?"

"Lucy?"

Carol had gotten up and was standing across from me with Dad on one side of her and Bernie on the other, all of them watching me expectantly. My elbow had stopped bleeding and was capped with a clean white bandage. No one said anything. They just watched me. In the movies, a vampire can't enter your house until you give it permission. It was like that with this, too. I had to open the door. I had to let in whatever was waiting outside.

Who's gonna be a brave girl?

The remote control was sitting by the Scrabble board. I picked it up. It was still warm from someone's hand. I pointed it at the TV and turned it on. I didn't understand what I was looking at, or rather, why I was looking at it. The scene playing out on the TV was one I'd seen a hundred times before. A thousand times. A wave of refugees trying to escape a famine or a heat wave or a storm or a war. These refugees were making their way out of some bombed-out city. All around them were crumpled street signs and smashed windows. Buildings that had been reduced to one or two crumbling walls. Here and there were odd remnants of what the city used to be. A strangely intact shop window. An elegantly painted café sign. The refugees themselves were faceless, coated head to foot in ash that was darkened here and there by patches of blood and sweat. Their clothes were tattered. Some were barefoot.

Most were injured. The ones who were strong enough hauled their possessions in whatever they could. Suitcases. Backpacks. Shopping carts. Some, mostly women, carried frighteningly still, frighteningly quiet children.

Their way was lit by spotlights that were mounted on drones the news networks used. There was a small swarm of them, jockeying for position over their heads. The refugees shielded their eyes as they shuffled past. They said nothing, even as reporters shouted questions at them through the drones' loudspeakers. Questions in English, which meant the reporters were both stupid *and* American. Even if they could understand, what would be the point? It wasn't like we needed man-on-the-street interviews to know what was going on. Millions had been forced to flee their homes in the last twenty years. Whether they were from Somalia or Qatar or Bangladesh or Mexico or Vietnam, they were all desperate for the same things: safety, clean water, a little food, a place to sleep. It was awful. It was tragic. It was barely news.

One of the drones zipped higher, over the rooftops, then sped away. It sent back images of a river of survivors that was several miles long and made up of tens of thousands of people. It also gave a sense of the scale of the devastation they were trying to escape. That did seem unusual. I sat forward on the couch. It looked like an entire city was on fire. Vast clouds of smoke hung everywhere, and towers of flame flickered in a thousand different places at once, brightening block after block of rubble and flattened buildings. It was like some giant had swept its hand across a board game it was tired of playing and knocked everything to the floor.

"People saw the flash from sixty miles away. Felt the ground shake from thirty."

It was Bernie. She had her arms around Carol, who had started crying.

"Four kilotons," Dad said. "At least."

My mind snagged on that word. *Kiloton.* That meant—

"They've got radiation sensors that are supposed to be able to spot nukes," he went on. "Even small ones. But . . . I don't know. They missed it somehow."

"They probably drove it into town in the trunk of a car," Bernie said. "Who knows. If they were sophisticated enough they could've gotten the damn thing into a suitcase."

I spoke for the first time. "Who's they?"

"We don't know," Bernie said. "No one's taken credit."

Dad moved through the newsfeeds and the picture shifted again and again. More shattered buildings. More smoke. More fire. A half-naked woman covered in blood and burns, screaming into the sky. Lines of body bags being laid out on the ground by soldiers in masks. They seemed to go on forever. A man standing in a field near the edge of a river with a microphone. His face was covered in soot and his head was bleeding badly. He was talking about how emergency services had been overwhelmed for miles in every direction. He said something about casualties, but the numbers didn't make any sense. They were too big. The picture changed again. More drone footage. Smoke parting to reveal white marble scorched black. A domed building. A broken, needle-shaped tower. A tall man sitting in a chair gazing out over the destruction.

Dread filled my stomach like concrete. I turned to Dad. "Where is this?"

He looked at Carol and Bernie. No one said anything, but they didn't need to. A scarlet banner appeared at the bottom of the screen. It said, in gold letters, all caps: WASHINGTON, DC.

FOUR

DAD TURNED OFF the news a little past six that morning, shocking us all out of our daze. The sudden silence made my ears ring. It was too warm, and the air was still. I sat up slowly, achy from having been in one position for so long. Carol had gone to the kitchen a couple of times in the night and brought back drinks and food, but they sat on the coffee table — crowded in with the previous night's Scrabble board and half-filled wine glasses — untouched. Glasses of flat soda and melted ice. A block of cheese gone sweaty with grease. We sat there for a long time without moving or speaking, and then Dad got up and headed toward the front door. We all followed him, first Carol then Bernie then me.

The sun was starting to make its way over Mr. Giolotti's roof across the street. The morning was bright and unusually cool. A relief from the airlessness of the house. We stood on the front lawn for a while in silence. A single car went by. My feet were aching. I looked down and was surprised to find myself still in my heels and prom dress. My makeup was like a clay mask, and my hair was crunchy and hot from all the product I'd used.

"What about fallout?" Carol asked. "Isn't that — isn't that a thing?"

She was standing a little ahead of us, one hand curling under the swell of her belly as she looked up at the clouds. Dad turned to me, worry cutting lines into his face. They'd discussed the fallout a half a dozen times. Carol had been right beside us.

"The wind is blowing the plume out to sea," I reminded her, as gently as I could. "But even if it turns north, they don't think it'll make it much past Baltimore."

"Right," she said, then turned back to us. "And what's happening at noon again? Sorry. My head's all . . . fuzzy."

"Press conference," Dad said. "Military, I think. The president. If they can figure out who the president is by then."

"I thought they said it was the secretary of the interior."

"She's a naturalized citizen. Not eligible."

"So who's next in line?"

"Agriculture. Secretary of agriculture. But nobody knows where he is."

Carol looked over her shoulder at Bernie. "They've gotta have a plan for this, right? The military. Just in case. I mean, they must have something filed away."

Bernie was staring at her phone. For hours, she'd been trying to get in touch with her mom, who was in this assisted-living place up in Canada, but hadn't been able to get through.

"Bernie?"

She didn't look up. "Yeah. Course they do."

"Well, what is it?"

"I was a corporal, honey. They didn't exactly share those things with me."

"I *know* what you were," Carol snapped. "I thought that since you were actually *in the military* you might have a slightly better idea what's going on. And if you don't, you could —"

Bernie stopped texting and rushed over to her wife. She tried to reach out to her, but Carol batted her away.

"I don't need to be held, Bernie. I need to know what the fuck is going *on!*"

The last shout seemed to exhaust whatever fight she had in her. The next time Bernie went to hold her she didn't resist. She took a shaky breath and lowered her head.

"I'm sorry. I'm — I keep trying to get Reggie and Alex on the phone, but . . ."

I suddenly remembered that Carol had gone to college in DC. Her best friends, Reggie and Alex, still lived there.

Bernie rubbed Carol's back. "I know, babe. The lines will clear up soon. We'll get them."

"Did you talk to your mom? Is she okay?"

"I haven't been able to get her yet, but I'm sure she's fine."

"Do you think she'll understand what's going —"

Bernie shook her head. It was quiet for a while after that. Next door, the Walkers came out of the house and stood on their front lawn just like we were standing on ours. They looked worse than us, hollow-eyed and trembling like it was the middle of winter. Did they have family in DC? I tried to remember, but couldn't. Dad waved at Mr. Walker and then the two of them met halfway between our houses and conferred quietly.

"What did he say?" I asked when Dad returned.

"I don't know," he said quietly. "It didn't . . . it didn't make a lot of sense."

Mr. Walker had gone out to stand in the middle of the road, head back, staring up into the sky. His arms were limp at his sides, but his hands were both twitching like wounded birds. His cheeks and the collar of his shirt were wet with tears. We all watched him for a moment; then Mrs. Walker went and got him. She gave us a tight smile as she ushered him back inside and closed the door. A police car appeared up the block and crept slowly past us. Two jets crossed the sky, leaving knifelike trails of white. I remembered I had my phone in my hand. I checked it for a message from Luke. Nothing.

Dad said, "Carol, what was that thing Mom always used to make us?"

Carol wiped at her eyes. "What thing?"

"You know. For Christmas. That pie."

"Oh," Carol said. "Mincemeat."

"Mincemeat. Right." Dad turned to me. "Luce, it was the worst. Pork and kidneys and all these weird spices. And fruit. She made it every Christmas."

Carol sniffed. "All of us hated it, but she was so damn proud of it."

"*Her* mom made it," Dad said. "And her grandma. And her grandma's grandma."

"So none of us would tell her that we hated it. We let her make it every year."

"Dad fed his to the dog under the table."

Carol managed a small laugh. "Who then promptly went out into the backyard and puked. What made you think of that?"

Dad rolled his shoulders. "Dunno. All of a sudden mincemeat pie sounded kinda good."

Carol drew Bernie's arm tight around her, over her belly. "Yeah. I guess it does."

Bernie kissed her softly and rubbed her back. I wondered where Luke was right then. What he was doing. I wanted to call him, but when I'd tried before, I'd gotten no answer.

"We should try to get a little sleep before the press conference," Dad said. "We've been up all night. Guest room's still made up from last time you guys stayed, Carol."

Carol nodded and the three of them shuffled back inside. I stayed where I was, staring at the blue sky as the sun rose into it. As I was standing there an image came into my head as hard and sudden as a punch — a girl in a daisy-yellow dress, her back to the camera. She was standing motionless in the remains of some kind of shop that sat along the road out of DC. The floor around her was a sea of shattered glass and bits of wood. Her dress was torn and covered in ash, but other than that, she seemed unharmed. Until she turned around, anyway. When she did, it became clear that the right side of her face and her shoulder had been utterly burned away. Gleaming white showed through charred skin.

"Lucy? You coming?"

I shook the image out of my head. As I turned away from the street, I looked down at the fake diamond on my finger. I wrenched it off and let it drop into the dewy grass beside my feet. It hit with a thump and disappeared. I turned and followed the others inside.

Carol and Bernie were lingering at the foot of the stairs. I went into the kitchen and stood by the dishwasher but immediately forgot what it was I'd gone in for. Soon the sound of the TV filled the house again. I came out of the kitchen to see Dad on the couch. Carol and Bernie slowly filtered back into the room and took their places. I went to join them, but stopped at the sound of my dress rustling. The dusky red satin was ugly in the morning light, rumpled and cheap-looking. I ran upstairs and traded it for sweats and a T-shirt before tossing it on the floor of my closet and shutting the door.

I slipped into my place downstairs. Carol had cleared the table and drawn the curtains to cut the glare on the TV, leaving a murky gray light. Dad picked up the remote and turned up the volume. Jessica Ramos was on the screen wearing a crisp blue suit, calm as ever.

". . . estimates suggest that the death toll within the city is likely to rise well above twenty thousand, with more than twice that number wounded. While there are still no claims of responsibility, American forces are gearing up for a massive counterattack against targets throughout Asia, the Middle East, and the Russian border states. It's unclear at this time who would have the authority to give that order. For more on that, we go to . . ."

FIVE

Τhat night I woke up to the feel of something vibrating down by my feet. My phone! I dove beneath my sheets and flailed until I found it. Blue light stabbed my eyes.

Need to see you. Hurry.

It was Luke. I texted him back but got no response. Hurry? Why hurry? Luckily, I hadn't bothered to actually get undressed that night, so all I had to do was throw on a pair of shoes and get moving. Luke's house was only three streets over from mine.

The Vaughns' driveway was packed with cars, and more parked in long lines down both sides of the street. Unlike the rest of the neighborhood, Luke's house had every light on, spilling a flood of yellow light across the hedges and into the front yard. I crept up onto the lawn. The living room curtains were wide open, so I had a good view inside. Dozens of well-dressed people sat on folding chairs arranged in neat lines — women on one side, men on the other — all facing the fireplace in the corner. Mr. and Mrs. Vaughn sat behind them, perched on the very edge of the couch, backs straight as boards, their hands clasped together. She was wearing a black dress buttoned to the neck and he was wearing a black suit and tie. Like everyone else in the room they were rosy-cheeked, ecstatic.

The object of their rapt attention was standing in front of the fireplace between a set of bronze andirons — Pastor Todd. Todd had come into the Vaughns' life after Mr. Vaughn's second DUI, which cost him his job and his driver's license and consigned him to court-appointed nights of drinking burned coffee in church basements with other jittery but determined alcoholics. AA taught Mr. Vaughn that the only way for him to get better was to turn his life over to the care of God. God turned out to be fairly elusive, so when Mr. Vaughn met Pastor Todd as he climbed out of the basement at Bethany Congregational one day, he decided to turn his and his family's lives over to him instead. Not long after that they joined Todd's Council of Deacons, which meant lots of meetings like the one going on in the living room just then.

The Vaughns' own personal Jesus was a waxy-faced body-builder with slicked-back yellow hair and these weird gray eyes that seemed too cold and too intense at the same time. At the moment, those eyes were shut and his arms were raised over his head as he addressed the congregation. I could hear him wailing straight through the glass.

"There are signs of his will everywhere! We have seen forests burn and farmland reduced to blowing sand. We stood witness as whole cities, entire nations, sunk beneath the waves. And now, on our very doorstep, twenty thousand burn in the heat of his divine regard. Are there any among you who doubt that this is but a prelude to *his* glorious return!"

The audience cheered and amened and hallelujahed. Suddenly

the urgency of Luke's text wasn't such a mystery. If I'd been locked up in the middle of all of that I probably would've called in the Navy SEALs for immediate evac.

"Pssst! Weaver!"

Luke stood in the light at the top of their driveway. He was in a black hoodie and jeans. His eyes had the red and puffy look of someone who hadn't slept in days. I raced up the driveway and threw my arms around him. He held me tight and, God, did I need it. Since the moment we'd left prom it was like everything inside me had burst its seams and come unraveled.

"Damn, Vaughn," I said when we separated. "The holy rollers are in rare form tonight. I think Todd's about two minutes away from pulling out the arsenic and the rattlesnakes."

"Come on," he said. "Let's get out of here."

He waved me into the passenger seat of the "limo," then took his place beside me. His door slammed. The engine turned over.

"How's Carter? Does he understand what's happening?"

"Mom and Dad made sure of it," Luke growled. "I had to give him half of one of Mom's tranquilizers to calm him down."

"Got the other half on you by any chance?"

That got me a sliver of a smile. I thought I deserved better, but given the situation, I'd take what I could get. Luke pulled out of the driveway and headed toward Main Street. Most everything was closed up for the night except for Saint Joachim's, Bethany Presbyterian, and three bars. Each one of them was so full their patrons spilled out into the streets. Town faded away and the humpbacked silhouette of Bethany Ridge rose ahead of us. Luke drove up the mountain, then parked in our favorite spot and cut the engine. It clacked and wheezed to a stop. He stared straight ahead, hands gripping the steering wheel, jaw grinding.

I reached for his hand, but before I could touch him he pushed open the driver's-side door and rolled out of it. There was a crunch as his feet hit gravel; then the door slammed shut again. The car dipped as he settled onto the hood, looking out into the forest. I didn't move. Didn't make a sound. It was airless in the car and hot. The insect chatter out in the woods seemed overly loud. I knew I needed to follow Luke outside, needed to find out what was going on, but I couldn't bring myself to open the door, to break that seal. Maybe he needed some time to himself. Maybe if I gave him his space, he'd work through whatever he was feeling, then get back in the car, and we'd drive home, or maybe to the Yankee Clipper for some late-night burgers. I had my keys to the Beth; we could even sneak in and cue up *Blood Canyon* for a private screening. My phone buzzed. It was Dad. He'd noticed I was gone and wanted to make sure everything was okay. Of course I was okay, I wrote back; I was with Luke.

My door squeaked as I opened it. Luke continued staring out into the woods, motionless. I came around the car and situated myself between him and the trees.

"What's going on?"

No answer.

"Luke?"

"Todd had a vision."

A laugh practically exploded out of me. Was *that* what all this was about? "Oh, of *course* he did!" I crowed. "Wait. Don't tell me. It had something to do with his flock's mission to move out to the desert, where they can dodge taxes, collect guns, and procure underage girls. I mean, seriously, why does God's divine plan always seem to center around some middle-aged creeper's access to teen boobies?"

"It wasn't that."

"It was some kind of weird group-sex thing, wasn't it?"

"God told him the end of the world was coming."

Another laugh. "Oh, did he? And did Todd happen to mention to his buddy Jesus that this prediction might've been a little more helpful, I dunno, three days ago?"

Luke ignored me. "He said when the end does come, his flock has to be in Brazil."

"Brazil?"

"Some village out in the rainforest. Todd says that's where the second coming is going to happen."

I stutter-laughed. Clearly, he was messing with me. Luke's expression didn't break.

"Wait, are you not — are you serious? And your parents — I mean, they're not going to do it, right?"

Luke said nothing.

"Oh my God, of *course* they are. Ever since your dad crashed his car into that funeral home, something like this was probably inevitable. But hey! This might actually be a blessing in disguise!" I left my spot and sat beside him on the hood. "If your parents want to traipse into the jungle to find God with a failed used car salesman, more power to 'em! You can stay with me and Dad this summer; then we'll head out in the fall like we planned."

"Lucy —"

"No, it'll be totally fine. Dad loves you. I mean, he might be weird and make you sleep on the couch at first, but he'll come around eventually and we'll —"

"Lucy!"

"What? Luke, this will totally work! We just have to —"

"I'm going with them."

The first and only time I was ever punched in the face was in freshman-year gym class. Cheryl Crain. She'd had it in for me ever since the first day of school, so when I bumped her in the middle of a soccer game, it gave her all the excuse she needed. She came back at me with a punch to the jaw so hard my knees turned to putty and I slumped to the ground. When I came to, Coach Bell was leaning over me. I could see her lips moving, but none of it made any sense. Who was she? Who was I? Was she speaking English? Later she told me that I'd been in shock. It was a defense mechanism, she said, a sort of gray room the mind retreated to when something was going on that was too intense for it to handle. I recognized the concept instantly. It might have been the first time I'd been punched, but I'd been a resident of that room before.

Luke kept talking, but it became this buzz of words swarming around my head. The next thing I knew, I'd left the parking lot and started walking straight down the hill and into the woods. There was no trail, and it was dark, and the forest floor was covered with leaves and rocks and spiny branches that threatened to send me sprawling. I didn't care though. I barreled along. The doors to the gray room were shut tight and locked. Soon I was far enough down the mountain that I couldn't see the stars or the moon or the lights of Bethany. I moved like the walking dead, legs stiff, hands groping at the dark. There was a rush of water below. I decided to follow it.

Eventually the trees broke, revealing a moonlit clearing. The remains of someone's old campsite sat on the bank of a trickling stream. I fell to my knees beside it.

Luke and I had met on the bus. It was halfway through our junior year. Up until then his dad had been driving him. That first day he climbed the stairs past Mr. Crawley, the bus driver, and came to a total standstill, looking down the aisle with what was clearly mounting horror. He didn't look anything like the Luke I'd go to prom with just over a year later. He was easily a foot shorter, with shapeless, floppy hair and a T-shirt-and-jeans wardrobe that I thought of as suburban camo. He would've disappeared completely in any semi-large gathering of teen boys. He looked as lost as he could be.

Crawley yelled at him to move it, so Luke shuffled along, clutching his backpack's strap. To make matters worse, everyone on the bus immediately began the oh-so-familiar dance of moving to the outside seat and refusing to make eye contact. It wasn't entirely about people's natural desire for personal space, either. Everybody knew about Luke's drunk dad and his weirdly intense shut-in of a mom. People think stuff like that is contagious, more than enough for a good old-fashioned shunning. Lucky for him I was there and knew the ropes better than anyone. I sat up a little straighter and scooted over to the window to let him know my seat was a safe harbor. Luke fell in next to me, mumbled a thank-you, then stared at the green vinyl seatback in front of us. We were pulling onto the highway when he said, "You know that scene in *Nightmare on Elm Street Two* where they all get on the school bus, but it turns out Freddy's driving it and they end up in the desert?"

He kinda seemed like he was talking to himself, but I wasn't about to ignore a conversational opening like that.

"Uh . . . yeah. Totally."

Luke turned to me, utterly straight-faced. "I'm starting to think that might be a best-case scenario."

He smiled. That was the first time I got a close-up look at his eyes. Emerald green and speckled with brown. There was a great whoosh, like a jet plane taking off, as we moved from one world into another.

Dead leaves crunched behind me. Luke was standing beside a tree a little ways up the hill, head down, hands stuffed in his pockets.

"They're taking Carter with them," I said. "Aren't they?"

Luke nodded.

"We can talk to somebody," I said. "The police. A lawyer. Or — what is it? — Child Protective Services. He's a kid."

"They're his parents."

"But you could become his guardian. Like we talked about. Or my dad could, or —"

"This isn't just about Carter."

"What do you mean it isn't just about Carter?"

Luke left his spot on the hill and sat cross-legged beside me. There was a beer bottle half-buried in the muck by the stream. He slowly wrenched it back and forth as he talked.

"When I was in middle school we had this rocketry club. Mr. Grayson — he was the club's sponsor — he'd help kids build these rockets and then they'd take them out to Butler Park and set them off. When I mentioned it to my dad, it turned out that when he was my age *he'd* been in a club that did the exact same thing."

Luke freed the bottle he'd been working on. It was intact, clear glass with pebbled ridges down the side of it. Luke carefully wiped the mud off.

"So for the next six months we built rockets together in the garage, and then every weekend we'd meet the rest of the club and spend the day launching them in the park. We'd do it all day long, rocket after rocket, and then Mom would show up with Carter in his stroller and the four of us would all go get pizza together at Mr. Tony's."

When the bottle was clean, Luke set it in the water. It bobbed and spun, then raced away into the dark.

"My family wasn't always messed up," he said. "If there's a chance we can fix things before —"

"Before what?"

He looked at me steadily, like he was willing me to hear his thoughts. I practically exploded.

"Nothing's going to happen! Luke, this will blow over and then you and I will — we'll . . ."

Whatever strength I had left rushed out of me all at once. Luke didn't say anything either; he just looked at me, eyes big as moons and twice as bright. A thousand arguments swirled around in my head, a thousand ways to back him into a corner and stop him from going, but I couldn't give voice to a single one of them. How could I?

We sat by that little stream until the sun started to rise up through the trees. Smoggy haze and low, thin clouds made it look deep red, like molten stone. Its light seeped out and filled the sky.

Luke took my hand; then we climbed back up through the woods and he took me home.

THE GRAY ROOM

SIX

SCHOOL WAS CANCELED for the next few days. When it started up again I told Dad I had the flu and he let me stay home, even though it was painfully obvious I was lying. I spent most of my time in bed with the shades closed and the lights out, alternating between working my way through the movies of Alejandra Aguilar for the hundredth time and engaging in my preferred method of self-torture — obsessively checking my phone for messages. There were plenty of texts from our friends wanting to be supportive and commiserate (I swiped through them all without responding, an evil, bitter voice inside me insisting that this was *my* tragedy, *my* loss, not *ours*), but ever since he'd reached Brazil there'd been nothing from Luke himself. I subscribed to every South American newsfeed I could, but didn't see anything about a bunch of Americans setting off on some wacko pilgrimage up the Amazon. I sent Luke emails and texts and left him voicemails until I was ashamed of myself, and then I did it a little more, and then I stopped.

—

One morning I woke to a silent house. I had no idea what day it was. I felt like I was covered in an inch-thick layer of mildew.

Extreme measures were called for. I peeled myself out of bed and staggered into the bathroom. The shower nozzle screeched as I cranked up the heat. The room filled with steam. My body seized when I stepped into the stall, but I refused to budge. I stood there, hissing through gritted teeth, as the water seared my skin, turning it an angry, lobster red. When I finally couldn't take it anymore I got out and sat naked on the edge of the tub, folded in half over my knees. My skin was so hot it throbbed.

The previous summer we'd taken a day trip to the Finger Lakes. At first it was going to be me and Dad and Bernie and Carol, but Luke conned his parents into believing he was doing this all-day charity thing and joined us. While the four of them went to walk around town I found a little beach and lay out in the sun, hungry for a tan. I must've fallen asleep, because by the time they came back I was sunburned from my forehead to the tips of my toes. On the drive home Dad cranked the AC and Luke laid me out in the back seat and spread aloe over my burning skin. He sang "Rock Lobster" the whole time. I somehow managed to laugh. Wince and laugh. Laugh and wince.

Sitting on the edge of the tub, I imagined the heat from the shower seeping down through my skin and bones and gathering into a ball in the space between my lungs. It would grow hotter and hotter until there was a chain reaction and I was consumed in a flash of light and flame, leaving nothing but a pile of cinders and an ash silhouette on the wall.

I got dressed and went downstairs. The house was empty. Dad must have already gone to work. Habit made me reach for the TV remote, but I knew there wasn't much point. No one, not even our steely goddess of information, Jessica Ramos, had any idea who was responsible for the sixteenth. Theories ranged from the al-Asiri to the Russian Federation to one of a hundred different terrorist groups that could've gotten hold of a nuke after China fell apart — Southeast Asian Communists, Mexican Guerillas, maybe even a group of homegrown white supremacist shit weasels. Our lack of information hadn't stopped us from getting a little sweet revenge though. Without a president or a congress to get in the way, the military enacted a plan that might best be described as, "bomb the shit out of anybody we think even *might* be responsible, plus a few we've been wanting to bomb for a while now anyway." I kept expecting to see retaliatory mushroom clouds of our own, but they never came, which I guess meant they were showing at least a *little* restraint. Still, in every statement the military made you could hear how ready, how *eager* they were to let it rip and damn the consequences.

Meanwhile, the death toll in DC climbed. Twenty thousand. Twenty-five. Thirty. They couldn't even count the number of people injured or the number of people without homes. The National Guard set up refugee camps in Maryland and Virginia.

I didn't have the attention span to read a book or watch another movie, and the hundred-degree heat made taking a walk a no-go. I decided to clean the house. *Why not?* I thought. It worked for Carol.

I started with my room. My seclusion had left the place reeking of stale skin and old hummus. A vinegary shut-in stink. I threw open the windows and got rid of the crusty plates and the half-filled glasses. I stripped the bed and washed the sheets and all my clothes. By then I was on a roll. I attacked the ceiling fan, dusting the blades and the housing, then polishing the wood parts with

Murphy's Oil Soap and the brass fixtures with a metal cleaner so caustic that I had to wear heavy rubber gloves and a surgical mask. Next I scrubbed the walls with a solution of water, baking soda, and bleach, moving from the ceiling down to the baseboards. When I was done with that I hauled our steam cleaner up from the basement. It must have weighed fifty pounds. The muscles in my arms screamed as I pushed it back and forth across my carpet. Every few minutes I had to dump a load of gag-inducing brown water down the sink, refill the reservoir, and start again.

The room gleamed, but I wasn't done. Not even close. On my way out to start on the kitchen, I paused by my closet door. It was closed, had been ever since the night of prom. I hesitated, my hand on the knob, but decided I wasn't ready to deal with what was in there. Not yet.

The kitchen walls looked okay, so I dropped to my knees on the linoleum and started to scrub. I came across a yellowy slick of egg that had congealed under the fridge sometime when I was in grade school. I pulled out a knot of steel wool and went at it so hard that at one point my hand slipped, driving a fingernail into the linoleum and snapping it down to the quick. I sucked away the blood and kept going, my finger stinging with every wipe and polish. I hit the living room next, vacuuming, dusting, cleaning last winter's ashes out of the fireplace. By the time I was done, my shoulders and back were like scraps of paper someone had crumpled up and tossed away.

I was hungry for lunch at that point, but I didn't want to slow down, didn't want to stop, so I went to the second floor and pulled down the folding steps that led to the attic. All the heat of the day had concentrated in that small space, making it feel like I'd stepped into the burning head of a match. I changed into a sports bra and shorts and got to it. There were boxes everywhere, all of them overflowing with crap. Extension cords. Halloween and Christmas decorations. Junk my grandparents had given us. Dad's and Carol's baby things. I tore into every unruly box — consolidating, throwing away, repacking — and then made neat stacks of newly taped-up and labeled boxes at the far end of the attic. I was almost done when I came to one box that was still sealed tight. I turned it around, trying to figure out what it was, and came to a single word printed in Sharpie in Dad's messy handwriting.

It said, simply, *Laila*.

I stood there awhile, breathing heavily, sweating profusely, debating. I bent down and yanked at the edge of the tape. It came up with barely a touch. When I opened the flaps, a smell came out that was like old paper mixed with something sweet and spicy. Sitting on the very top was a dinner plate–size piece of wood. It had been worked into a kind of crest shape and painted powder blue with white and yellow trim. In the center of the crest were hand-painted flowers surrounded by the words *The Weaver household. Laila and Roger. And baby makes three?*

I picked it up and turned it over in my hands. I'd forgotten about it entirely. My Great-Aunt Jean had made it for Mom and Dad as a wedding present. It had hung in our kitchen above the sink when I was little. I vividly remembered trying to climb up onto the counter and grab it so many times that Mom and Dad eventually had to move it to the other side of the room. But it was strange. I didn't remember Dad taking it down and packing it away. Maybe it was one of those things you got so used to seeing that you hardly even noticed when it was gone.

I set the crest aside and went through the rest of the box. It was full of old clothes and knickknacks. A set of empty perfume bottles. Three silver-backed hairbrushes and a mirrored platter. At the very bottom was a huge photo album bound in fake leather with fake gold trim. I had to laugh. Even though Dad had been born at the beginning of the digital age, he'd never been a digital guy. No matter how much I tried to convince him of the absurdity of his position, he stuck to a real camera and real film. Even when it got to the point that he had to beg, borrow, and steal to get film and have it developed, he kept at it. It was a point of pride. Had to respect that, I guess.

I dug out the album and opened it to the first page, marveling, exactly like I had when I was little, at picture after picture of two strangers who'd gone on to become my parents. They'd started the album not long after they met as freshmen at Florida State. She was studying law; he was studying art. Back then, Dad was deeply tanned, with a full head of dark, curly hair and a huge, paint-speckled beard he insisted was fashionable at the time. Mom was a pixie blonde with a round face and pearly skin and a never-ending wardrobe of brightly colored vintage clothes. She'd have looked like a fairy princess come to life if it hadn't been for the combat boots she always wore, and the mischievous gleam in her green eyes. There were pictures of them at the beach and in their dorm rooms. Pictures on campus. Pictures in bars. In almost every one of them they were making goofy, grinning faces, or kissing.

The backgrounds transitioned from sunny beaches to hard winters and New York City skyscrapers while Mom was in law school and Dad worked at a museum. (It always broke my heart to see him in his old artist mode, back before the demands of single Dad-hood forced him into the life of an accountant. He always insisted he was fine with it, happy even, but I couldn't help but feel guilty.) Their wedding was by a lake in the Adirondacks. Mom had wildflowers woven into her hair; Dad looked like he couldn't believe his luck. They moved to Bethany right after Hurricane Enrique turned parts of lower Manhattan and Brooklyn into a kind of American Venice, full of winding canals and buildings only a few years out from slouching into the sea forever. After that the album quickly shifted to pictures of me. Me as a baby. Me as a toddler. Me walking. Me sitting, triumphantly, on the potty. Every single year of my life was represented, right up until my last year of middle school, anyway. After that, the album was blank. I guess we had more on our minds than picture-taking after that. Nothing any of us wanted to remember anyway.

I flipped backwards, pausing on my favorite picture. A close-up of Mom standing beside a Ferris wheel. It was taken at a state fair a year or so before I was born. She was in a strapless dress the color of violets with freckles on her cheeks and her bare shoulders. The wind had made her golden hair into a messy crown. She had a rapidly melting ice cream cone in her fist and was holding it out toward the camera, toward Dad, grinning madly. It was almost hard to believe it was her. I still pictured her as she was years later, after she'd shaved her head, after the gleam in her eyes had been replaced with something hard.

The heat seemed to have risen twenty degrees since I'd come up the stairs. Sweat was rolling off my forehead and making a little puddle at my feet. The cut on my finger stung as the salt poured into it. I packed everything back into Mom's box and put it with the others before closing up the attic, slathering myself with sunscreen, and heading outside.

It was hot and the sky was a pale blue. Down the street, Mrs. Ivanchuk was trimming her rosebushes. I waved to her, then headed for the backyard, instantly freezing at the sight of Luke's car sitting in the driveway. My heart leapt, but then I remembered why it was there. He'd insisted I take it, the morning he left — signed the title over to me and everything. When he handed me the keys, he made me promise I'd use them to cross as many places off our list as I could.

I brushed my hand along the driver's-side door. It was rough due to multiple coats of black spray paint, quickly applied. The sun flared in the windshield. Part of me wanted to dive into the back seat, roll up the windows, and shut the doors, but instead I skirted around it and made a beeline to the shed. I entered the code into the pink combination lock — it was from my old middle school locker, but Dad had appropriated it after one of his chainsaws got stolen — then dragged out the lawnmower, a rake, a shovel, a large keg of weed killer, several small gardening tools, and a wheelbarrow full of black mulch.

I wiped the sweat from my forehead and got to work.

—

When Dad got home he found me collapsed on my back in the front yard.

"You, uh, you okay there, Goose?"

My head was throbbing. I grunted something semi-coherent. Dad had his briefcase in one hand and a large shopping bag in the other. He put them down on the grass and sat next to me.

"Seems like you got a little work done today."

I groaned. Dad twisted around and looked back at the shed.

"Lucy, did you — did you wash the *lawnmower?*"

"Had to," I said. "Dirty."

Dad took off his tie, then picked at the freshly cut grass between his knees. "Guess you haven't heard anything more from —"

"Uhn-uh." I cut him off before he could say the name. There was nothing left in our house to clean, and I was afraid that if I let him finish, Mr. Giolotti might come downstairs to find me steam-cleaning his drapes.

"You know," Dad said, "I was reading that all the cell towers are overloaded, and there's been some hacking, I guess. A lot of networks are down. They thought they fixed it, but, you know, international calls."

He must have known how lame that sounded, since he abruptly switched direction.

"Hey! How about we get you up?"

"Ungh-ay."

Dad put his arm under my shoulders and hauled me to a sitting position. My head did a loop-de-loop. Everything started to go dim, but I took a breath and the world came rushing back in. I looked down at myself. I was covered in sweat and dirt and grass clippings.

"Bet you could use some dinner," he said. "Pasta?"

I nodded. "Are Carol and Bernie coming?"

Dad shook his head. "They're dealing with some stuff for Bernie's mom."

"She all right?"

"Fine," Dad answered briskly. "They're coming over Monday night. Dinner in an hour?"

I nodded weakly. Dad swung the shopping bag over his shoulder and headed up the walk.

"Oh, and hey," he said, pausing at the door. "We also have to talk about school. It's fine that you've been out, but any more absences and I think I'll get one of those 'Get your daughter to school or we'll call the cops' letters. So Monday morning, everything goes back to normal, okay?"

I nodded. The screen door squeaked open and shut. A few minutes later, Jessica Ramos's voice filtered out into the front yard.

"The al-Asiri Empire promised severe retaliation today as American and allied drones continued to pound their strongholds in Saudi Arabia and Yemen. Meanwhile, The Russian Federation announced their intention to resume nuclear missile tests in response to what they're calling the West's heightened aggression . . ."

Her voice mixed with the clatter of pots and pans as Dad started dinner. I looked out over Mr. Giolotti's house and up into the blackening sky.

Yeah, right, I thought. *Everything goes back to normal.*

SEVEN

MONDAY CAME. I wouldn't say I exactly bounded down the stairs that morning, but as soon as I woke up I found myself weirdly looking forward to going back to school. Sit at a desk. Listen to a lecture. Move to another room when a bell rings. Even the prospect of gummy lunchroom pizza and soggy fries was strangely comforting.

Dad was usually gone by the time I left for school, but when I passed his home office that morning the door was shut and there were sounds of movement coming from inside. Weird. Even when he worked at home he rarely used the office, preferring to hang out on the couch downstairs. I went to knock and was struck by an odd smell. It was clean and sharp.

"Uh . . . Dad?" There was a *tra-thump* of something falling; then Dad's voice came back, shaky and a little muffled "Yeah. Hey! Good morning."

"What're you doing? What's that smell?"

The door flew open. Dad came out and closed it behind him. His clothes were disheveled and he looked like he hadn't slept.

"You okay?"

"Fine. Good. Yeah. I spilled some coffee on the wall and

started to paint over the stain, but then the color was a little off so now I have to repaint the whole office. It's a mess in there."

"You need help?"

"No. Thanks. I'm good. Gonna finish this up, then get to work. In fact, I better hustle. And you better get to school." He edged the door to the office open and was easing back into it. "Remember, dinner with Carol and Bernie tonight!"

"Uh, yeah. Okay. I'll —"

He was inside with the door shut before I could finish. There was a muffled shout of "Have a good day" and then more unidentifiable sounds. I backed away, slightly unsettled. Dad was like clockwork. Had been since I was little. He worked. He came home. He made dinner. He went to bed. Worry twisted around in my gut, but I cut it off. The whole world was currently having one big collective freak-out; why should good ol' Roger Weaver be excluded?

I went downstairs, grabbed Luke's keys, then stepped out the front door. Not even eight a.m. and already it was nearly a hundred degrees. Luke's car sat in the driveway like some massive black hole. The windows gleamed in the sun. Out of habit, I headed for the passenger side, but course-corrected halfway there and threw open the driver's-side door. The smell of the car hit me in a wave. Oil. Hot plastic. The remnants of a hundred junk-food meals eaten on the fly. The musk of old clothes balled up and discarded on the back-seat floorboards. It made me weak in the knees. Ever since Luke had gotten the car at the end of our junior year, I'd ridden in it to school every morning, slumped down in my seat, fiddling with the music while he drove. The thought of getting in and driving all the way to school alone in that car made me feel like I couldn't breathe. I darted my hand inside and swiped Luke's sunglasses off the dash. With them on, the world turned a shade dimmer. Blunted. Manageable.

I slammed the door and started the walk to school.

—

Halfway there, I was dripping with sweat and my caffeine levels were dangerously low, so I stopped by Bethany Square and got an iced coffee. I figured school could wait awhile. After that I walked around aimlessly for another hour or so, eventually ending up across the street from Saint Joachim's. The front doors were open and the pews were nearly full.

I crossed the street for a closer look. Candles glimmered in the cave-like church, casting a glow over a handsome young priest who stood at the pulpit. His voice was buttery warm. I was about to go inside, figuring I'd sit in the back and let that voice lull me to sleep, but I got distracted by the sound of glass breaking somewhere behind me. Across the street from the church was Jimmy's Irish Pub, door shut and windows dark. A narrow alley ran alongside it. There it was again: a crash, like a sheet of plate glass breaking. This time it was followed by a laugh. Someone appeared in the gap of the alleyway, arms raised over his head, hopping up on his tippy-toes.

It was Toby Wolfowitz. Because of our names, we had the same homeroom, which made him one of those people you aren't really friends with but who's always had a weird kind of presence in your life. Someone you're aware of without actually knowing. He was big, easily over six feet. Not skinny, but not athletic, either.

He always wore those blue Dickies pants that rockabilly guys and car mechanics liked, along with engineer boots and one faded band T-shirt or another. Since the last time I'd seen him, he'd shaved off every scrap of his shoulder-length blond hair, turning his head into a gleaming white globe.

Toby scooped up a rock off the ground and hurled it out of sight. There was another crash and he let out a whoop. What the hell was he doing?

I slipped off Luke's sunglasses as I made my way down the alley to a small courtyard. It wasn't much more than a couple dumpsters sitting on a stretch of filthy concrete. The air was thick with the smell of old beer and even older cooking grease. On the far side, Toby had propped five sheets of glass against a brick wall. They stood side by side, each one about the size of a coffee table. Three more were in shards next to them. He turned when I stepped out of the alley.

"Oh. Hey, Weaver. How you doing?"

He said it like we had just run into each other in the library or something.

"Uh, fine. How *you* doing, Toby?"

He shrugged. "You know. Want a beer?"

He pointed to a half-empty case on the ground by one of the dumpsters.

I held up my iced coffee. "I'm good. But don't let me stop you."

"Suit yourself."

Toby wound up, then threw another rock at one of the panes of glass. It practically exploded.

"So where'd the glass come from?"

"Don't know," he said as he hunted around for more rocks. "It was here when I woke up."

"You slept in the bar last night?"

"No, in the alley."

"In *this* alley?"

He chuckled to himself. "Yeah, I got pretty hammered, then stayed up until, like, three a.m. talking transcendentalism with this French biker dude. Jimmy has a couch in his office, but it was a nice night with the stars and all, so I slept out here."

Another pane of glass exploded. It was strangely musical, pretty once you got past the shock of it.

"So you woke up in the alley, found these panes of glass, and decided to throw rocks at them."

Toby drained his beer and tossed the empty into a dumpster. "You want a go?"

"Who? Me? No."

"You sure?" Toby stood there, bouncing a rock in his hand, grinning. That's when I noticed that he'd shaved not only his head, but his eyebrows too. He was utterly hairless. You'd think it would've made him look weird or off-putting, but all it did was highlight his startling blue eyes. It was like someone had hooked up jumper cables to his neck and sent a million volts of electricity running through them. I looked from him to the remaining panes of glass.

"Well, whose glass is it?" I asked. "Jimmy's?"

"No idea."

"Well, someone must want it. Right?"

"Dunno. Maybe."

I glanced down the alley behind me. Nobody on the sidewalk or the street. The crash of the breaking glass replayed in the back of my mind. I put down my coffee and took the rock out of Toby's hand. He jumped back, delighted, and leaned over with his hands on his thighs, watching me like a coach.

"Straight down the middle, Weaver. Hard as you can." The sheet of glass gleamed. I rotated the rock in my hand. A little voice started up inside me, insisting that this was stupid, that I needed to leave. It was making some decent arguments, but in the end, I cocked my arm and let the rock fly. It streaked across the courtyard and hit the glass dead center. Bright shards exploded and rained down on the concrete.

"Nice!" Toby shouted. "Here. Do another one."

He tossed me another rock and I threw that one too. The next sheet of glass cut neatly in half. The top part seemed to hover for a split second and then it hit the concrete and broke into a thousand pieces. Toby took out the last one with a perfectly placed shot. I have to admit I was a little jealous; it was like he got to eat the last cookie in the package. He grabbed another beer and chugged it. The hum ran from the top of my head all the way down to my fingertips and there was a weird ache in my right arm, like a craving. Why had it felt so good?

Toby broke me out of my trance. "We should go check out those model homes they put up down on Azalea Street."

"What? Why?"

He grinned, devilishly. He had the rest of the beer in one hand and a huge rock in the other.

"Oh! No, I — no. You go ahead though."

"You sure?"

I heard glass shatter again. It was like a song I couldn't get out of my head. I swallowed hard. "Yeah. Definitely."

"Okay," he said, and then, "You want to take a ballroom dance class with me?"

I stared at him. Had I misheard that? I rewound the movie in my head and listened to it again. Nope. He'd definitely just asked me if I wanted to take a ballroom dance class with him. And now he was standing there waiting for an answer. All I could say was, "Uh . . ."

"See, I saw this movie about it when I was a kid and ever since then I've been sort of obsessed with ballroom dance. The moves. The outfits. But I always kept my desire buried deep inside of me because, you know, ballroom dance. Who does that? But now that the world's probably going to blow up I figured it might be my last chance. And I thought you might be a fun person to try it with. It doesn't have to be a big deal. There's a class down at the rec center. It's on Tuesdays and Thursdays. At six thirty."

He stood there, waiting patiently, his blue eyes bright and eager as a puppy's.

"I, uh, think I'm going to pass, Toby," I finally said. "But thanks."

"No problem. If you change your mind, you know where to find me."

Toby ambled down the alley and out to the street, tossing the rock in the air and whistling as he went. Once he was gone, the courtyard was silent. The mounds of broken glass sat on the greasy concrete, glittering in the sun. I knelt beside them and ran my finger along one of the pieces, hard enough to feel the edge but not enough to break the skin. I didn't know why, but it quieted something inside me, made me peaceful in a way I hadn't felt in days. I looked around for something else to break.

Lights came on inside the shop next door to Jimmy's. Voices spoke in Spanish. I hustled out of the courtyard and into the alley. For some reason I expected things to be different when I emerged onto Main Street, but it was all exactly as I'd left it. The street was still empty. Most of the stores were still closed. The priest was still at his pulpit, arms out, smile wide. I couldn't hear what he was saying, though. My ears were filled with the crash of broken glass.

—

Not long after that, I found myself sitting alone on a hillside out behind the school. My low-grade anticipation had ended roughly ten minutes after I'd walked in the door. The place was museum quiet. Cemetery quiet. In room after room, teachers taught their lessons while well-behaved kids sat at their desks, taking notes and asking perceptive questions. Even Tilly Jacobs, usually a varsity level class skipper and time waster, was sitting in the front row of her Trig class scrawling notes like her life depended on it.

Announcements were piped in over the loudspeakers. A blood drive for DC in the cafeteria during all lunch periods. A change in venue for a meeting of the yearbook committee. Sure, there were anomalies, a few blank-eyed hallway wanderers, a few bathroom stall criers, but overall it was aggressively normal, *desperately* normal. Even though that was exactly what I'd wanted when I'd gotten up that morning, it made me feel like someone's hands were wrapped around my throat. Hungry for air, I'd ducked out one of the back doors near the old metal shop and ended up on a weedy mound that ran between the soccer field and the woods that surrounded the school.

Objectively speaking, it was a fairly crappy spot. The ground was hard and the thin tree cover meant there was virtually no protection against the hundred-degree heat. When the rare breeze blew, it carried with it the brutal stink of an overflowing dumpster out near the teachers' parking lot. All of that was worth it, though, since it meant I was almost completely alone. Just me and a foursome of pot-toking neo-hippies playing Hacky Sack out in the middle of the field.

I covered myself with SPF one million sunscreen and hid my eyes behind the mirrored lenses of Luke's sunglasses. I figured I'd watch something on my phone, or maybe try to nap, but after a few minutes there was this sharp tug inside of me and I ended up swiping between various newsfeeds on my phone. I didn't really *want* to look, but it was like when you were a little kid and you had a loose tooth. Your tongue went to it no matter what, pushing and probing, wondering if that was the moment it would fall out for good.

"Nearly two hundred US soldiers were killed yesterday when a truck packed with explosives crashed into a mess hall at a military base in Bulgaria. Further reports of—"

swipe

"—despite allied bombing, al-Asiri forces are reported to be massing near the Iranian border in a show of—"

swipe

"— *gunmen believed to be associated with the increasingly popular, fascist New Dawn party broke into a refugee camp outside Paris early this morning and killed nearly three hundred* —"

swipe

"— *Russian President Vladimir Orokov has officially opened diplomatic talks with the al-Asiri empire, suggesting that an alliance between the two countries will be a vital check against what he calls unnecessary US and European aggression* —"

I lost myself in the madness. Sometime later the double doors by the metal shop were flung open. I stiffened, guessing it would be one of the campus security guys, come to chase me and the Hacky Sackers back to class. But it wasn't. It was another refugee from academia. He came straight across the field, striding purposefully. I lowered my sunglasses and could make out blocks of color through the rippling waves of heat. Khaki pants. Sky-blue button-down. Black hair. Red backpack. He threw the pack down by the goalpost, then dropped to his knees and started tearing through it. Behind me, someone shouted,

"Yo! Anybody down for more Hacky?"

While I'd been looking at the news the stoners had retreated to the woods for a nap. They roused themselves and staggered back onto the field. There was a good deal of bumbling, and then they found a spot barely five feet away from me, chuckling it up and kicking that stupid little ball back and forth. When one of them started a Bob Marley sing-along, I grabbed my things and headed for a bit of shade at the far end of the field. My new perch brought me a little closer to the goalpost and the kid in the blue shirt. He'd pulled a thick textbook and a pad of paper from his backpack and was hunched over them, pen in hand, writing feverishly. He was so intense about it that it was almost impossible not to watch. He looked familiar, but I was having trouble placing him.

It might've been because he was such a mess. His black hair was sticking up in random spikes and swirls, like he'd slept on it for three nights running. And then there were his clothes. They were nice enough — expensive, even — but badly rumpled and dotted with sweat marks that looked like they hadn't necessarily been deposited that day. There was a stain on his collar. Ketchup. Maybe jelly. He'd clearly tried to wash it off, but it was still there.

Ba-da-bump, ba-da-bump, ba-da-bump-BA-BA!

The kid reached into his pocket and pulled out his phone. After checking the ID he silenced it and dropped it to the ground. Then he ripped out the page he'd been working on, crumpled it up, and threw it into his backpack with a growled "god*damn* it." His ringtone replayed in my head, *Ba-da-bump, ba-da-bump, ba-da-bump-BA-BA. Ba-da-bump, ba-da-bump, ba-da-bump-BA-BA,* and something clicked. The night of the prom. The first phone I heard ringing. Was that Jay Karras? It didn't seem possible, but another look confirmed it. It was him. Mr. Straight A's, Mr. Student Government, with his pressed clothes and tidy hair and firm handshake, had been reduced to a filthy wreck sitting in the dirt and scribbling in a grubby little notebook.

I settled in and watched. He'd fill a page, then rip it out and throw it away with a curse before starting again. He did it over and over. Was he taking notes? If so, on what? And if he wanted to study so bad why wasn't he inside with the rest of the zombies?

Inside the building, bells rang. One period moved into the

next. Jay's sky-blue shirt turned navy with sweat. Finally, he shut the notebook and, in what looked like a fit of frustration, hurled it onto the field. It landed not far from where the Hacky Sackers sat, loose-limbed and grinning, passing around a bowl, their white-boy dreads swinging behind them.

Eventually, the bell rang for the end of the day. I gathered my things and set out across the fried yellow grass of the soccer field. Jay had collapsed onto his back, eyes shut. He looked even worse close-up. Patchy stubble on his cheeks. Skin gone the color of old bologna. An angry sunburn was forming on his forehead and along the bridge of his nose, which had a slight bend to it, like it had been broken once and was now slouching forever to the left. Not being completely heartless, I dug a tube of sunscreen out of my bag and tossed it onto his chest. He woke with a start, looking pissed.

"It's sunscreen, dummy. If you lie there any longer you're going to turn into beef jerky."

Jay sat up, but didn't say a word. Not so much as a grunt of thanks. He tore the cap off the tube and squirted a puddle of lotion into his hands. He rubbed it all over his face and arms, wincing when he touched the burns that were already there.

"What are you doing out here, anyway?" I asked.

"Nothing."

"Doesn't look like nothing."

Jay put the cap back on the tube and thrust it out to me without meeting my eyes. "I want to be alone. Okay?"

Out on the other side of school, bus engines started turning over. I snatched the sunscreen out of his hand.

"Your wish is my command," I said, adding, in my head, *asshole*.

When I reached the building and opened the door, I took one last look behind me and caught Jay scurrying out into the soccer field to retrieve his notebook. Once he had it, he retreated to his spot by the goalpost and continued to write furiously.

EIGHT

OUR DINNER with Bernie and Carol was supposed to be something simple, but as soon as they arrived, a piece of news broke that changed the whole thing into a big celebration. Turned out we had ourselves a new president.

"He walked *right* up to General Barrington's headquarters in Maryland," Dad recapped for what seemed like the twenty-third time, wine sloshing in his glass, as we sat around the table. "Right up to the front gates! Knocked on the guardhouse door."

Dad raised his fist as if knocking on an invisible door. He put on a shy, hesitant voice.

"Uh, excuse me, my name's Hank Chin and I think I'm, well, I think maybe I'm the president?"

The three of them shrieked with laughter, so sudden and so loud it was like an icepick shoved in my ear canal. Dad and Bernie had already dispatched one bottle of chardonnay and were working on a second. Their faces were pink and jolly. Dad raised his glass.

"To Henry Paul Chin, fifty-first president of the United States."

"Hear, hear!"

Glasses clinked.

"What was he the secretary of again?" Carol asked as Bernie topped off her glass with sparkling cider.

"Health and Human Services," Bernie said. "Eleventh in the line of succession. He was in Chicago when the bomb went off."

"But his wife and his son . . ."

Bernie nodded grimly. "Both in DC."

"That poor man," Carol said. "No wonder it took him so long to show up."

Dad scoffed. "That and he was probably scared of Barrington."

"Oh, come on," Bernie said. "I served with people who knew Barrington. They said he was an all right guy."

"An all right guy who *really* likes bombing things."

"The al-Asiri want to invade Iran, Roger. If those lunatics take Tehran they'll have a nuclear arsenal. Do you want that?"

"No, but what I'm saying is, Barrington's deciding these things all on his own. Who elected him?"

"It's *not* all on his own," Bernie said. "The other generals agreed."

"Oh, well! The other generals agreed. I feel so much better knowing that a military junta is in charge. We're gonna fit right in with those New Dawn fascist assholes. Sis, help me out here."

Carol didn't look up from the table. "I don't like it either, but things are different now. After the sixteenth —"

"Carol, we still don't even know who planted the bomb in DC."

"Oh, please."

"We don't! We *think* we do, but —"

They kept going, but I couldn't take it anymore. A vise was

tightening around my brainstem. I poked at my dinner with the back of my knife. Dad's chicken had always been one of our favorites, but as I sat at the table that night, temple throbbing due to forced good cheer, it looked like someone's spleen that had been removed, partially dissected, and covered in a creamy dill sauce. My chair squeaked as I pushed back from the table.

"Can I be excused, please?"

Everyone turned to me. Carol lowered her glass. "What's wrong, Luce?"

"Nothing. I—"

"You haven't eaten a bite," Dad said. "It's your favorite!"

"I'm not—"

Dad hopped out of his seat, staggering a little. "Hey! If you're not feeling the chicken, let me get you something else. Anything you want. Seriously. Your call. It's a celebration!"

"I'm fine. Dad, really. I just want to—"

"Oh! I know! Grilled cheese!"

Bernie piped up. "Rog, you are far from the condition where you should be grilling anything. You probably shouldn't even be standing right now."

Dad blew a wet raspberry in her direction, then stuck one finger in the air like some kind of old-timey orator.

"Consider, if you will, the humble grilled cheese. You say it is a mere sandwich, but I say it is a monument to the ingenuity of mankind. For what is the grilled cheese but the ultimate expression of the domestication of animals, the advent of agriculture, and the harnessing of fire? It's the history of our species laid out on a plate, our rise from savagery into the warm and gooey embrace of civilization. They should put one in the Smithsonian. The Hall of Sandwiches! Damn, now that I think about it, I'm making one for myself, too."

Dad stumbled into the kitchen, and there was a crash of pans. Bernie laughed and shook her head.

"Sorry, Goose. We get a little rowdy."

"We're just relieved," Carol said. "After everything that's been going on, a bit of normalcy is precisely what the doctor ordered. But, as usual, I'm glad your father left, because Bernie and I wanted to talk to you."

Carol swung her chair around to be closer to mine. Bernie leaned in too. I was surrounded.

"We know it's a difficult time," Bernie said. "With everything that's happened, you must be feeling —"

"I'm fine," I snapped, dreading the prospect of my aunt telling me how I was feeling. "Just tired, that's all. Maybe I'll go lie down. Okay?"

Carol took my hand to stop me from leaving. "Me and Bernie and your dad, we figured you've probably been thinking a lot about what you'll do in the fall now that things, well, now that things have changed so much."

Bernie chimed in. "We know you don't really have a focus, like a career kind of focus. But there's still time for college, you know. Maybe not a four-year school, but you could sign up for community college and then transfer."

Carol nodded. "It could give you time to explore. Figure out what you want to do. Who you are."

"Guys, I don't want to go to community college."

"Then maybe some kind of internship," Carol offered. "With your dad or with me. Not that you want to do what we do necessarily, but to start getting some experience. And who knows, you might even get inspired." She leaned in close, head tilted with concern. "All we're saying is, we know how scary this has been, Luce. But we're going to get through it together. God knows we've done it before, right?"

"Things are going to start getting back to normal now," Bernie said.

"Exactly," Carol agreed. "And we know that Luke leaving has made all of this even harder, but we want to make sure you know that there are good things waiting for you on the other side of *all* of this, *great* things even, and —"

"God! How fucking *stupid* do you people think I am?"

As soon as the words left my mouth, all noise in the house ceased at once. You would have thought I'd punched Carol in the jaw. I couldn't help it. Everything that had been building up in me over the past few days had finally exploded.

Bernie recovered first. "No one thinks you're stupid, Lucy. We think —"

"What? That some guy you'd never even *heard* of before today is going to snap his fingers and magically fix everything?"

"No, we —"

"The world has been fucked since you people were in kindergarten and you didn't do shit about it!"

"Lucy!"

Before they could say another word, I headed for the front door. Behind me, Bernie shouted my name and then Dad did too. I ignored them, grabbing my phone and the keys to Luke's car on my way out.

"Where are you going? Lucy! Come back here! We're not done!"

"Yes, we are!"

I let the door slam behind me as I ran to the car. Dad charged out of the house and onto the front steps.

"Lucy Rose Weaver!"

I threw myself into the driver's seat and cranked the engine. Dad yelled my name again. I peeled out of the driveway. I didn't have a plan at first. I just drove, slaloming from street to street and neighborhood to neighborhood. Everything came at me in a hyperreal blur timed to the throbbing in my head. The lights were all extra bright, and the lines of houses and shops were like cut glass. It hurt to look at them. Eventually it all got to be too much and I found myself parked on some side street where nothing looked familiar. I let my head fall against the seat, trying to breathe but feeling like there was a steel cage locked around my chest.

I swear, Weaver, sometimes you are such an asshole.

Luke's voice was so clear in my head that it was like he was sitting beside me. When I turned, I could even see him there with his feet kicked up on the dash, popping Peanut M&M's into his mouth while the wind mussed his already-mussed hair.

They're out of their goddamn minds! I countered.

Who the hell isn't? Dream Luke chuckled. *You?*

I'm the only one who's not living in a fantasy land. Community college? Seriously? That's their genius plan? That's where their minds are going in the middle of all of this?

Luce —

And they're bringing a baby into this nightmare. A baby!

They're doing what they think is best, Luke said. *It's all anyone can do.*

Even if what they think is best is total bullshit?

Yes. Even if it's what Lucy Weaver of Bethany, New York, thinks is total bullshit.

Is that what you did? I demanded. *What you thought was best?*

In my mind Luke turned away from me, stung, looking out the window and into the dark for a long time. I wanted Dream Luke to admit that he had made a terrible mistake, that he and Carter should have stayed with me. But Dream Luke was beyond my power, just like the real one.

My phone pinged. There were four texts — three from Dad, one from Carol.

Dad: Walking out was not acceptable. We need to know where you are, Lucy.

Dad: That wasn't like you at all. You really hurt your aunts' feelings.

Dad: Call me, Lucy.

Carol: Your father is worried sick. Call us, Lucy.

I could imagine Dad at home on the couch, bracketed by Carol and Bernie, sending messages out into the void, praying that someone would tell him that everything was okay, that his world wasn't broken, only bent a little. Easily repaired. That everything would be back like it was soon enough. My thumb hovered over the keys, but as much as part of me wanted to give that to him, and to Carol and Bernie, I couldn't bring myself to lie.

I tried to think of somewhere to go, something to do, but nothing seemed right. I sure as hell wasn't going home. I closed my messages and scrolled through my contacts, but I realized that most of them were actually Luke's friends, not mine. I deleted them one by one. Tilly Jacobs. Carrie Dunn. Jim and Navi. Ernie Wright. Gone. When I was finished, one contact remained. It sat there in front of me, glowing. I didn't know if the number I had would still work, I hadn't used it in years, but as I stared at the name, a weird feeling of rightness settled around it and I knew I had to try.

need to meet asap, I typed. yankee clipper. 10 mins. emergency!

It seemed like forever until those three little dots popped up, then turned to words.

Lucy? Uh . . . ok. See you there. 10 min

I dropped the phone, put the car in drive, and took off.

NINE

THE YANKEE CLIPPER was nearly deserted when I got there, just an elderly couple at a back table and some girl in a red hoodie who was staring up at a TV behind the counter. A white-haired news guy was reading the headlines.

". . . and on the same night as the new president's first speech, deadly explosions rocked the streets of Mumbai. The Indian Prime Minister is blaming the attack on Pakistani terrorists who found inspiration, he says, in the recent attack on Washington DC . . ."

I took a booth by the window and kept an eye on the street. It was impossible to sit still; the idea I'd had on the way over was so good my bloodstream was filled with firecrackers. I drummed my fingers against my notebook and tapped my feet. A waitress brought over a pot of coffee. The last thing I needed was caffeine, but I nodded and she filled my cup. I threw it back, wincing as the burned sludge hit my stomach.

"Lucy?"

The girl in the red hoodie crossed the diner and dropped into my booth across from me

"Uh, I'm actually waiting for someone, but —"

She pulled back her hood, revealing a peaches-and-cream face and an upturned nose. "You text me out of nowhere and tell me to meet you here because it's an emergency. And then you walk in, look right at me, and go sit at another table. What the hell, Weaver?"

The engine revving in my gut crashed to a halt. I squinted across the table.

"*Jenna?*"

"Uh, *yeah.*"

The world went screwy for a second and then snapped back into focus. The shape of her face said it was definitely Jenna Pearl, but nothing else did. Her vampire complexion was gone, replaced with a farm-girl glow. No black eye shadow, black eyeliner, or black lipstick. Her hair was still dyed but it was skull-free, gathered up in a loose ponytail. Her clothes were different too. No more goth dominatrix wear: she was in a ragged pair of camo shorts and a tank top. The hoodie looked like something you'd get at Target.

"What, uh, what happened to you?"

"Nothing happened to me."

"But —"

The waitress returned and slid a plate of curly fries and a Coke between us. Jenna squirted a mound of ketchup and dredged some up with one of the fries.

"So, what's the emergency?"

I stammered for a second, unable to get over the feeling that I'd fallen into a scene from *Dawn of the Body Thieves*. I fumbled with my pen and notebook. Where was I? What had I planned to say?

"Uh, okay. Right. So. I was thinking about how we were

talking at prom, which was great, by the way, and how it sounded like you weren't a hundred percent sure what you wanted to do next. After making a few hundred million dollars, I mean."

Jenna ate another fry. "Right."

"Well, it gave me an idea."

"What idea?"

I turned the open notebook around to face her. "Ta-da!"

Jenna looked at me quizzically, then pulled the book to her. The waitress swung by and warmed my coffee. I loaded it up with cream and sugar. While Jenna read, I turned toward the TV. Men and women crowded a city's streets, wailing as bodies on stretchers were carted out of a demolished building. Two hundred and eighty-three dead. The picture switched to green-tinted video, strangely pretty, of missiles being launched from the deck of a ship.

There was a soft clap as Jenna closed the book. She looked like she was about to say something, but I jumped in before she could.

"Okay, see, I was thinking about when we were kids," I said. "How we would hang out all the time and watch movies and stuff? Movies *no one* watched but me and you. But then we kinda went different ways. Not that those ways were bad, necessarily, but I think maybe sometimes when we think we're getting on track, what we're really doing is getting off track. You know what I mean?"

Jenna laid the book on the table and eased back in the booth. She took a sip of her Coke. "I heard about Luke."

My caffeine-fueled heart punched me in the chest. I dug the tip of my spoon into the tabletop.

"Yeah, well, you know. He had things he had to do."

"You hear from him?"

I forced out a small laugh. "Boy can't stop texting. It's a real problem."

"Lucy—"

"He made a choice," I said. "Right? There was choice A and choice B and he went with B. That's the way things are. No hard feelings. And, hey, maybe the fact that he made the choice he did says something. Like maybe we weren't really as compatible as we always seemed. Or it wasn't meant to be. You know?"

Jenna nodded, her eyes locked on mine. "And now you want *me* to come with you," she said. "On this trip."

I practically leapt across the table. "Think how amazing it would be! Me and you? On the road together?" I grabbed the notebook and started tearing through the pages. "Look. I remember how you said you always wanted to go to that Winchester Mystery House where there are all those fake rooms and ghosts and stuff. Oh! And Roswell, New Mexico. There's this whole alien museum down there and it's supposed to be so cool."

"Lucy—"

"Wait a second. I have to show you this. This is amazing. In California there's a whole—"

Jenna laid her hand down on mine, pinning the open notebook to the table.

"Lucy, we've barely talked since the eighth grade."

"Exactly! That's the whole point!"

"You can't just *summon* me here and then start going off about how we're going to travel the world together. What? Do you think we'll be besties like we were when we were kids? Do each other's hair and giggle about boys?"

"When the hell did we ever giggle about boys?"

Jenna dropped a handful of bills on the table. "Look, it was great seeing you at prom and talking again. Seriously. And I wish you all the luck in the world, okay? I hope you have a truly amazing time. But I have to go."

"Jenna, wait!"

She was out the door and a block away by the time I caught up with her. I grabbed her shoulder and spun her around.

"Are you seriously going to go make a bunch of money, then head off to college? *Now?*"

"No."

"Then what?"

Farther down the block, two college-age guys stepped out of a mud-splattered Land Rover. One of them shouted, "Jenna! Let's go!"

She waved to them, then turned back to me. "I'm going to do something useful," she said.

I reached for her as she started to leave. "Jenna. Wait."

"Sorry, Lucy, I have to go. Enjoy being a tourist."

Jenna hurried down the sidewalk toward the guys. They opened the back door to the Land Rover and ushered her in. A second later they took their places in the front and drove away.

—

I left Bethany without a destination in mind, simply following the streams of mostly autonomous traffic until they led me out toward this car-dealership-and-chain-restaurant hellscape way out on the edge of town. While most people sat back and read or watched movies projected on the inside of their windshields, I swerved and weaved my way through traffic, gunning the engine to get through yellow lights and ignoring the blaring, computer-generated horns all around me. After a while, the shops petered out, replaced by tracts of boarded-up buildings and warehouses. At one point, I passed a knot of fire engines, ten of them at least, parked on the side of the road. Their emergency lights filled the sky with an ominous red glow. I slowed and a cop waved me by. As I rolled past the trucks, a vast, low building appeared. It was a shuttered mall, maybe, or an old office park, and it was entirely engulfed in flames. I could feel the heat through my windows and smell the thick, slightly sweet smoke. The firefighters had all their hoses focused on it, sending fountains of water in high arcs, but it didn't seem to be doing a bit of good. A section of wall crumbled as I passed, sending the flames even higher.

Soon that was gone too and I was on a quiet road turning through the trees. No signs. No exits. No cars in either direction. All I could see were my own headlights wedging open the darkness ahead.

It occurred to me that I could keep going. Why not? I had my phone; I had the clothes on my back. The little bit of money Luke and I managed to squirrel away was safe in the bank. I pressed down on the accelerator. The engine strained for a second, then got with the program and dropped into a steady hum. Sixty miles an hour. Seventy. Trees whipped by.

Jenna Pearl didn't know a goddamn thing. Luke and I didn't want to be fucking tourists. We'd spent our entire lives watching the world fall apart, watching cities drown and forests burn and farms that seemed to stretch from horizon to horizon turn into deserts. We watched people starve and we watched them tear each other to shreds over bits of land and puddles of water. What we'd learned was that colleges and careers and making money was pointless, a stupid game people played because they thought that's what they were supposed to do. Luke and I didn't fall for it. Not for a second. We were going to see everything we could see, and do everything we could do, before it was too late, before it was all gone. We were going to live. Wasn't that important too? Wasn't that worthwhile?

At eighty miles an hour, deep vibrations moved up from the tires, through the frame of the car, and into my chest. The guardrail beside me became a blur. Maybe as long as I kept the pedal down I'd keep going faster and faster. A hundred miles an hour. Two hundred. Three. Eventually I'd break the sound barrier and then the speed of light. Maybe I'd find that there was another barrier out there too, one that no one had ever seen before. And if I broke that, what then? Where would I end up?

A horn sounded. I was halfway across the center line with a tractor-trailer barreling right at me. There was no window at the front of the rig and no driver, just a flat gray wall of plastic and steel. The horn blared again and I wrenched the steering wheel to the right. All I remember of what came next is the whoosh of the truck as it rocketed by, then the car shooting off the road toward a field. I screamed and yanked the wheel again, kicking off a long, panicked slide, followed by a crash of glass and metal. The car jolted to a stop, throwing me forward until my seat belt jerked me back hard and knocked the wind out of me.

After that there was the sound of my own breathing and the engine's *tick-tack-tick* death rattle. I fumbled with the seat belt, got it off, then threw my shoulder into the door. It popped open and sent me tumbling into the weeds. I got up and managed to walk a few steps before my knees turned to rubber and I went down hard on my ass.

The clouds shifted, letting a little moonlight through. I was sitting in the middle of a field about twenty feet from the edge of the highway. There were some trees in the distance and a low fence. I crawled toward the front of the car, looking for what it was that I'd hit. I found a gnarled tree stump, two feet high and as fat as a trash can. The passenger side had deformed around it, almost like it had turned to liquid at the moment of impact, flowed around the stump, and then frozen that way.

I turned over and threw up into the grass — just ropy strands of spit and acid, since I barely had anything in my stomach. When I was done, I made my way back to the driver's-side door and climbed into the front seat. The keys were dangling in the ignition. I turned them, but nothing happened. Not so much as a groan. The glove compartment had opened in the crash, spilling everything inside onto the passenger seat. The owner's manual. A tire gauge. Our trip journal. I tipped it into the moonlight and turned through the pages.

It was all there. Our future sketched out in multi-colored ink. Lists of cities. Itineraries. Attractions. Luke's hand-drawn maps. Page one was all about the Pacific Northwest. Seattle and Portland, mainly. We'd written down facts about each city along with the best times to visit and things to do. At the bottom of the page Luke had drawn stick figure me and stick figure him hand in hand, dwarfed by towering redwoods. A giant, grinning salmon flew over our heads, above the trees.

Flipping through the pages was like moving back in time.

We'd added Ottawa the night we stood in a hailstorm outside a Brinn Lightly show praying for a scalped ticket. The first time we slept together happened to be on Marie Curie's birthday, so that's when Paris got its own page. Luke had lain on his belly in a shaft of afternoon sunlight, sketching Curie's face in the journal while I dozed and traced tiny hearts on his arm with one fingernail. A few weeks later I ended up sitting in a Wal-Mart bathroom, petrified, fumbling with a pregnancy test while Luke sat in the stall next door singing Beatles songs at the top of his lungs to distract me. When we got home we made a page for Liverpool, England and Bentonville, Arkansas.

I turned to the last page. Antarctica. Stick-figure Luke in bright green, a crown on his head, being hoisted into the air by his waddling subjects. I remembered lying in the back seat of Luke's car, his breath velvety hot on the back of my neck, as I drew it. His voice was in my ear, a husky whisper:

Hey. Weaver. You wanna go to prom with me?

I slapped the journal shut, then got out of the car and threw it as hard as I could. It sailed over the dark grass and disappeared. A trio of eighteen wheelers — driverless just like the one that nearly killed me — whooshed by on the road behind me. I reached back into the car and found my phone on the passenger side floorboard. There were no new messages. No new calls. There was nothing left to do. No other choice. I opened a contact and hit call.

"Daddy," I said, voice shaking when he answered. "I think I need help."

TEN

BERNIE AND CAROL were gone by the time Dad and I got home. He went inside, but I stood on the steps staring at the empty patch of driveway where Luke's car had sat just that morning. The tow truck driver had diagnosed it as a lost cause, so Dad had him take it to the nearest scrap yard. I imagined it sitting there the next morning, surrounded by all the other wrecks. Its windows cracked and the front end crumpled up like a scrap of paper, exposing the mangled engine. I looked down. In my hand were Luke's sunglasses. I'd grabbed them from the wreck just before it was taken away. The silver frames looked dull in the dim light. One lens was slightly cracked.

Dad called from inside the house. I turned and went in, letting the door slam behind me. He was in the kitchen sitting at the little table. He didn't look up as I took a seat across from him. The refrigerator hummed.

"Were you drinking?"

I shook my head.

"Lucy, if you were, you—"

"I wasn't."

"And you're sure you don't need to go to the ER. Sometimes

when you're in shock you don't feel everything right away. Something could be broken or —"

"I'm fine."

"If anything happened to you I think I'd —" His voice caught. I grabbed his hand. His eyes were red, surrounded by ashy circles. "I've always tried to — I've always wanted things between us to be —"

"I know."

"We *talk* about things, Lucy. Even now. With all of this. We don't walk out the door and disappear like —"

Dad stopped short. Head down, he pushed one hand through his scraggly, graying hair. There was a tiny smear of white paint on the side of his hand and on the cuff of his shirt, from his office painting endeavor. It was oddly endearing. My slob dad. I got up from the table and took down two glasses from the cabinet. I filled them both with OJ and slid one over to him.

"I think I have to ground you or something."

I drained my glass and poured another. "Seems reasonable."

"And you have to call your aunts," he said. "You have to apologize."

"I know. I will."

We drank our juice in silence awhile.

"How was the speech?" I asked.

"Speech?"

"The president's."

"Oh. We didn't — we were —"

"Busy looking into how to give up an eighteen-year-old for adoption?"

Dad grinned. A ray of sunlight through storm clouds. I took my glass and got up from the table.

"Come on," I said. "I'm curious. We'll turn the TV off right after."

Dad and I usually sat on opposite sides of the coffee table when we watched TV, but that night we both claimed the couch. I turned on the TV, then navigated around until I found the speech. The video began in a nondescript room. An old man with a steel-gray buzzcut and an army uniform was standing at a podium.

I said, "He looks fun."

"That's Barrington," Dad said. He took the remote and turned up the volume.

"The death toll has now stabilized at just over twenty-six thousand," Barrington said. "With more than double that number injured. A little over a hundred thousand have also been displaced from their homes. There is still no claim of responsibility for the attack, but the FBI and CIA are pursuing multiple leads. Turning to current military operations —"

A young man in a uniform appeared and whispered in Barrington's ear. The general nodded, then turned back to the screen.

"Ladies and gentlemen, the president of the United States."

Barrington stepped to the side as a door opened behind the podium. A slight, young-looking man, some kind of aide, I guessed, stepped through it. Struck by the lights, he stopped immediately, stuttered left, stuttered right, clearly unsure where to go. I looked behind him, waiting for the president to come out, but the door closed, leaving the man and General Barrington. The general whispered in his ear and then ushered him to the podium. This was him. The president. He stood there a moment, looking into the camera and tugging nervously at his jacket, which seemed too big for him.

"He lost his wife," I said. "Right? And his son."

Dad nodded. President Chin began to speak.

"Hello," he said, then quickly glanced at General Barrington, who frowned. "I mean . . . greetings, my fellow Americans. My name is Hank Chin. Henry Chin. Most of you probably don't know me. Until, uh, until this morning I was the secretary for Health and Human Services, which is eleventh in the line of succession to the presidency. When it was determined that everyone — that all others in the line before me, were either —" He took a breath and started again. "That they were either killed in the attack or otherwise ineligible, I was sworn in as the fifty-first president of the United States by Chief Justice Richard Ortega."

He looked over at General Barrington, who gave an almost imperceptible nod toward something in front of him.

"Oh. Yes."

The president lifted several pieces of paper off the podium. He cleared his throat and read from one of them.

"In regard to the chaos overseas. Let it be known that we will not stand idly by while other countries take advantage of the tragedy in our nation's capital. That's why, on the advice of General Barrington and his colleagues, I'm moving more of our forces, both conventional and nuclear, into staging areas in Eastern Europe, Asia, and the Middle East. We will also continue working with our allies to root out and destroy terrorist networks throughout the world. To the enemies of the United States, I say that further escalation of these already dangerous conflicts will be met with overwhelming force and resolve."

He returned the papers to their place, then stood there considering them a moment, brow furrowed.

"I've admired Amanda Hargrove, President Hargrove, for a long time. Ever since we were in college together." He smiled slightly, to himself. "She had one of the most brilliant minds I've ever known. I was so proud when she asked me to join her administration. My family was too."

There was a glass of water sitting at the corner of the podium. He took a drink from it and set it down again.

"That said, we sometimes disagreed. One of those disagreements was about what I saw as the over reliance on the use of military force, and how it could make already dangerous situations worse." He looked up into the camera. "Maybe if we could all just sit down together, if we could *talk*, then maybe we could come to some kind of —"

Barrington moved toward the podium and took hold of the president's arm. There was a tense, whispered exchange between them and then the general returned to his place, scowling. When President Chin spoke again his voice was slow and halting.

"When my son — when Caleb turned four, he started having nightmares. We didn't know why. He was a happy kid. He had friends. His mom and I, we both . . ." His voice gave out. He swallowed then continued. "But for some reason every night when he went to bed he had the most horrible dreams. Night after night he'd wake up screaming, inconsolable. He said whenever he shut his eyes there were monsters in the darkness and ghosts. He saw my death and the death of my wife played out a hundred times in a hundred different ways. But the worst nightmare, he said, was one where he found himself completely alone. The location always changed. One night it would be on a beach. Another it would be in a huge empty building, like a warehouse. But he was always alone and it was always just beginning to get dark. In his dream he'd run and run, calling our names, calling his grandparents' names and the names of his friends, but no one ever answered and no one ever came. No matter how loud he screamed, no matter how much he cried and begged, there was never anyone there. Just him. Just Caleb."

President Chin's eyes and face reddened and then tears emerged and spilled down his cheeks.

"I want to say to all of you, whether you're down the street, or across the country, or across the world, whether you love this country, or hate it . . . you're not alone. People you love are all around you. Even if you don't see them. Even if you can't touch them. They're there. You're not alone. None of us are alone. There's no reason to be afraid. There's no reason for us to keep fight —"

There was some kind of commotion offscreen, a shuffle of bodies and harsh, whispered voices, and then the video cut out abruptly. There was silence for a moment and then a gleaming studio appeared onscreen. Jessica Ramos sat in the center of a chrome desk, a stack of papers in front of her. For the first time, she didn't seem to have any idea what to say. The TV went off with a click. Dad dropped the remote. We sat in silence until the air conditioner came on with a long exhale. I found Dad's hand and held on as tight as I could.

—

When we headed upstairs, Dad stopped outside his office and said he had some work he wanted to catch up on. I pointed out that it was nearly one a.m., and he threw his hands up in mock helplessness. That was Dad for you. The world descends into madness and his first instinct is to fiddle with someone's investments. I hugged him good night, then hobbled into my room. Wrecking Luke's car seemed to have tied every muscle in my body into knots. I shut my door and, instead of going to bed, made my way through the dark to the closet.

The light came on as I opened it, spreading a small glow into the room. I eased myself down to the carpet and sat cross-legged in front of the door. My prom dress was lying there, balled up and wrinkled. I pushed it out of the way, along with a pair of worn-out running shoes and some T-shirts I didn't wear anymore. Behind it all there was a white cardboard box, the kind Dad used to file away his clients' papers. I pulled it toward me and lifted the top.

The box was filled with mementoes, old pictures and report cards, trophies from when I was a kid. I dug down to a cigar box at the bottom. Mom and I had picked it up on one of our treasure hunting expeditions, which is what we called trips to secondhand stores and antique shops. It was a thing we did. A mother and daughter ritual.

I undid the brass latch and opened the box. Inside were seventeen letters Mom had written me, single sheets of paper tucked into white envelopes. Mostly they contained descriptions of everyday things. Meals eaten. Books read. TV shows watched. Hot afternoons spent sitting in a concrete-and-steel courtyard looking up at an enormous blue sky. It was only in the last few letters that

Mom said anything about the fact that I'd never written back. She wasn't angry about it — at least, she didn't let on if she was — and she wasn't "disappointed" in some passive-aggressive mom kind of way either. Usually, all she wanted to know was if I was okay. She said that late at night, when she couldn't sleep, she'd lie in her cot and think about the life she was supposed to have had. Dinner parties and game nights with me and Dad and Carol and Bernie, going to my graduation and then seeing me off to college, living for the holidays when I'd come back home. Meeting the person I'd marry. Becoming a grandparent. Sometimes, she said, it seemed like that life was still happening in some parallel universe, one that ran right alongside our own, so close she could almost, but not quite, touch it.

I know that losing out on that life was my choice, she'd written in her last letter. *I won't make excuses. I hope you know that everything I ever did, I did for you.*

I put the letters back in the box and shut the closet. There were a few envelopes and some paper in my desk drawer. I leaned over a blank sheet for a long time, gripping the pen hard, wondering what to say. Everything that came to mind seemed too small to fill the gap of all those years. I was about to give up when the right thing finally struck me. It was only one sentence long, but it was something I thought she deserved to know. The only thing I wanted to say.

Everything you said was going to happen is happening.

It didn't excuse anything she'd done, it didn't say she was right, but it was true. I couldn't deny that. I went back and forth over how to sign off. *Best wishes. Sincerely. Love. Your daughter.* Eventually I just wrote *Lucy.* I sealed the envelope and turned it over. The return address on Mom's last letter was printed neatly in big block letters. I copied it as carefully as I could.

Laila Weaver — Inmate #357120
Berryridge Federal Prison
Westerly, CA 90867

I'd mail it first thing in the morning.

SHANGRI-LA

ELEVEN

WHEN I GOT to school the next morning, I didn't go right out to the soccer field. Instead I wandered the halls aimlessly awhile, dipping into classes here and there. I sampled a bit of early Roman history, some calculus, and a lecture on Dickens. Mr. Cash, the biology teacher, was talking about a theory that dinosaurs, rather than having gone extinct, had evolved into birds.

I was over near the lunchroom when Principal Tusso rounded a corner. I slipped away through a nearby set of double doors. It was dark on the other side and quiet. I stood with my ear against the door, listening to Tusso's footsteps slap against the tile. He passed right by without so much as a pause. I breathed a sigh of relief, then turned and looked out into the auditorium, waiting for my eyes to adjust.

Rows of empty seats were laid out in arcs in front of me, the aisles between them lit by glowing safety lights. Up onstage there was a set that resembled a large, overgrown forest complete with strikingly realistic papier-mâché trees, so tall they disappeared into the rafters. Flowered vines hung from the branches like Christmas garlands. The stage floor had been made into a rolling hillside covered in a carpet of what looked like grass and moss and scattered rocks. A backdrop continued the woods in forced perspective, and beyond that was a low sun done in gold and orange. This was the setting for Shakespeare's *A Midsummer Night's Dream*. The drama department always did Shakespeare in the spring. It was one of the things I'd been most excited about when I finally graduated from middle school. I'd be a teenager and I'd do Shakespeare. What could be more wonderful than that?

I drifted down the ghost-lit aisle toward the stage. I still loved the feel of an empty theater, the hushed churchiness of it, the soaring darkness. I took a seat in the first row, right by the railing around the orchestra pit, and craned my neck to look up into the trees. I'd walked into the auditorium for the first time on day one of freshman year. I was a raw nerve back then, steam-coming-out-of my-ears pissed one minute, a gray-room zombie the next. Mom's trial had just finished. I'd hoped that would be the end of the whole thing, that people would finally stop talking about it, but the judge had ordered life without parole and there was another round of outrage. Most people wanted death.

Back in middle school, theater was like being wrapped up in a world within a world. Despite the constant bustle of action, despite the spontaneous singing of show tunes, and the vocal exercises, and the line memorization, and the stage-crew crash and bang, the theater was calm and still. Safe. One day in class — this was when Mom had only been listed as missing, before her arrest — Jamie Barker said something mean to me about how she had probably left us for a better family somewhere far, far away, and Mr. Cronin took him down *hard*. Sent him right to the principal's office, where he got three days' detention. Later on, Cronin pulled me aside and whispered in my ear in this jokey Old West accent that was totally lame and incredibly cool at the same time, "We take care of our own on this here ranch, pardner."

But when I'd walked into Drama 1 my freshman year at Bethany High, Ms. Bowers, the teacher, just stared at me, unblinking, with small, cold eyes. After class, I worked up enough courage to go to her desk and ask about auditions for the fall musical, which was going to be *Les Misérables*. I wanted to know if freshmen were up for leading roles or if we'd only be considered for background characters and walk-ons. She pursed her thin lips and told me she thought it would be best if I didn't try out for a play at all that year. Not for the musical or the spring Shakespeare, not even for the one-acts the seniors did in their advanced-directing class. She said she'd already discussed it with Principal Tusso and he'd agreed. When I asked her why, she said, "Things being what they are, we feel that your presence would simply be too distracting. Better for everyone if you found another after-school activity. Maybe one that's a little more . . ." She paused, searching for the right word. "Solitary."

I got up from my front-row seat and climbed the steps at the side of the stage. Close up, the forest set was even more impressive. Richly detailed. Solidly built. I took a deep breath and smelled paint and sawdust and the faint odor of the chemicals they used in the fog machines. I lit the flashlight on my phone to get a better look. *A Midsummer Night's Dream* was about two pairs of young lovers who find themselves in an enchanted forest ruled by Oberon, the king of the fairies. As I moved across the stage, I noticed that the faces of smiling elves had been subtly painted into the knots of trees. Not only that, but statues of winged fairies had been placed here and there, hidden in tufts of grass and flowers. They were minuscule details that almost no one in the audience would ever notice, but they made it feel more real, more beautiful.

All the way stage right, near the wings, there was a bed of artificial flowers painted in alternating bands of yellow and orange and red. Each one had been sprinkled with dots of resin, which had hardened into what looked like glass beads. In the full lights of the show they'd sparkle, making the flower patch seem kissed with dew. I imagined Oberon and his queen, Titania, reclining near them, spouting poetry in otherworldly gowns of gold and silver.

I thought about Ms. Bowers, with her icy, beady eyes, and the muscles in my calf vibrated like plucked guitar strings. I imagined raising my foot and stomping that bed of flowers to pieces, the pipe-cleaner stalks crunching as they collapsed. The larger flowers were supported by thin, wooden dowels. I bet they would go off like gunshots, like snapped bones. Maybe when I was done with the flowers I'd get a hammer from the scene shop and take down the whole damn set piece by piece.

The bell rang for the next period. A second later the auditorium doors flew open and a horde came flooding in.

"Lights! Somebody get the lights!"

I took a last look at the flowers and then I escaped into the darkness of the wings.

—

"Pssst. Hey. Weaver."

I turned to find that Toby Wolfowitz had joined us. He was squatting in the dirt between me and a contingent of pot smokers out in the woods. The ranks of soccer-field lurkers had swelled since President Chin's speech the night before. There were now eight or ten others spread out all along the field and in the trees behind me.

"Hey, Toby. What are you doing here?"

"Couldn't resist AP Calc this morning," he said. "But we were reading the Beats in American Lit so I decided to come out here instead. They're a bunch of pretentious phonies."

That was the funny thing about Toby. He might've looked like a burnout freak, but he was straight A's, all the way. I'd heard he was in the running to be valedictorian.

"Hey, who are you going to be for Halloween?"

Halloween? "Uh, unless there's been a schedule change no one told me about, that generally happens in October, Toby."

He plopped down beside me. His bald, sunburned head gleamed. An odd smell wafted off him. Sweat? Booze? No, there was something chemical about it. Sweet, but sharp at the same time. What was it?

"Right," he said. "But Tyler Greenbaum figured since we'll all probably be living in a post-apocalyptic wasteland by October we should go ahead and have Halloween now. Me and Tina Fielding and a friend of hers are going as the Teenage Mutant Ninja Turtles, but we need a fourth."

"Green's not really my color."

"Cool, cool. Oh, I found this old tree house out in the woods. Wanna go out there and take some horse tranquilizers? Maybe play a game of Candyland?"

"That's sweet, but I was right on the edge of a nap here."

"No problem." He turned and called out across the field. "Yo! Karras! What about you? Candyland?"

Jay was over by the goalpost again, still keeping to himself, still scribbling in his notebook and glowering.

"No thanks," he grumbled.

"I was just kidding about the horse tranquilizers!"

Toby turned to me and shook his head to indicate that he was most definitely *not* kidding about the horse tranquilizers.

"Fine," he said, then peered into the trees. "Hey! Fong!"

A second later Toby and Gary Fong were hurrying into the woods. The strange smell lingered after he left. It took a second, but what it was finally hit me. Gasoline. Why did Toby Wolfowitz smell like gasoline?

The bell rang for the next period. A few kids drifted across the field and into the school while others came out and took their place.

"We're heading in for some chow, Lucy. Want us to bring you something?"

The Hacky Sackers gathered in a little arc in front of me. A swampy fog of hemp and patchouli odor hung around them. I'd learned their names earlier — Wade, Lorenzo, Stank, and Cooper — and discovered they were actually nice enough guys. They even stopped singing the Bob Marley songs when I asked them to.

"Lunch ended more than an hour ago," I said. "They're not serving now."

For some reason that elicited a round of throaty chuckles.

"Oh, no worries," Wade, their apparent leader, drawled. "One of those new lunch ladies is crazy in love with Stank here. She's like Polish or something. Twenty-two years old. Fled the Russian Army in a goddamn goat cart. She says her and Stank's souls are perfectly entwined."

Stank was the littlest of the foursome. A five-foot-nothing senior with dreamy green eyes and a patchy beard. I had no idea what his real name was.

"Is this true, Stank?"

He blushed adorably. "I got Svetlana's name tattooed on my *heart*, Lucy."

"Great. You can use it to remember her by when she's in prison."

"Oh no, it's not like that," he said. "Our love doesn't exist on the physical plane. It's a spiritual thing."

Cooper and Lorenzo busted out laughing. They jostled their friend around and sang a chorus of "Stank's in looooooove!" while the little guy giggled.

"Anyway," Wade said, pushing the other three aside, "Svet's happy to supply under-the-table comestibles if you care to partake."

"I'm good, guys. Thanks, though."

"No worries. Okay, guys! Let's do this! Cheesy fries, here we come!"

They ambled off into the school, leaving me and Jay largely on our own. He went on writing, one hand clutching his forehead, the other holding his pen in a death grip. If anything, he looked even worse than he had the day before: more grease in his hair, more stubble on his cheeks. The dark circles around his eyes were fast approaching living-dead level. He'd changed clothes — a pink button-down with khakis — but it looked like he'd pulled them right out of the hamper. There wasn't a square centimeter that wasn't wrinkled. Even with his sunburn, he still kind of looked like he had some kind of wasting disease.

Whatever, I thought. He wasn't my concern. I scooted back to the edge of the woods and laid my head against a tree trunk. I was exhausted. When I'd woken up that morning, the muscles in my body were screaming, wrenched into knots by the impact of the car crash. I'd considered asking Dad to take me to the doctor so I could get something stronger than aspirin, but he was locked up in the office again, working away.

I shut my eyes behind my sunglasses, my sore body desperate for sleep. In between bells it was quiet out by the field, nothing but the murmurs of my fellow skulkers and the scrabbling of Jay's pen. The voices faded into the background as I drifted off, but the sounds of Jay's work — *scratch scratch scratch, rip, crumple, scratch scratch scratch* — followed me all the way down into the dark.

—

I woke up some time later, crusty, dripping with sweat, and even more achy than I'd been before. It was weirdly quiet. The woods behind me were empty and so was the soccer field. Everyone had left. Except for Jay Karras, that is. He'd barely moved, just exchanged his notebook for a textbook, and was reading intently.

I grabbed my phone and woke the screen. Two thirty. I'd slept through the rest of the school day. Every muscle complained as I struggled to my feet. I started for the roundabout but quickly realized that the busses would be gone too. *Damn it. Damn it. Damn it.* I had a long, painful walk ahead of me. Unless . . .

"Hey, Karras. You got a car?"

Jay grunted in a way that might have been affirmative. Why, oh why, was fate conspiring to make me constantly have to deal with this jerk? I sighed, resigned.

"Think I could get a ride home?"

Nothing. Not a word. I figured he was trying to come up with a good excuse so he could turn me down, but then he glanced around to make sure we were alone and said, "Could you do me a favor first?"

"What is it?" I asked, wary, praying this wasn't the moment I found out Jay was some kind of creep. But no. All he did was hold his notebook out to me with a grimly determined look on his face.

"Seriously Jay, I'm the last person in the world you want checking your homework for you."

"It's not homework."

"Then what is it?"

He pushed the notebook at me again. "Just read it."

I shot him a glare and he must have thought better of his tone because he instantly softened it.

"Please? I don't — I don't have anyone else I can ask."

I turned toward the road that led off school grounds. How far was it to my house? Two miles? Three? I'd walked it before, but not with my body all jacked up from a car crash. I sighed and took the book out of Jay's hand. When I opened it to the first page, I expected to see notes, maybe some kind of essay or something, but it wasn't that at all.

It was a poem.

"Uh . . . I'm not really an expert on —"

"You don't have to be," he said. "You just have to be honest. Okay?"

I sat down and dropped my sunglasses to the ground beside me. It was a short poem. Twenty lines arranged into five four-line stanzas. It was about a flock of birds he'd seen one morning rising out of the fog and into the sunrise near a small lake behind his house. But it was about more than that too. It was about his family. And war. And time. I read it through twice, then closed the notebook.

"Jay?"

"Yeah?"

"That was the worst poem I've ever read in my life."

Jay dropped his head into his hands and groaned. "You know what the *really* shitty thing is?"

"What?"

"That's the best one."

"Seriously?"

"Turn the page."

I did and found another, longer poem called "Ghost Lights." It was about looking up at the stars on a beautiful summer night and realizing that they'd all burned out millions of years before. It touched on themes of loneliness and isolation and wondered how humanity could ever find meaning in the random enormity of a hostile universe.

"God," I said. "You're right. That's awful."

Jay slammed shut the big textbook he'd been reading. I finally got a good look at the cover. *Masters of Modern Poetry.*

"I've read every word of this stupid thing," he said. "Read every poem. Studied every lesson. It didn't make any difference."

"So maybe poetry isn't for you. You could try something else."

"Turn to the back."

Full of dread, I did what he asked. I found a series of drawings. Ten pages of them. Mostly still lifes. Bowls of fruit. The view from a window on a rainy day. An old woman's hands. They were even worse than the poems.

"I have another whole notebook of songs, too."

"And I take it they're . . ."

"I can't even look at them."

"Okay, so you're not an artist," I said. "It's not like the world's dying for more artists at the moment."

He snatched the notebook out of my hands and shoved it in his pack. "I know. I'm just running out of options."

"What do you mean?"

Jay's phone buzzed in his pocket. Thank God — at least he'd turned off that stupid ringtone.

He pulled it out and checked the number. "Damn it."

"What?"

He quickly gathered his things "Nothing. I gotta go. If you still want that ride I have to stop by my locker first."

Inside school the halls were empty. The only sounds were a few distant voices and the hum of janitors buffing the floors before the next day's assault. I paused to get a drink of water at one of the fountains while Jay kept going and turned the corner. I couldn't help but chuckle. The idea of Mr. Straight A's sweating it out over a series of truly awful poems was more than a little ridiculous. Sweet, maybe, but still ridiculous.

I was wiping my mouth with the back of my sleeve when I heard what sounded like a library's worth of books hitting the floor.

"Oh man!" Jay yelped. "Sorry!"

I rounded the corner to find him sprawled out on the floor. A girl was on her knees near him, gathering up a pile of books she'd dropped when, I guessed, she and Jay collided. Jay scrambled to his feet and tried to help her.

"Sorry," he said again. "I didn't see you. I didn't mean to —"

Jay and the girl stood up at the same time, each with a book in hand. The second Jay looked at her, he froze solid, speechless, pale. I didn't know who the girl was, but I couldn't blame Karras for getting all moony-eyed. She was tall — *statuesque* was probably a better word, actually — with ridiculously long legs, painfully cute freckles, and long golden hair that hung down her shoulders like something out of a high-end shampoo commercial. Basically, she was the sort of accident of genetics that drove girls like me to develop sparkling personalities.

"C-Clarissa," Jay stuttered when he sort of regained the power of speech. "Hey. Hi."

Clarissa's eyes scrunched adorably. It seemed that while she was clearly burned into Jay's memory, the reverse was not true. Part of me wilted inside.

"*Hey,*" Clarissa enthused without a trace of recognition. "How's it going?"

"Good. Good. Oh. Your book."

He smiled bashfully and handed her the book he was holding.

"Thanks," she said, then pointed one delicate fingertip behind him. "You, uh, dropped some of yours, too."

Jay spun around. "Oh. Right. Ha. Ha."

I cringed as he scrambled to pick up his backpack and its contents. In his haste he re-dropped half of them, so he had to lean over again and take another crack at it. I had a nightmare vision of this going on for hours, days, while Clarissa and I watched with steadily mounting embarrassment. But no. Jay finally got himself together, and then he stood up and . . . nothing happened. Like literally nothing. He just stood there, speechless, trapped in one of those failed social interactions where the only escape seems to be mutual suicide. It was so God-awful awkward that I had to step in.

"Okay!" I said, giving Jay a slap on the back. "Me and *Jay Karras* here have to get going. Say goodbye, Jay Karras."

"Uh, yeah. We gotta . . . yeah. See ya. Clarissa."

"Bye, Jay!"

I had to give her credit; it was a decent save. Clarissa took her things and glided away on a cloud of fairy dust. Jay was abjectly motionless. I didn't know what to do, so I laughed at him. He grimaced, grabbed a couple books out of his locker, then bolted down the hall. But he wasn't going to get away that easy.

"So-o-o," I warbled as I followed, barely restraining my desire to skip. "Who's the lovely lady?"

"Nobody."

He quickened his pace, but I kept up, not taking my eyes off him for a second. He sighed heavily.

"She's nobody. We had gym together in middle school."

"Ah, middle school gym, the beginning of every truly great love story." I slipped on my sunglasses. "So, were you as smooth then as you are now?"

Jay punched through the double doors that led out to the parking lot.

"Pretty much."

—

Jay's car was more or less what I expected — A generic, spotlessly clean compact with a whisper quiet electric engine and an autonomous feature he actually used. When Jay, or rather Jay's *car*, pulled up to my house I initiated an exchange of contacts in case I needed a ride again and then he sped off down the street without a word. I went inside, where I was immediately greeted by a blast of air-conditioning.

And a cat.

On the coffee table.

"Dad!"

Upstairs, there was a rustle behind his still-shut office door. I heard him pop out and quickly close it behind him, then he came into view at the top of the stairs.

"Hey! Sorry. What's up?"

I looked up at him.

"What?"

I pointed at the table. "Something you want to tell me?"

He clapped his hands. "Oh! Right! Sorry. That's Copperfield."

At the sound of its name the scrawny, ginger-colored cat let out a tiny squeak. Dad came down the stairs and dropped to his knees by the table. He stroked the cat's head until it was blissed out and purring.

"I was out doing some grocery shopping this afternoon and almost ran the little guy over in the parking lot. I followed him to make sure he was okay. Turned out he was living behind the store in this little nest made out of trash. You should have seen him when I got him home. Filthy. Fur all matted."

"Looks okay now."

"Yeah, I put him in the shower."

"How'd that go for you?"

Dad held up his right arm. I hadn't noticed that it was wrapped, from forearm to elbow, in a white bandage. "It was not without incident."

Copperfield jumped up and planted his paws on Dad's chest. He laughed, delighted, and rubbed the cat's ears.

"What about your allergies?"

"Picked up a boatload of antihistamines."

Copperfield hopped off the table and started to make figure eights around my ankles. I stepped away from him without really thinking about it.

"You okay with this, Goose?" Dad asked.

The cat looked at me with his big green eyes and let out a puzzled meow.

"Uh, yeah," I said, despite a strange uneasiness. "Sure. Of course. The more the merrier, right?"

"My thoughts exactly. I have some more work I need to do up in the office, so I was thinking I'd order Thai for dinner. That okay?"

"Sure. Fine. Just gonna do some homework first."

As I headed upstairs, Dad stretched out on the floor near the fireplace. The cat climbed up his chest and nuzzled him. Watching them, my sense of unease grew. It was like I was looking at a stranger. It was crazy, I knew that, it was just a cat — but a voice in my head reminded me that the biggest changes sometimes started out small.

"Who's a good little boy?" Dad cooed as he stroked the cat's side. "Who's got a home of his very own?"

———

After dinner Dad closed himself up in his office again and I went to my room. I tried to read but lost track of the story after only a sentence or two. When I queued up *Emperor of Bones* it was the same thing. Ten minutes in and my mind was wandering. I swiped over to my newsfeeds. There'd been a poison gas attack on a train in Berlin and American drones had fired on a wedding party in Iraq, killing everyone present.

My phone vibrated. I moved to my messages.

Have you been able to sleep lately?

It was Jay. Weird. One sorta-kinda okay interaction with the guy, and now he was messaging me? I almost ignored it, but since I didn't have anything better to do, I decided to tap out a response.

not really
you?

I just lie here, staring at the ceiling.
Midnight. 1am. 2am. 3am.
My dad gave me a tranquilizer last night,
but even then all I got was an hour or two.

were you at least tranquil?

Made me kind of paranoid. At one point
I became convinced the house was on fire.

how long's that been going on?
the no sleep thing

How long has it been since the sixteenth?
A week? More?

I was surprised to find that I didn't know. The last few days had been such a blur. How long *had* it been?

something like that.

they say if you go too long without sleep,
you start hallucinating
that started yet?

Depends.
Earlier today were there four rasta meerkats
having a polka dance party on the soccer field?

I laughed, then typed.

most definitely

Well then, I guess I'm fine.

I smiled to myself, surprised to discover Jay Karras was at least slightly amusing. Down the hall, Dad's office door opened and shut. The stairs creaked as he went to the kitchen and poured a glass of water. A few moments later, his office door opened and closed again and the house was quiet.

my dad went to the grocery store today and
came back with a stray cat
he found in an alley

There was a pause. I was a little embarrassed, thinking maybe Jay and I were done and I hadn't realized it, but then there were three blinking dots and he said,

Nice of him.

                                                            i guess

???

                    idk. he's allergic to cats. he's never wanted
                            one before. then today he brings one
                                            home out of nowhere?
                        also, since DC he's spending all this time
                                            shut up in his office
                            when he's never done that before
                                                    it's weird

My Aunt Halla has been baking a lot.
It's all she does when she gets home from the gallery
Cookies. Pies. Cakes. Bread.

                                at least you've got cake

Good point.
I also just read about a guy who owns
a chain of grocery stores in the south.
He had his suppliers reroute
all the deliveries for his locations
to the DC refugee camps.
Says he's going to keep doing it until
all of his money runs out.
He's worth about three billion dollars.
And the governor of Wisconsin just proposed
building a landing strip for the UFOs he thinks

are going to come once
we all start firing nukes at each other.

what's your point?

Three little dots blinked, then disappeared then blinked again as Jay tried different responses. Finally, he said,

I think maybe
none of us are sure who we are anymore.

I sat with that for a moment, reading it over and over, feeling the weight of it in my stomach, and then I wrote,

true.
some of us have even resorted to writing
deeply shitty poetry.

🖕

I laughed. There was a scratch at my door. I dropped my phone and let Copperfield in. He stalked around the room, sniffing everything in sight, then took a spot on my windowsill. A little sentry. I got out of bed and stood next to him. The night was deep and quiet. Next door, Mr. Walker was standing on his lawn looking at the stars, unmoving, a solitary statue. He'd been doing it a lot lately. Dad went out to try to talk to him from time to time, but Mr. Walker never said a word.

I picked up my phone and leaned against the window frame.

do you think it's really going to happen?

What?

I searched around online until I found a looping video of nuclear bombs going off. It was a compilation of sun bright flashes, mushroom clouds, and smoking ruins. I sent it to Jay. There was a pause and then he wrote,

I don't know. Maybe. You?

I swiped over to my newsfeed and stood there looking at my phone. Nightmares in twelve-point font scrolled by. I wrote,

sometimes I think it's what we deserve

Nothing. No response. I felt stupid. It was getting late, so I tossed the phone onto my bed and went to the bathroom. Washed my face. Brushed my teeth. I called good night to Dad, and his voice came through the walls of his office, muffled. I went back into my room, threw on some pajamas, and got into bed. I picked up my phone to set an alarm. That's when I saw what Jay had written. It was just one sentence.

Feel like skipping school tomorrow?

TWELVE

JAY PICKED ME UP the next morning and we drove out of Bethany. I had no idea where we were going and didn't ask. I kept expecting him to suck the mystery out of the whole thing with an explanation, but he didn't say a word.

I put my feet up on the dash and picked through the bag of trail mix he'd brought, looking for chocolate chips.

"I couldn't sleep last night," I said. "So I watched *Black Suitcase* again. For the first time, I got to thinking how maybe the suitcase isn't really a suitcase at all. It's a *door.*"

I popped a handful of chocolate into my mouth. The car signaled a turn and took us onto the highway. Even though the car was doing the driving, Jay kept his eyes on the road and his hands on the wheel. Very responsible.

"What I mean is, it *acts* like a door," I said. "So one second Esperanza's feeding pigeons in the park, right? And then this weird black suitcase appears. For some reason she gets up from her bench, takes it by the handle, and walks away. And as soon as she does, nothing makes sense anymore. *Nothing.* Her brother *looks* like her brother, and her dog *looks* like her dog, but somehow we know, and she knows, that they're not. But what are they?

And what do they want? And those trees? By her apartment building? God! I still get the shivers thinking about them. And when she goes to the dance club and meets Mr. Fernando, how does she know about his back room, since as far as we know she's never been there?"

I leaned on the console between us.

"See? When she took the suitcase, it was like she was walking through a door. But a door to where? Another world? Hell? What?"

I waited for an answer. Jay checked his side-view mirror as the car passed a truck in front of us.

"So?" I asked. "What do you think?"

"I have no idea."

"That's fine. We're just theorizing. What do you *think*?"

"I think I've never seen *Black Suitcase*."

I nearly dropped the bag of trail mix. "Wait. Seriously?"

"It's a TV show?"

"It's a movie!"

"Is it good?"

"*Good*? Is it *good*? Jay, it's the pinnacle of new-wave Spanish horror directed by the master of the form, Alejandra Aguilar!"

Jay shrugged. My mind felt like it had been blown into a million pieces, but then I thought, *Right. Of course.* The night before he'd displayed a rudimentary sense of humor, and keeping quiet about our destination that morning suggested he had a certain appreciation for drama, but he was still Jay Karras.

"Okay, maybe that one's a little obscure," I said. "What about *Bonebreak Symphony* by Cho Sun Pak? Surely you've seen that one."

"Nope."

"*The Jack Dog*? *Cannibal Creek Massacre*? *The Secret Letters of Mina Harker*?"

"You can keep naming horror movies as long as you want; I won't have seen them."

That's when it hit me — the awful truth. "Wait. You've *never* seen a horror movie?"

"Does *The Wizard of Oz* count?"

"No, *The Wizard of Oz* doesn't count! Why would *The Wizard of Oz* count?"

"When I was a kid those flying monkeys scared the hell out of me."

I flopped back into my seat. How could somebody go through life without ever seeing a spurt of arterial blood as directed by a master like Pak, or felt the brain-grinding tension Katherine Jefferson created in *The Stone Bible*? To have never experienced the mind-bending, reality-warping horrors of *Black Suitcase* . . . it was like never having seen a sunset before, or a rainbow.

"Well, there's no way around it," I said. "I'm going to make the ultimate horror watch list for you. Must-sees. Lesser-known gems. It'll be like horror university."

"Uh . . . okay."

I started putting together a syllabus in my head, but got stuck on whether I should do a chronological arrangement — so he'd get a sense of the evolution of the form — or a more thematic one. In the end, I decided to keep it simple and focus on the monster. We'd do sections on zombies, vampires, ghosts, and serial killers. And then we'd finish up with a deep dive into my favorite monster of all — creeping, existential dread. This arrangement was really the best, given that each type of threat had its own unique thematic underpinnings, *and* — since what we're afraid of changes with the times — they fell in a kind of rough chronological order anyway. Jay had no idea how fortunate he was to have lucked into a teacher like me. He was on the verge of a total mind expansion. I almost envied him.

We crossed a river and moved off the highway and onto a two-lane road that wound through small-town main streets. When the towns petered out we were left with sunlit woods and mossy granite hills on either side of us. I rolled down the window and let warm air fill the car.

After we came around a sharp curve, Jay took over control of the car and slowed us to a stop in the middle of the road. To our left, a narrow, dirt-and-gravel trail led off into the woods.

"This is probably a good time to tell you that what we're doing is technically illegal."

He was really doubling down on the drama. I had to respect that. I tossed a handful of peanuts into my mouth. "Let's do it."

The car thumped off the asphalt and onto the trail. The going was slow as we moved up a long and steady grade. Leafy sunlight passed over us for a while, but then the woods grew heavier and older, choked with fallen trees and vines. Water was rushing somewhere ahead of us. I sat up higher as we bounced along. When I looked back over my shoulder, the main road had disappeared completely.

Obviously, I'd seen this movie before. Hundreds of times, in fact. Seemingly normal guy, maybe a little *too* normal, invites a girl on a hiking trip that quickly turns into a depraved kill fest. I gave Jay a steady, appraising look as he drove. He'd cleaned himself up a good bit since the last time I'd seen him. Stubble gone. Fresh clothes. Hair messy, but clean. The dark circles under his eyes were still there, but they'd faded a touch. Paired with his slightly bent nose, they gave him a pleasantly sleepy look. No. He wasn't *too* normal. He was freaked out and he was sad — both of which were reasonable, given the circumstances, and both of which could have been used to describe me — but he didn't feel like a threat. Besides, tucked away in my backpack I had the can of pepper spray Dad had given me for my last birthday. If by some chance I was wrong, I was pretty sure I could take him.

Twenty minutes later we came to a stop. A heavy chain stretched from tree to tree ahead of us, a rusty PRIVATE PROPERTY — NO TRESPASSING sign hanging from the center of it. On the other side of the chain, an even narrower trail led deeper into the woods. We got out of the car. The air was thick with the smell of foliage and the sound of buzzing insects.

Jay went around to the back of the car and popped the trunk. It was spotless too, not so much as an oil stain inside, nothing but a spare tire and a small day pack. He undid his button-down shirt, folded it neatly, and put it in the trunk. This left him in a white tank top and a pair of khakis that hung low on his hips. Unexpectedly — shockingly even — he was actually kind of ripped underneath his business casual attire. Not body builder–ripped or anything, but enough to make a person sit up and take notice. Ropy muscles coiled around his arms and the shadows of abs showed through his shirt. His shoulders were also way broader than they'd seemed. With the muscles and that slightly bent nose of his, he looked more like a boxer than the future mid-level executive I'd taken him for.

"What?" he asked.

I suddenly realized I'd been staring. "Nothing. I just — Nothing."

Jay looked down at himself. His cheeks went pink with embarrassment.

"Oh. That. I heard that being on a team looks good on your transcript so I did water polo for a while. It's kind of a dumb sport."

"And so cruel to the horses."

Jay gave me a courtesy laugh, but it was a Dad joke, and a bad one at that. What was wrong with me? Was I trying to impress Jay freaking Karras? Before I could humiliate myself any further, I slipped on my sunglasses and headed for the trail.

"Come on," I said. "Let's get this show on the road. This way, right?"

After we went around the NO TRESPASSING sign Jay took the lead. After about a half mile or so, he turned off the trail and onto another one that wound up a wooded hill. At first, lingering aches from the crash had plagued me, but as we walked, I started to loosen up. By the time we got to the top of the hill, they'd faded away almost completely. We shared a bottle of water and a few handfuls of peanuts. My clothes were sticking to me and my hair was damp with sweat, and I could almost see a haze of steam rising up off Jay. The opposite side of the hill was steep and strewn with dead leaves and fallen branches. He capped the water bottle and we skittered down the slope sideways, grabbing at trees with each step. When we reached the bottom, he shocked me by breaking into a run.

"I think this is it!" he declared, galloping like a little kid through the trees.

I followed. The sound of rushing water got louder and louder and then we came to a break in the forest. Ahead of us was a gray, rocky shore and a fast-flowing river the color of steel. On the other side of it there was another steep hill, covered with a mix of boulders and scrubby trees that looked like they were holding on for dear life.

Jay stood in a patch of sunlight with his hands on his hips, grinning, hair blowing in the wind. His skin, which had looked almost ashen out on the soccer field, glowed.

"The state dynamited this valley over a hundred years ago," he said. "They were going to put a railroad through here, but then they hit all this water. Since they couldn't pump it out, they packed up and went home. Some rich guy bought up the whole area like twenty-some years ago and put up his no-trespassing signs. People sneak in anyway. I heard it was one of the best places to go in the state — everybody called it Shangri-La — but I'd quit collecting so . . ."

"And by collecting you mean . . . ?"

Jay dashed away down the shore. "Come on. I'll show you!"

We ventured downstream. After a few minutes, Jay dropped to his knees near the water. By the time I caught up to him, he was digging through a pile of rocks with his back to me. Exhausted, I sat down by a boulder and tried to catch my breath. The sun beat down on my back and sizzled against my earlobes. I put on more sunscreen. Drank some water. Jay had started separating rocks into three different piles I couldn't even guess the purpose of. A feeling of strangeness came over me as I watched him. It was kind of like that feeling you get when you wake up from a dream in the middle of the night and, for a few panicked moments, nothing in your room seems familiar. Two days earlier I'd never so much as said hello to Jay Karras, and now there I was, out in the middle of nowhere with him on some kind of weird adventure.

There was a splash as he plunged his hand into the water. He shook it until clouds of dirt floated away, and then he spun around and raised his closed fist.

"Hold out your hand," he said.

I did. Jay dropped something cold and smooth into my palm. When he drew his hand back, I said, "Holy shit! What *is* that?"

Half of the rock Jay had given me was gray, just like the others all around us, but the other half was nearly pulsing with color. I took off my sunglasses so I could see it better. Most of it was a pale rose, but there was an inner section that looked like an unbroken field of grass. It varied from a bright, almost translucent lime to a hunter green that was so dark it was nearly black.

"It's pink feldspar mostly," he explained. "The green is called hornblende. It's not worth any money or anything, but it's kinda pretty, right?"

I rubbed my thumb over the surface of the rock. It was warm, rough in places and glassy smooth in others. I nodded dumbly and tilted my hand so the light played over the rock's facets and made them sparkle. *Pretty* didn't cover it. Not even close.

"How'd you get into this?"

Jay went back to sorting through his piles. "My Aunt Halla. She was into rocks when she was a kid, so she took me the first time. I was six, I think. We were on this family vacation in Utah walking along a dried-up riverbed. I was bored. Complaining. Halla gave me her rock hammer to play with, probably to shut me

142

up, and I was just randomly smashing things with it because, you know, six-year-old boy."

He examined a rock. Tossed it aside.

"Anyway, Halla went around a bend in the streambed and I sat down to drink some water. There was this brown rock sitting by my feet, about the size of a softball. I started banging away at it, and after a few hits it broke in two, like an egg."

Jay looked back at me. His eyes were intense behind his glasses, bright with amazement.

"It was hollow. Inside were thousands of spiky, emerald crystals, like a forest had grown up inside the stone. I held it out into the sun and the whole thing sparkled. It was a geode, only I didn't know what that was at the time, had never even *heard* of one. I called my aunt but she didn't hear me, so for a long time I just sat there in the middle of the desert, all alone, with this thing in my lap that, I don't know, seemed like magic."

The rush of the river filled a span of quiet. Eventually he turned back to the water and washed off another rock. He put it in my hand, beside the first one.

"White quartz," he said.

It was like a dollop of whipped cream. Its surface was rounded smooth, cool to the touch.

"Why'd you quit collecting?"

Jay's eyebrows drew together as he considered. "I dunno. After my brothers and sisters came along, things got kind of busy. Seemed silly, I guess."

He selected a rock from one of the piles, examined it, then chucked it into the water.

"Come on," he said. "I heard there's garnet around here some-where."

We moved downstream and away from the river's edge where Jay found the mouth of a shallow cave cut into the hillside. He sat and began sifting through the piles of rocks. I took a place nearby and watched the river flow. In the shade, the sweat I'd worked up evaporated, raising goose bumps along my arms. The sky was cloudless and the trees made a green wave in the breeze.

From where we sat I had a better view across the river. The bank on the other side rose up over the forest, a gray mound topped with green. I told Jay I was going to take a look around, then started back the way we'd come. After a while, the river wid-ened and slowed. The crash of the whitewater faded behind me. The trees were heavier there, crowding the bank and leaning out over the water where tiny, translucent fish darted around beneath the surface. Everything was shadowy and cool. I pushed on until I found a place where the river narrowed again. Boulders marked out a path to the opposite shore. I hopped from one stone to the next until I made it to the other side.

Once across I started up the hill, reaching from tree to tree or from one small stone outcropping to the next. By the time I got to the top, my legs ached again and I was glazed with a new coat of sweat. I dropped onto a pile of rocks near the edge of the cliff and squinted up into the bright sky, then out toward the horizon. The forest blanketed low, rolling hills, interrupted here and there by lakes and ponds and the steel and ivory turns of the river. Farther out were pockets of gray: small towns like Bethany, and the roads that connected them. A hawk flew in lazy circles over my head, its wings wavering in the high-up winds.

We didn't start out as a particularly outdoorsy family. Sometimes Carol and Bernie would try to get me and Mom and Dad to go on a hike or a bike ride, but the three of us would always find something else of vital importance we had to do. Get the car washed. Return some library books. Mom was the one who turned us around. Well, turned *me* around, anyway. Dad remained unconvinced.

It started small. A walk around the neighborhood one summer day, which lead to this series of multi-hour rambles through local state parks. In the beginning we followed clearly marked paths of gravel or asphalt, flat, gently winding, packed with dog walkers and bicyclists. Eventually Mom declared that we might as well have been walking through a mall, so she graduated us to rough, barely there trails, where colored tags nailed to trees every hundred feet or so were the only things to guide us. It wasn't long until that wasn't enough either. Mom enrolled in an orienteering course, and we set off into unmarked woods with nothing but a map and a compass.

One day I came downstairs in my pajamas to find Mom in the living room surrounded by stacks of boxes. It was like a second Christmas. I waded in and tore them open. There were boots and backpacks and collapsible aluminum cooking gear. Meals in vacuum-sealed packages. Fishing poles. A hatchet small enough to fit my hand. Mom led me out to the backyard, where she set up our tent, a sleek, two-person dome in green and black. That very weekend, she said, we'd be driving to a state park several hours away. This was no place for joggers or power-walking senior citizens. This was serious. We'd be gone for two whole days. We'd hike and fish and sleep out under the stars, just the two of us.

I was nervous but excited as we packed up the car before dawn. What if we got lost? What if no one ever found us? What if there were rabid bears or werewolves lurking out in the trees and we had to fight our way to freedom? Dad stood on the front steps in his robe, coffee in hand, as we pulled away. I waved and he waved back and soon we were on the highway, speeding through a foggy morning to our destination. We rode in silence. No radio. No movies streamed through the dashboard set. Mom said that weekend was about leaving the world behind.

The park wasn't a park: it was a forest, huge and crowded with trees so big it hurt my neck to try to look up at them. There was no one there but us and nothing even remotely resembling a trail. She unloaded our gear and helped me put on my backpack, which was a small, kid's version of her own. Once I was ready, she slipped into her pack and we set out from the little parking lot.

We moved fast, Mom striding forward, pausing occasionally to check her map and compass. I struggled to keep up. The forest closed around us. Within minutes I couldn't even see the car, just green trees and sun filtering down through them. We hiked until twilight, then set up our tent in a small clearing while Mom, after a few frustrated tries, built us a fire by shooting sparks from a piece of flint into a pile of twigs. Her plan was that we'd have fresh fish for dinner, but neither of us had any luck. I didn't mind so much. It meant we got to dip into the emergency food stash Dad had packed for us. Hot dogs and s'mores cooked over the campfire.

We were exhausted from the long day of hiking, so we got in the tent around eight. The woods came alive with the sounds of insects and hooting night birds. Every now and then something would move out in the trees. Mom said it was probably raccoons or deer, but I imagined black bears and shambling undead horrors.

"Get some sleep, Goose," Mom breathed, barely conscious. "Got to hike all those miles again tomorrow."

I turned on my side and threw my arm across her belly. Mom put her hand over mine and laced our fingers together. I listened to the in-and-out of her breath and the calls of the animals, imagining what it would be like if we *didn't* walk all those miles again the next day. What if the two of us, mother and daughter, took our map and our compass and just kept on going? Drinking out of streams. Learning to fish and forage. I imagined us as characters out of a little kid's book, the kind I'd recently gotten too old for: a wilderness family, swinging from vines, making clothes out of leaves, talking to bears and raccoons in their own language. We'd miss Dad and Carol and Bernie, and Jenna and all our friends, but what would the two of us see on that journey? Where would we end up? Who would we become? My head spun. I fell asleep dreaming about it.

The sun had barely risen when I woke the next morning. Even so, it was hot and airless in the tent. I turned over to tell Mom about my fantasy from the night before and was surprised to find her gone. Her pack was still there, along with most of her things. Only her clothes were missing. I unzipped the tent and stepped out. The forest was quiet. The fire we'd made was a small pile of dark ash. Leaves crunched underfoot as I walked around our campsite, peering into the trees and calling out. No sign of her. No return call. She'd probably gone off to pee or maybe to try her luck at fishing again. Nothing to worry about. I yawned and turned back to the tent.

A sharp crack out in the woods stopped me in my tracks. It was like the sound a piece of kindling made when the flame hit an air pocket inside it and it exploded, but louder, echoing through the trees. There was another one and then another. Curious, I found my boots and followed the noise away from camp.

The cracking sound got louder, and then there was a pause when I thought I heard voices. I must have been nearly a mile from our campsite. I came to another clearing, bigger than the one our tent was in, grassier and hilly. There was another crack, the loudest one yet. I knelt down by a big old stump and peered around it. My mom was standing in the clearing, but she wasn't alone. There were two men with her. Big-bellied guys in baseball caps and flannel shirts with the sleeves cut off. New York rednecks, my mom would have called them. She handed one of them something; I couldn't see what it was. The man took it, then nodded to his friend, who knelt down in the tall grass.

Mom shaded her eyes and turned all around, like she was admiring the scenery. Who were these men? What was she doing? And why hadn't she told me she was going to leave? I was about to come out from behind the stump and ask her myself, but then the man in the grass stood up. He had something in his hands. It was jet-black, a little longer than a baseball bat, thin on one end and flared on the other. A handle sat in the middle. A rifle. It was a rifle. The kind I'd seen soldiers carrying on the news. Mom took it from the man, then tucked the stock into her armpit. She gripped the handle and lowered her head to look down the thing's length. The men stepped back. Mom breathed slow and pulled the trigger.

That same crack filled the clearing, so loud this time I had to stick my fingers in my ears, so loud that flights of birds erupted from the trees and tore away into the sky. Mom fired again and again, leaning into the rifle as she did it. Smoke filled the air, and across from her a thick tree with a target nailed to it splintered. When the last echo faded, Mom lowered the gun. The men whooped and applauded, but Mom had no reaction. She nodded to the first man, then handed him something from her pocket. A white envelope. The man took it and the gun. After a little work he'd partially disassembled it and packed it away into a black case, which he handed Mom. She walked away without another word. She was headed right in my direction. I turned and ran as fast as I could.

By the time Mom got back to our tent I was lying on my side, eyes shut, pretending to sleep while the moment in the woods ran through my head in a loop. Mom leaning into the black rifle, one eye squeezed shut, the other sharp. Her finger on the trigger, pressing gently, followed by a sudden crack and an almost liquid sounding echo. It didn't make any sense. My mom took me to play rehearsal and made mint chocolate chip brownies for bake sales. She and Dad spent Saturday nights with Carol and Bernie, playing endless games of Scrabble. Why was she out there with those men? What did it mean?

Mom closed the tent flap, then emptied her backpack onto the ground. I opened my eyes. The gun case was smaller than it had seemed from across the field. It was a deep, pebbled black with heavy clasps along one side and a thick handle. There were two small cardboard boxes sitting on top of it: red, white, and blue with drawings of bullets on the side. The gun case and the bullets went inside her pack and then she refilled it, straining to close the zippers. When she was done she opened the tent flap again and sat down next to me. Morning birds were chirping. The sun was high and strong.

"Let's keep this between you and me. Okay, Goose?"

She turned and caught me with my eyes open. I nodded slowly. She smiled.

"Who knows," she said. "Maybe next time you can have a try."

In my mind I heard the crack of gunfire, rhythmic and sharp. I imagined what it would be like to have all that power in my hands, to feel the kick of it against my shoulder and watch as the target disintegrated. A strange churning started in my stomach. I looked up at my mom and said, "Yes. Please."

My phone pinged. It was Jay asking if I was okay. I looked at the time. More than two hours had passed. I made it down the hill and back across the river and found him barely a foot from where I'd left him, bent over a pile of stones near the cave. When he heard me coming, he spun around and waved his hand over his head like he was signaling a rescue ship, a goofy grin plastered across his face.

"Hey! Look at what I found!"

For a second I thought he'd cut himself, but what I took for blood pooling in the palm of his hand was really a pile of small, crimson stones, gleaming in the sun.

———

We stayed another hour or so and then we made the long walk back to the car. Our hike plus my impromptu mountain-climbing expedition had left me practically liquid, a puddle of a girl sloshing around in Jay's passenger seat. I rolled the three garnets he had given me around in my palm as the car took us back to Bethany. Soft music played on the radio. Synthy piano and drums. A distorted voice.

"What are we listening to?" I yawned, watching the trees on the side of the road fly by.

"You don't know this guy?" Jay reached over to turn up the music. "Mika Day. Performs as Snuggle Dungeon. I started listening to him last week. He's pretty great, right?"

My head flopped to the side. "Snuggle Dungeon? Seriously, Jay?"

"What?"

"I dunno. You don't exactly look like the kind of guy who'd be into a band called Snuggle Dungeon."

"And what kind of band do I look like I'd be into?"

"Something with a larger harpsichord section, perhaps?"

Jay laughed. "Seriously, though," he said. "He plays all these instruments one by one, sampling each of them as he goes and layering them on top of each other. When it's done he sings over top of it. He's playing in Harlow soon. You wanna go?"

"Yeah. Sure."

"Cool. Great. Awesome."

By the time we got to Bethany, school buses were making their afternoon rounds. Kids trudged along, backpacks pulling them down. *Suckers,* I thought.

We came to a stop at the back of a long line of cars. I lowered the window to try to see what was going on ahead of us. As soon as I did, a strong odor filled the car.

"What *is* that?" Jay opened his window. "Smells like smoke."

He was right. It did. But there was something chemical

beneath it, something familiar. As we inched forward, fire trucks came into view ahead of us, a whole army of them, parked on either side of the street with their lights turning. Firefighters grabbed their gear and ran down the hill, away from the road. Up ahead at the intersection a man in a blaze-orange vest stood in the middle of the road guiding traffic through the bottleneck. He held up a hand for us to wait as he waved the opposite lane through. I rolled down my window.

"Hey! What's going on?"

He nodded down the hill, where the firefighters were rushing toward another line of engines. Beyond them there was a small neighborhood. Newly built houses lined the streets. Six of them were on fire.

"Whoa," Jay said, echoing my sentiments.

The firefighters were quick to get into position, spraying the houses with water from the front-line trucks, but even I could see that it wouldn't be any use. The houses weren't houses anymore. They were walls of fire. Flames poured out of smashed windows and caved-in doors. The roofs were burning like the wicks of candles.

Jay shouted out to the guy directing traffic. "Was anybody hurt?"

"Nah, they were all empty, thank God. Abandoned. Guess whoever did it isn't a complete asshole."

"Somebody *did* it?"

Traffic guy looked down at us for the first time. "You don't smell that?"

"Smell what?"

"Gasoline. Houses were soaked in it! Second one this week."

I was surprised I hadn't recognized it before. Somebody behind us leaned on their horn. Traffic guy waved us forward.

"Okay! Move it along! Let's go!"

As we pulled away, I twisted around and leaned out the open window. Behind us, the firefighters had retreated and were gathered in a small arc a safe distance away, heads thrown back, watching. One of the houses had burned down to the studs, its bones showing black through the flames. Soon there'd be nothing but ashes and a vacant lot. I watched until the house passed out of sight behind us, but the smell of smoke and gasoline followed us all the way home.

—

I couldn't sleep again that night. Dad was shut up in his office, working as usual, and I was lying in bed, staring at the ceiling. Hours passed. I reached for my phone and called Jay. He picked up on the first ring.

"So," I said, not bothering with a hello. "What does your girlfriend think about your undying crush on Clarissa the beautiful?"

"What girlfriend?"

"The girl you were at prom with."

There was a brief but intriguing pause. "She's not my girlfriend."

"Then who was she?"

"Nobody."

"You hang out with a lot of nobodies, Jay. This mystery girl, Clarissa, . . ."

"You."

"Funny. But seriously. Who was she?" Silence again. "Come *onnnnnnnn*, Jay. Just tell me her name."

"Penny."

"Penny?"

"Yes, Penny."

"And Penny is *not* your girlfriend."

"Right."

"So what is she? Your social worker? Your bodyguard?"

"Lucy."

"Your accountant?"

"She's my cousin."

A laugh caught in my throat. "Wait. Seriously?"

"She's — hold on." He fumbled with the phone. "Marla, beat it!"

A young girl's voice in the background. "Who are you talking to, Jay?"

"Nobody. Go away!"

A door slammed, and then Jay was back in my ear with a deep sigh.

"The thing is, I didn't even want to go to prom," he said. "But my parents gave me this lecture about how it was a once-in-a-lifetime experience, and they didn't get to go to a prom when they were my age, and I'd regret it if I didn't. Not having anyone to take was my last line of defense, but Mom had Penny all queued up and ready to go."

"So how was it?"

"It was a nightmare."

I let out a squawk of a laugh. "I'm serious!" Jay insisted. "I barely even know her. She's like a third cousin, maybe a fourth. Plus, she's three years older than me, in college, with a boyfriend."

"Why'd she do it then?"

"Her mom made her! I tried to make the best of it. I mean,

we're there, right? We're *kind of* family. Might as well try to have fun. But we have nothing in common. Nothing. Eventually she started texting with her boyfriend. I couldn't even blame her. He's a really nice guy."

I laughed again, imagining his expression.

"And then, *then*, as if going to prom with my cousin wasn't bad enough, we get to the end of the night, I'm ten minutes from freedom, and my damn phone rings."

We were both quiet after that. I reached over and turned out my light. The shades were drawn so the darkness was heavy as a blanket. I could barely see to the foot of my bed.

"Who was it that called you?"

"My aunt," Jay said. "You know what's weird? I don't even remember the drive home that night."

"Me either."

"All I remember is sitting there with the TV on in this kind of daze, watching all those people trying to walk out of the city. There was this one girl in a toy store wearing a yellow dress. Her face—"

I sat up in the dark. "Wait! You remember her too?"

"Do *you*?"

"I haven't been able to get her out of my head. That was a toy store she was in?"

"They made custom dollhouses," Jay said. "The girl was the owner's daughter."

"What was she doing there in the middle of the night?"

Jay said he didn't know. When I asked if she was okay he didn't know that either. Apparently she'd disappeared in the days after the attack, lost in the waves of injured and homeless. Not even her family knew where she was. I lay back down with my head on the pillow, gazing at the ceiling, the phone warm against my ear.

"Lucy? You still there?"

I said I was.

"What are you doing?"

"I was just . . . she must have thought it was any other night. You know? She goes to work. She has to stay late. Maybe she has plans the next day, with friends, or with her boyfriend. Maybe she's going to sit in her pajamas all morning and watch old movies. But then—"

My throat closed up. I shut my eyes and there was a blinding yellow flash. After a long quiet moment, Jay said, "You know, Chin ordered the bombing to stop. And the raids. He's trying to calm things down. He's calling for peace talks."

"Is anybody listening?"

Jay was silent. There was a rustle and then a creak of bedsprings. His voice came back soft, husky.

"Somebody posted a map online," he said. "It has all the likely targets on it with fallout patterns and stuff in case it actually— you know. We're far away from any big cities, which is good. Military bases too."

"Sweet, we'll live out our days in a nuclear wasteland, fighting off mutants."

Jay chuckled. "I see you as the scrappy scavenger type. Dressed in rags. Living in an old dumpster."

"Yeah well, you're going to be one of those weird hermit dudes, hoarding old books and muttering to yourself about Puggle Dungeon."

"Snuggle Dungeon."

"Whatever."

I curled up on my side. Jay yawned.

"Maybe the radiation will give us superpowers," he said, voice thick with sleepiness.

"Mmm. I want gills."

"Gills?"

"I plan on building an underwater empire. No boys allowed."

"Honestly, I just hope my glasses don't break. The post-apocalypse is really gonna suck with severe myopia."

I laughed, throat aching from being clenched for so long. Jay's breath was slow and steady. The door to Dad's office opened and shut. His footsteps were quiet as he made his way to bed.

"It's getting late," Jay said. "Maybe we better —"

"Tell me something about rocks."

That caught him off-guard. "What about them?"

"Anything," I said. "Just talk."

He was awkward at first, stumbling over his words, but then he got in the zone. He told me about star sapphires and cursed diamonds and something called shocked quartz, which was made when asteroids crashed into the earth millions of years ago. His voice was soft in my ear. It was like he was lying beside me in the dark. He started talking about ancient magicians who spent their lives trying to turn base metals into gold and I found my hand moving across my bedspread, reaching out, like it was searching for his.

THIRTEEN

THAT SATURDAY I TEXTED Jay and told him it was time to kick off his education in horror.

Fine, he texted back.

> But we have to do it at your house.

> > but you said you had a sweet
> > home theater in the basement

> We do, but my house can be a bit . . . much.

> > > ???

> I have brothers and sisters.

> > > so?

> I have A LOT of brothers and sisters.

This was intriguing.

how many?

I sat at the edge of my bed waiting for a response, but nothing came.

jay? did you have a stroke?
do I need to call the paramedics?

Three little dots, then,

Damn it.
7.

I almost dropped the phone.

7?!? you have 7 brothers and sisters? seriously?
are you a mormon and forgot to tell me?

Ha.
Seriously though. It's like
the monkey house at the zoo over here.
Damn it. I just made you want
to come even more, didn't I?

!!🙊🙈🙉🙈🙊🙉🙈!!

Dad was locked away in his office again that morning, but I got shouted-through-the-door clearance to break the terms of my grounding. Jay picked me up an hour later. He was silent during the whole rainy drive to his house. Brow furrowed. Teeth grinding. Bethany Books appeared up ahead. Jay turned at the corner and headed down Willow Street toward Queen's Mill, a sprawling subdivision on the east side of town. We rolled through the gates and down the wide streets. His house was big. Three stories with a neat yard, at the end of a quiet street. He brought his car to a stop behind a white minivan. Rain pattered on the roof. He stared at the house, like a determined general facing a hopeless battle.

"We got lucky with the storm," he said, carefully surveying the yard. "Otherwise the whole pack would be out here. They'd have taken us down before we made it out of the car."

He pointed to a door at the far end of the driveway.

"We go in through the basement," he said. "Then lock the door leading upstairs from the inside. That should keep them out for a while. Just promise me, no matter what you hear up there: Do. Not. Leave. The. Basement. Understood?"

I threw him a crisp salute. Jay rolled his eyes, then opened the car door. We fast-walked up the driveway, heads down against the rain, Jay keeping us close to the wall so we wouldn't be visible through the first-floor windows. He was reaching for the doorknob when his phone started to ring.

"No no no no no."

"What?"

He yanked the phone out of his pocket and put it to his ear. There was a low peal of thunder.

"No, I — but Mom, I —" Jay drew in a resigned breath. "Yeah. Fine. Okay. I said okay!"

He hung up. The phone dangled from his hand. Rainwater flattened his hair and dripped down his glasses.

"My mom says she wants to meet you."

I started laughing. Jay turned his back on me and headed for the front door.

"You think it's funny now . . ."

We came around the side of the house and climbed the steps. From the other side of the door came the crash of shattering glass followed by a chorus of voices screaming at the top of their lungs.

"YOU MEANT TO DO THAT!"

"I DID NOT! YOU'RE JUST STUPID!"

"I'M NOT STUPID! YOU'RE STUPID! AND A BABY!"

"I'M NOT A BABY — YOU'RE A BABY! MOM!"

"MOM!"

"MOM!"

"MOOOOOOOOOOOOM!"

Jay pushed the door open, exposing a large marble-tiled entrance hall. There was a scream as a small mob of children tore across it from right to left. There must have been fifteen or twenty of them, all bound up together in a boiling scrum of flailing limbs, snotty noses, and screeching voices. As soon as they disappeared down the hall to our left they were immediately followed by a pack of five barking dogs the size of small ponies, which were in turn followed by a single toddler, who ran with his arms outstretched, giggling madly. Halfway across the room he slipped, fell flat on his face, then got up and kept going, crying instead of laughing.

"Jay, that's more than seven."

He'd turned pale. His happy glow from the day in Shangri-La, gone. "Saturday," he said. "They brought their friends. Stay close. This could get ugly."

I followed as Jay moved carefully into the house. All around us was what could only be described as an explosion of humanity. Everywhere I looked there were raging packs of kids. Kids playing video games, kids watching TV, kids listening to music — all with the sound turned way up — and in one corner kids involved in what looked like an MMA-sanctioned brawl. Toys and books and discarded clothes littered every available surface, and it seemed like half the walls in the place were decorated with crayon scrawls. When they saw Jay, it was like a feeding frenzy. Half of them dropped whatever they were doing, or destroying, and ran to him, pawing at his legs and shouting.

"Jay! Gloria broke my snow globe!"

"I did not!"

"Jay! I need a snack!"

"Jay! Ralph's diaper is full."

"Jay, who's the girl?"

"*Jay!*"

"JAY!"

"*JAY!*"

Jay kept his head down and powered through even as a handful of the kids attached themselves to his arms and legs and he had to drag them along. I followed in his wake and we eventually made it to the stairs that led up to the second floor. The narrow passageway had the natural effect of knocking some of the kids off him. They tumbled away and past me, laughing and squabbling all at once. I turned back. There was a dog pile of them at the bottom of the stairs and they were all trying to get to their feet and give chase. More were coming behind them, eyes wide and fingers sticky.

"Don't look back!" Jay shouted. "Keep moving! They can smell fear!"

We made it through a door at the top of the stairs. Jay slammed it shut the second I got through and put his back to it, panting.

"We did it," he said. "We're safe."

"JAY!"

The voice came from somewhere down the hall. Not a kid's voice this time. A woman's. Jay's mom, I guessed. He grimaced and pointed forward. Along the way we passed a boy no older than three or four, who was completely naked and struggling to do a handstand.

"Eric, go put on some pants!" Jay said. "We have a guest."

The kid giggled and ran away.

The woman called out again. "Jay? Is that you? Come in here!"

We passed through a dining room and into a large living area. There were two women there who looked like sisters. Both were tall and striking with angular faces and thick black hair. One, slightly older, I thought, was in a sharp gray suit, while the other wore all black and had a brightly patterned scarf tied around her neck.

"Mom, Halla, this is Lucy. Lucy, this is my mom and my Aunt Halla."

Halla, the woman with the scarf, waved and smiled. Jay's mom stepped forward and stuck out her hand. "Amina Karras."

I took it, suddenly feeling like I was interviewing for a job at a bank. "Lucy Weaver."

"You two were planning on watching movies today," Ms. Karras said. "Horror movies, I think."

"Yes."

"Do you know the work of Farouk Ibrahim?"

I looked to Jay, who seemed vaguely mortified. "Uh . . ."

"Egyptian filmmaker," Ms. Karras said. "He doesn't make horror movies though. He makes documentaries about the current state of the Middle East."

"More or less the same thing now, sis," Halla commented.

Ms. Karras slung her purse over her shoulder. For the first time, I noticed that she had a deep scar that ran from the corner of her right eye onto her cheek. "Very true."

"Well," I said. "I'll . . . check him out."

"Excellent," she said with a nod, then pivoted toward her son. "Jay, I need you to take your brother Wendall to the hospital."

"What?" Jay said. "Why?"

Ms. Karras pulled her keys out of her purse and grabbed an umbrella. "He broke his finger practicing karate with Gloria."

"Mom, we have plans!"

"It won't take long," she said. "You can watch movies when you get back."

"But—"

Halla stepped back and yelled up the stairs. "WENDALL! YOUR BROTHER'S HERE TO TAKE YOU TO THE HOSPITAL!"

"OKAY, AUNT HALLA!"

"Mom. Seriously. You *know* his finger isn't broken."

"Oh, are you a doctor now, Jay?"

"No," he said, clearly grasping for patience. "But you *know* Wendall's a big faker. He does it for attention."

"Don't say that about your brother!"

"But—"

"What if it's like that episode of that show?"

The voice came from behind us. I spun around to find a staggeringly pretty black-haired girl who was maybe twelve years old. She had her hands on her hips and a sour look on her face.

"Remember?" she said to Jay. "The one where the guy broke his leg and they fixed it, but bone marrow had leaked out of the break and it got in his bloodstream and he went crazy and died."

Jay had both hands pressing into the sides of his skull like he was trying to keep his brains in. "Don't be an idiot, Marla."

Marla squealed. "Mom!"

"Don't call your sister an idiot, Jay!"

Jay sighed and turned his back on Marla. "Mom, come on, Wendall's finger is *not* broken."

"Just take him to the ER and see!"

"Why can't you or Halla?"

"Sorry, kiddo," Halla said. "Your mom's got an important meeting and I have a thing at the gallery I can't miss."

"But it's Saturday!"

"The world does not stop revolving just because it's Saturday," Ms. Karras said.

"What about Dad? He could at least say if it was actually broken or not."

Halla nodded toward a small room off the kitchen where a man — the spitting image of Jay twenty-five years in the future — was dead asleep and snoring in a recliner. He was wearing green doctor's scrubs and had a headset stuck in one ear.

"Your dad didn't get home until four a.m. and has to be in again tonight," Ms. Karras said as she and Halla moved toward the stairs. "He needs his sleep."

Marla wailed from behind us, "But Mo-om! Jay has a movie date!"

Then she howled with laughter. When Jay feinted like he was going to punch her, she ran away giggling. Ms. Karras handed Jay an insurance card and a credit card and she and Halla swept out of the room and down the stairs. Just then an angelic-looking boy appeared. He was maybe seven or eight, but small for his age. He had rosy cheeks and hair so blond it was almost white. His chubby cheeks were glistening with tears. Wendall held up his right hand, which had been wrapped several inches thick in what looked like a mix of toilet paper and tape.

Jay rolled his eyes and waved him along faster. "All right. Come on. Let's get this over with." He turned back to me. "I'll take you home on the way. We can do the marathon another time."

"That's okay. I'll come."

"You want to come to the ER with us?"

"Nothing else happening. We'll start the marathon when we get back."

Wendall wailed. "Ja-ay! My finger! Hurts!"

Jay shut his eyes and drew in a long, deep breath, the kind you take when it's either that or you start ax-murdering people. When he was settled, he pointed his brother toward the door.

"All right, ya little creep, let's get moving."

—

A couple of hours later Jay and I were on the way back from the ER. Wendall was in the seat behind us, sound asleep, his finger wrapped in gauze and a metal brace. It wasn't broken, but it was sprained, which had allowed the little guy a tiny measure of satisfaction.

The rain was falling harder, a steady gray rush. The windshield wipers swished back and forth.

"So," I said. "Can I ask you about something that isn't remotely my business?"

"Does it have anything to do with how I came to have seven brothers and sisters, none of whom look anything like me or my parents?"

"Well, I would've found a *slightly* more delicate way to phrase it than that."

Jay took off his glasses and polished them on his shirttail while the car merged onto the highway.

"My folks met at a refugee camp in Algeria when they were kids. Dad's from Greece. Mom and Halla are Egyptian."

"How'd they get here?"

"It was before the worst of the bans. And Dad has a distant uncle in Wisconsin who sponsored them. Anyway, they had me and then, when I was seven, they started adopting other refugee kids who'd lost their parents. Marla from Vietnam. Paolo and Gloria from Mexico. Ahmed from Bangladesh. Eric from Kenya. Parviz from Pakistan. Wendall's from Florida. His folks died in Hurricane William."

I turned around. Wendall was in his seat, softly snoring, his white blond hair like snow.

"Does he remember?"

"Not really. He has bad dreams sometimes. Most of them do."

"That's amazing," I said. "That your parents did that."

Jay slipped his glasses back on. "Yeah, it made us *super* popular around the neighborhood," he said. "Threats online. Angry phone calls all night. Dad used to come out every single morning to find his tires slashed. He was probably the only person in history to buy spares in bulk."

"Did it ever stop?"

"Not until we moved," he said. "This was back in Georgia. We lived there until I was eleven."

The car glided off the highway and onto the road that led to Bethany. Shops flickered by as we came down Main Street. Jimmy's. The Beth.

"So your mom and dad's families . . . ?"

"Dad lost most everybody in the famine," he said. "I think there are some cousins left, but no one's heard from them since the New Dawn got voted in. Mom and Halla's parents were university professors back in Cairo when the al-Asiri took over."

He didn't say more. Didn't need to. I wondered if they'd killed them after his mom and her sister had escaped, or before.

"It's just me and Dad at my place," I said. "And the cat now, I guess. My aunts come over a lot too. My Aunt Bernie used to be a marine. She fought in Korea. She and my Aunt Carol are about to have their first baby. They were adamant about not finding out the gender. I'm hoping for a boy."

I was a little surprised at myself. I generally made it a rule to avoid talking about family stuff since it almost always led to questions about Mom, but sitting there with Jay, it came out before I gave it a thought. I braced myself, but all he did was kind of smile and say, "Well, if you ever want to trade places . . ."

"Sure," I said. "Your parents adopt kids like it's a bodily function. Why not me?" He laughed. It was small and breathy, a kind of stealth chuckle. Nothing at all like Luke's big, booming HA! The way Luke laughed, it was always a little bit like he was performing a laugh. Jay just laughed because he thought something was funny. Because he thought *I* was funny.

The car turned onto Willow Street at Bethany Books. A few minutes later we were pulling into his driveway again. Jay undid his seat belt and turned to Wendall.

"Hey. Jerkface. Let's go."

The kid didn't stir. Jay rolled his eyes. I followed him out of the car and around to the back door. He tried to coax Wendall awake, but the kid was out cold, so Jay strained to lift him up onto his hip. Wendall fussed for a second, then draped his arms around his brother's neck.

"Finger hurts, Jay."

Jay lowered his head so their foreheads touched. "I know, buddy," he whispered. "We'll get you to bed, okay?" Wendall nodded, then rested his cheek on Jay's shoulder. He drifted off again, lips puffing in and out with sleepy breaths. Jay held him close.

"I'll tuck him in; then we'll go downstairs and get a movie going," he said quietly. "We're starting with *Cannibal Creek Massacre*, right?"

There was a warm, sleepy grin on his face. His hair was mussed and his glasses were askew. It's strange how things happen. Ever since the 16th there'd been this knot inside me, tightening more and more every day. But in that second, standing there with Jay in his driveway as he held Wendall, smiling like a dope, it gave way. I found myself smiling too.

—

Hours later, we were a pair of lumps sitting side by side on a leather couch in their basement rec room. We'd made it through *Cannibal Creek Massacre*, *The Midwife*, and *Bonebreak Symphony*. A true marathon of horror. I'd wanted the experience to wash over him uninterrupted — no analysis, no discussion, no escape — so we hadn't talked about the movies as we'd watched, just jumped from one to another. When the last image of *Bonebreak* faded I was practically jumping out of my skin.

"So? What did you think?"

Jay was silent. The only light in the room was the dim glow of the TV screen. He rubbed his eyes and dropped his glasses onto his lap. Over the course of the marathon, the distance between us had slowly closed. He turned and lay his cheek against the leather of the couch, facing me.

"We've gotten this far without lying to each other," he said. "Right?"

"As far as *you* know."

He smiled. "I think maybe I'm not a horror guy."

"Why not?"

"It's possible," he said, "that I'm a coward."

I laughed.

"I'm not kidding! During *The Midwife* when that guy came home from work and found her alone with his daughter, and he didn't know she had a knife behind her back the whole time?"

"*Such* an amazing moment!"

"Let's just say I was doing everything I could to keep from whimpering like a little baby."

"Oh, come on!"

"No, seriously. You were this close to seeing me without my usual aura of macho calm."

"Yeah, right," I said. "Macho calm. This from the guy who listens to Snuggle Dungeon."

"Hey, only someone with a firm grip on his masculinity can listen to music that weepy."

I patted his arm like a doting aunt. "Don't worry, dear, we'll watch a nice Disney movie next time."

"Anything but *The Little Mermaid*. Ursula the sea witch freaks me out."

Jay went to the mini fridge in the corner and pulled out a couple more sodas. When he sat down again, our knees were only inches apart. He opened one of the bottles and handed it to me.

"So, what got you into them?"

"Horror movies? Me and my friend Jenna used to watch them when we had sleepovers."

"Jenna Pearl? We had AP Calculus together. I heard she joined some kind of cult."

I rolled my eyes. "There are always rumors about Jenna. Don't listen to them. Anyway, she was into horror and got me into it too. It was fun, but just kid's stuff back then. Watching things I knew I wasn't supposed to. But later on . . ."

I stopped myself. The TV screen was frozen on *Bonebreak*'s final image. Mr. Yoon, bloody ax in hand, baring his teeth. His white suit was covered in splashes of blood.

"Later on, what?" Jay asked.

I squeezed the icy bottle in my hand until it stung. I was about to make a joke, blow it off and talk about something else, but for some reason I didn't. "When we were kids, Jenna's parents used to fight all the time. She'd wake up to them screaming at each other in the middle of the night. Saying horrible things. She had to call the cops a couple of times. The whole thing really messed her up. She told me she started watching horror movies because they were the only thing that could make her feel something other than what she was feeling."

Jay waited, listening. Above us I could hear the sounds of his family moving from room to room.

"I guess there was a time freshman year when I needed the same thing."

I held my breath, expecting the obvious follow-up questions — When did you know about what your mom did? Did she really do it? — but Jay didn't ask. He slouched deeper into the sofa, erasing even more of the distance between us. Upstairs, someone turned on music and started to sing. Jay picked at the leather of the couch.

"Ever since the sixteenth there's been this" — his eyes narrowed like he was trying to see something in the distance — "this empty place. Right here." He put his hand over the center of his chest. "It aches. You know? I pick up a book or I watch a TV show, but after five minutes the words don't look like words anymore and the actors all seem like they're running around screeching at each other. I want to sleep, but I can't even do that. Until last night, anyway."

"What happened last night?"

Even as I said it, I knew. It was me. I'd happened last night. Or we had, I guess. Our two voices in the dark. We'd talked until almost dawn, but still, when I woke up I couldn't get to the phone fast enough.

Jay's hand was beside mine, palm up, fingers slightly curled.

It was crisscrossed with lines and little highways of veins. A thin white scar cut across the base of his thumb. I traced the length of it with my fingertip.

"When'd you get this?"

"Fifth grade. I was running away from some kids who wanted to kick my ass and I fell into a pile of broken glass."

"Was that when you broke your nose?"

He grinned. "No. That was another time. And thanks for noticing."

"No problem." The muscles in my neck stretched as I lifted my chin to show him my scar. "Fell into a coffee table."

Jay reached out with his other hand. His touch was light but warm as he brushed his finger back and forth over the ridge. A tingling sensation bloomed beneath my skin, moving down my throat and into my chest. Was that the first time he'd touched me?

"Guess we're both pretty clumsy," he said.

"Guess so," I agreed, my voice thick.

I lowered my chin and we were face-to-face, inches apart. I really noticed his eyes for the first time; they were a warm, sunny brown, like chestnuts or autumn leaves. As I looked into them I felt the same snap of connection I remembered from prom. The feeling of something invisible moving between us. I could hear my blood rushing in my ears and there was this nervous, jittery feeling in my stomach. Jay's gaze dropped to my lips. Everything else in the world seemed to disappear. I felt myself lean forward and then, just as suddenly, I felt myself stop.

"Jay, I . . ."

Every light in the basement snapped on at once. Glaring

fluorescents pouring down from overhead. The shock of it sent us reeling back to opposite sides of the couch. His mother called down from the top of the stairs.

"Jay! Dinner's almost ready. Halla made molokhia. Your friend is welcome to stay!"

After a pause Jay hollered back, "Okay! Thanks, Mom!" His voice sounded thick too.

The door to the basement shut with a clap. Mr. Yoon continued to grimace on the TV screen.

"What do you think?" Jay asked. "Molokhia's this Egyptian thing they loved when they were kids. I looked at the recipe once. It literally said, 'cook until slimy.' It's not to be missed."

He sat there looking at me, his expression unreadable, waiting. With all the lights on, everything in the basement looked flat and cold. A different world from the one we'd inhabited seconds before. Jay started to say something else, but I dug my hands into the cushions and pushed myself up off the couch.

"I think I better get going."

He jumped up. "I'll drive you."

I waved him off. "No. That's okay. I've got a movie hangover. Walk might do me good. It's not too far, right?"

Jay sat again and looked up at me in this curious kind of way, almost like he was looking at someone he thought he'd recognized, but now wasn't sure. He put his glasses back on and said, "No. It's not too far."

Neither of us moved. Jay stared at the floor. I stood at the end of the couch. The jittery feeling in my stomach had faded, but it was still there, sending tingling tremors through my body. My heart kicked. I was lightheaded. I saw myself dropping back onto the couch beside Jay, but when I started to move, it wasn't to go to him, it was to flee out the door to the driveway. It shut with a smack and I stood there trembling despite the warm night. Wind moved through the trees and air-conditioning units hummed. Inside the house, the sound of his family coming together for dinner was like a stampede. Kids laughed and squealed. Jay's mom shouted for him again. I heard him call back, "Coming!" A few seconds later, all the lights in the basement went out. I stood there a bit longer, listening to the sounds of their voices, and then I hurried down the driveway, past Jay's car and out to the dark street.

MAYBE THE WORST IDEA I EVER HAD

FOURTEEN

 BACK AT SCHOOL the following week, I skipped the soccer field and hung out in the old engineering shop, a big concrete-floored room filled with junked computers, 3D printers, and old welding gear. It hadn't been used in years — ever since a kid named Greg Wayland nearly burned his face off with an acetylene torch — so it was largely forgotten. I generally staked out a spot behind the desk in the abandoned teacher's office, plugged in my earbuds, and watched a movie on my phone. That's what I was doing the next time I saw Jay.

It was a Tuesday or Wednesday. Dance music was thumping in my ears as Esperanza Belén walked into that club for the first time, so I didn't hear him when he came in. All I caught was a flicker of movement by the door. My instinct was to dart into the shadows and hide, like I did when one of the security guards walked by, but I wasn't fast enough. He saw me the second he opened the door. I was stuck. Jay crossed the floor toward the office, hands in his pockets, eyes on the floor. I hadn't seen him since we'd watched movies at his house. Hadn't talked to him either. He'd texted me a few times — To say hi. To offer me a ride to school. — but when he did, I sat there staring at the phone. I didn't know what to say so I said nothing.

I hit pause on the movie and pulled my earbuds out, holding them close in that way you did when it was only temporary. Jay stopped in the office doorway.

"Wanna see a magic trick?"

I was too thrown by the question to answer it. He dropped into the seat across the desk from me and produced a deck of cards from his back pocket. He fanned them with a flourish and held them out.

"Pick one."

On my phone's screen, Esperanza was frozen on the dance floor. I figured the best way to get this over with quickly was to do what Jay wanted. I took a card. It was the ten of diamonds.

"Now," he said. "Remember your card and put it back in." I leaned forward. "No! Wait until I look away first."

He turned and looked back into the shop. The cards hovered in front of me, shaking a little. From nerves? I slipped mine into the deck. Jay turned back around, collapsed the fan, and set about shuffling. After a few seconds of silence, he said, "You been walking to school? Taking the bus?"

"Walking," I said quietly.

"Hot, right? I was about to have heat stroke out on the soccer field so I went back to class. Calculus was a ghost town. A *lot* of people are skipping. You can tell the teachers are wondering why the rest of us are even bothering at this point."

He cut the cards, bridged them, and let them fall, all in one fluid motion.

"I found this magic site the other night when I was bored.

All how-to videos. Really amazing stuff. I thought, *Who knows? Maybe I'm a magic guy and don't even know it.* Been practicing since then."

The cards danced in his hands, making a sound like someone riffling through the pages of a book. He was good.

"Wendall keeps talking about you," he added. "Apparently you made quite the impression. He really liked your hair, I guess? I dunno. Kids."

He set the deck in front of me in a neat stack.

"Cut 'em."

I cut the cards into two piles. Jay shuffled them all together one last time, then waved his hands dramatically over the deck, eyebrows furrowed, lips moving like he was silently intoning some kind of ancient spell. "Ala . . . kazaaam!"

In a flash Jay whipped out a card and held it up so I could see. It was the queen of clubs. He stared at me, wide-eyed, expectant. I looked from the card to him and back again. I nodded.

"It *is? Seriously?*" He turned the card around and looked at it. "Are you messing with me right now? Lucy Weaver, you *better* not be messing with me."

"No. That's it. That's my card. You got it."

Jay jumped out of his chair. "Ha! It didn't work at home. Not once! I did it for Parviz and Halla and Marla. They all laughed. Well, who's laughing *now*, suckers?"

Jay marveled at the card, his cheeks flushed with excitement. I couldn't help but smile.

"So I guess you're a magician now."

Jay tossed the card up in the air and caught it with one hand. "Goddamn right I'm a magician! I'm gonna go get me a *cape*."

The bell rang for first lunch.

"Oh man, I'm starving. Wanna get out of here? Get some nachos or something off campus? I'll pull a rabbit out of your hat."

Jay grinned. I imagined getting up from the desk and leaving with him. Getting in his car. *Maybe we could go back to Shangri-La. Maybe we could* — I cut myself off and held up my phone.

"Think I'm gonna keep watching this."

There was a pause. A flicker of disappointment passed over his face, but then it was gone.

"Yeah. Sure. Of course." He started to leave, then immediately turned back. "Oh! But before I go. Check out these bad boys."

Jay handed me his phone. On the screen were two tickets to the Snuggle Dungeon show. My stomach sank. The show was at the end of the week.

"You're still good, right?"

I stared at the tickets. I'd completely forgotten that I'd said I would go.

"Lucy?"

I handed him the phone back. Swallowed. "Uh. Yeah. Sure. Definitely."

"Great! Okay, I'm out of here. Man! I still can't believe that trick worked. Gonna go out and amaze the general population with astounding feats of prestidigitation! Ala-KAZAM!"

He kicked the door open, then let it slam shut behind him. The hallway was filled with people moving toward lunch, a riot of voices and bodies. I jammed the earbuds back in and hit play, but for the first time, *Black Suitcase* wasn't enough to blot out everything that was racing through my head. I swiped to another screen and found a familiar voice.

"— *elections throughout Europe today led to sweeping victories for the fascist New Dawn party in Spain, France, Germany and* —"

swipe

"— *Chin's moratorium on bombing has allowed the al-Asiri Empire, with assistance from the Russian Federation, to gain unprecedented ground in its assault on Iran, bringing the Empire closer than ever to its goal of securing that country's nuclear arsenal, which US sources have referred to as a 'bright red line in the sand.'*"

swipe

———

I hid in the engineering shop, mainlining catastrophe, until the final bell rang. Once the halls cleared out I stalked through the school, head down, trying to figure out what I was going to do about Jay. There was no way I could go to that concert with him, but what was I supposed to do? Call him? Send him a text? If so, what should I say? I pushed through the outer doors and started across the senior parking lot. *Maybe keep it casual,* I thought. *Start with a joke, and then come up with some kind of excuse. Something reasonable. Something—*

I was halfway across the lot when I looked up and I was struck by a lightning flash of inspiration. I stood there, gawking like a weirdo as all around me people got into their cars, honked their horns, and sped away. When the path was clear, I hitched my backpack onto my shoulder, took a breath, and strode across the blacktop to an adorable teal convertible. Its owner was about to start the engine. I walked right up to the driver's side and leaned on the door.

"Hi there," I said, as brightly as I could while still sounding sane. "I'm Lucy Weaver. We need to talk."

———

That night I texted Jay and asked him for a ride to school the following day. He agreed so fast it made my heart sink.

On the way there that morning he suggested we stop for some breakfast, and we ended up sitting at one of the outside tables at Bethany Bagel. Jay was chowing down while going on about some new card trick he was trying to learn. I was having a hard time paying attention because of the piece of paper that was sitting in my pocket.

"... the videos I've been watching say it's all about misdirection. Like that's helpful. I *get* that it's all about misdirection, but *how* am I supposed to misdirect someone? I'm starting to think..."

It was a half sheet of notebook paper folded up in a tight rectangle, like a little book. I could feel its outline pressing into my thigh. I slipped a hand into my pocket and ran my finger along its edge. The paper was smooth and warm.

"... and even if you don't have a way to hide it up your sleeve, you can still — "

Now or never, I thought. I yanked the paper out of my pocket and held it in the air between us. Jay abruptly stopped talking. He looked at the slip of paper, then at me.

"What's this?"

"This? This is an African elephant."

"What I'm asking is why are you —"

"God, just take it!"

I tossed the paper into his lap, happy to be rid of it. Confused, he tucked his cards into his pocket, then took an excruciatingly long time wiping some cream cheese off his fingers before picking up the paper and unfolding it. I snatched up my coffee and took a long gulp.

Finally, Jay said, "I don't understand. How'd you get this?"

"It's not exactly a state secret."

"I know. I'm saying—"

"It didn't require some kind of James Bond, Mission Impossible–style break-in or anything."

"Lucy."

"I didn't have to crack the vault at Fort Knox."

He glared at me.

"I asked her for it! Which, incidentally, is something you could have done yourself between sixth grade and now, but never mind."

Jay held the unfolded paper up in front of my eyes. "And what exactly do you expect me to do with Clarissa's number?"

I put my drink down and turned toward him, eagerly. "See? That's the thing! You don't have to do *anything*. I already did the prep work for you."

"What prep work?"

"I told her all about you!"

He stared at me, open-mouthed.

"No. It's fine," I said. "Trust me. I sung your praises like crazy, but, like, subtly, right? Like I was doing *her* a favor. Which I was! Anyway, I told her all about you, and all about this concert coming up, this Snuggle Dungeon thing, and she was totally interested. Turns out she's a fan."

"She is?"

"A *super* fan. Only reason she didn't have tickets already is she had this thing with her parents, but it got canceled. Anyway. All you have to do is call her, be briefly charming, and then boom! Your middle school dreams have come true."

He looked down at the piece of paper. Clarissa's handwriting was elegant and forthright, the kind you saw in Civil War documentaries when wives wrote to their husbands who were away at Antietam or wherever. It hadn't been all that hard to get the number from her, despite the fact that I'd been right about that one interaction I'd seen between them in the hallway. She barely remembered Jay at all. Still, after I laid it all out, she'd said "Sure!" then handed over her number before zipping away in that little convertible.

"It's just . . . I thought *we* were going to the concert."

My stomach churned. Now we were at the heart of it. The ugly, bleeding heart of it. Jay was staring out at the traffic zipping by on Main Street, shoulders slumped, Clarissa's number dangling from his fingers. In that second I wanted to take it all back — Clarissa's number, every stupid word that had come out of my mouth — but instead I lowered my head and fiddled with my nearly empty cup of coffee.

"I guess I thought this concert could be an opportunity for you to get something you really want. I mean, why not go with someone you're really interested in instead of with, you know . . ." I took a breath. "A friend."

The last word hung there. It was a punch. Hard, I told myself, but necessary. The door chime jangled behind us as someone came out of Bethany Bagel and headed for their car. Jay folded up the piece of paper and put it in his pocket.

"Guess we'd better get going."

"Yeah," I said, feeling a little sick.

After a painfully silent few minutes on the road we pulled into the school's parking lot. Jay cut the engine right as the first bell rang. All around us, crowds moved from their cars to the two main entrances, jostling and laughing. Jay watched them intently for a second with this strange sort of look on his face, and then he pulled out his phone and began hurriedly typing.

"What are you doing?"

He didn't even look up. "Getting tickets."

"For what?"

"The concert."

"I don't under — you already have tickets."

"Yeah, but you don't."

"Why do I need a ticket?"

"Because you're coming with us."

Cartoon tires screeched in my head. I turned and grabbed his arm. "Jay, no — third wheels are bad. Super bad."

"You're not going to be a third wheel."

"Why not?"

"Because I'm going to get you a date too."

"You're going to do *what?*"

He finished his business on the phone, then dropped it in his lap. "You wanted to help me, right? I mean, that was the whole point of this, wasn't it? Looking out for my best interests?"

"I —"

"Clarissa and I hardly know each other. This would be so much easier for me if it was a group thing. Besides, it's only fair that I return the favor."

"Jay, no. I'm not — I mean, that's sweet, seriously, but the concert is this week. You're not going to have time to find somebody for me to go with."

"Oh, I already found him."

"You did? Wait. Who? Jay, who?"

He didn't answer me; he was too busy laughing.

FIFTEEN

GATHER 'ROUND, GENTLE FRIENDS, and pay witness to a humble play presented in three acts. The title?

A Long Night in Harlow, New York, or
A Prisoner in the Snuggle Dungeon.

ACT ONE: HEY! THOSE AREN'T PORTOBELLOS!

Harlow was a city a couple of hours north of Bethany. We decided to take the train since the concert venue was just a short bus ride from the station. I ended up next to the window in the row behind Jay and Clarissa. Through the gap between their seats I could see that they were sharing a set of earbuds that were plugged into Clarissa's phone. When we'd met on the platform she'd been super excited about some Snuggle Dungeon bootleg she'd managed to get ahold of. The two of them had geeked out hard and had been listening to it ever since we boarded.

"You know, my whole life I've had this fantasy about riding on the top of a speeding train car."

I turned. My date, Toby Wolfowitz, grinned madly from

the seat next to me. He leaned toward me so our faces were only inches from each other.

"I think I saw a way we can get up there. You wanna come with?"

"Are you serious? What if there's a tunnel or something?"

"That's actually part of the fantasy. So? You up for it? We could play ninjas."

Clarissa took out her earbud and said something to Jay, who laughed. I couldn't make out what it was. Toby waited for an answer.

"I don't think so, Toby."

"But you're my date," he said, sounding oddly hurt. "Jay said so."

"Technically I'm your date for the *concert*. Since we're not at the concert yet, you're on your own when it comes to things like this."

"So if we were *at* the concert and I wanted to, like, rush the stage or rob the place or something—"

"Then I'd have no choice but to help."

Toby gave my knee a friendly pat. "You're okay, Lucy Weaver."

"Thanks, Toby."

He leaned out into the aisle and looked in both directions. "The coast is clear. I'm going to explore my options."

He got up. I grabbed his arm before he could take a step.

"Toby, just . . . be careful."

He gave me a wink and took off. Jay and Clarissa had gone silent, listening to their stupid band. I fiddled with my phone as trees and mountains and rivers shot by my window in a hundred-mile-an-hour blur. I'd gotten a special dispensation from Dad to go to the concert on the condition that I check in with him periodically. I texted him an update, then drummed my fingers against the armrest.

Jay and I had gotten to the Bethany station right before Clarissa and Toby. For a date I'd forced him to go on, he sure was nervous about it. He could barely keep still while we waited for her to show. And when Clarissa did come swanning up the stairs, all golden hair and supple skin, he'd practically bowed to her before stammering out a flurry of barely intelligible awkwardness. And, okay, the girl was model-level pretty, there was no doubt about that, but she was more like the sweetly grinning daughter you'd see on a billboard advertising a local family dentist, not a high-fashion model. Unthreatening pretty. Boring pretty. Was that really what Jay wanted?

The train came to a rest at a crowded station. Jay leaned over and said something to Clarissa. She swatted him on the arm and laughed a Disney Princess laugh, chirping and musical. Something about it made my stomach clench. What were they *saying* to each other? When the doors opened, the two people sitting in front of them got off. Before I knew it, I was out in the aisle, elbowing another couple out of the way so I could grab the seats first. As the train starting moving again, I turned so I was on my knees looking at Jay and Clarissa over the back of my seat.

"Hey, guys! What's happening?"

They looked up. The white Y of the earbuds cord they were sharing connected them, like a bridge. Jay seemed wary, but Clarissa beamed up at me. I swear to God, when I was little, I had an American Girl doll that looked *exactly* like her.

"Hey, Lucy!" she chirped. "Where'd Toby go?"

"Train surfing," I said. "So how's Muggle Dungeon?"

Jay narrowed his eyes. "Snuggle Dungeon."

"Snuggle Dungeon. Right."

"It's great!" Clarissa said. "We're listening to a bootleg of *Windswept Arcade.* Do you know it?"

"I do not."

"Oh! Well, Mika — that's Snuggle Dungeon's real name — and Master Mark made it as a charity thing after Hurricane William. It uses all these samples, though, and they never got them cleared, so the album got banned for years. Luckily my dad knew one of the producers, so he got me a copy."

Of *course* her dad knew one of the producers. Not only was she beautiful, she was probably rich, too. I wondered if the girl had ever had a negative thought or a sad experience in her entire life.

She plucked out her earbud and held it up to me. "You wanna listen?"

I waved it away. "I think I'll go in cold. Let the anticipation build. So! Clarissa . . . what's your last name again, Perin?"

"Perin. Yes."

I pointed at Jay. "Is this guy great, or what?"

Jay grimaced, but Clarissa didn't miss a beat. She nudged him in the rib with her elbow. "Yeah! He is. He's great!"

"Were you aware of his high level of expertise when it comes to rocks, minerals, and card tricks?"

She beamed, going along for the ride. "I was not."

"Oh, he knows everything. Don't you, Jay?"

"I don't really—"

"Come on," I said. "Don't be shy. Tell us something about rocks. A rock factoid. Or a mineral factoid. Your choice."

"Uh . . ."

He was clearly hoping for something like a train derailment to distract our attention, but I wasn't about to let it go, and since Clarissa had turned the full sunshine of her attention on him, he was stuck. He gently cleared his throat.

"Well, I've actually been reading about heavy metals," he said. "Like gold and iron. Did you know that all the gold in existence today, everywhere in the universe, was created in the first few milliseconds after the Big Bang?"

Clarissa reacted with what I thought was a pretty impressive simulation of interest. "No way. Really?"

"Uh-huh."

She was wearing a gold starfish necklace on a hair-thin chain. She lifted it off her tanned chest and turned it so it shone in the light coming in from the window.

"So this little guy had a front-row seat for the creation of the universe."

"And it's the same with iron, too," Jay said. "Even the iron in your blood. It's like there are these parts of us that have existed forever."

"Whoa."

I tapped my fingers against the headrest, impatient. "Whoa indeed. Good history lesson, Jay. We'll skip the magic, though. Now! Clarissa, I have some questions for you designed to make sure that you're an appropriate concert companion for my friend Jay."

Jay sighed helplessly, but Clarissa laughed and sat up straight like I'd called on her in class.

"Okay, shoot!"

"Great. Let's see. Best subject in school?"

She wrinkled her nose prettily. "I'd say English."

"Extracurriculars?"

"Spanish club. Cross Country. And there's my church's youth group. We mainly do charity type stuff.

"Your take on the current state of international relations vis-à-vis the looming threat of all-out nuclear war?"

"Uh . . ."

"Insightful. What are *your* career aspirations?" I held my hand up before she could answer. "No! Let me guess. Marine biologist! No! Veterinarian! You totally want to be a veterinarian."

Clarissa smiled again, but it was a different kind of smile, a hard one. I swore I could see the muscles in her cheeks working to pull the corners of her lips upward and set them in place.

"Well, I *did*," she said. "One time our cat got really bad asthma and it was my job to give him his medicine. So every day after school I put this little mask over his face and sprayed in this stuff for him to breathe. After a week he got better, which I, of course, attributed to my genius-level doctoring. So I downloaded applications to all the top universities in the country with vet programs and presented them to my mother. I was five."

Jay laughed a little more than was necessary. I scowled at him.

"And now?" I asked.

"Well, I'd planned on studying business or marketing, but now I'm thinking I want to do something more service-oriented. Like Habitat for Humanity or Amnesty International. Maybe something in government."

Jay angled himself toward her, which had the side effect of partially shutting me out.

"I know what you mean," he said. "I was planning on doing pre-law, then going into corporate tax law —"

"You *were?*" I said, shocked, but Jay ignored me.

"— but now it seems like, what's the point, right?"

"I know! Where were you going to go to school?"

"Yale. But I sent them a letter saying they should give my slot to someone else."

What? Mind blown, I interrupted him again. "You *did?* Jay, how did I not know this?"

He turned from Clarissa like he'd suddenly remembered that I was there.

"Oh. I guess you never asked."

The door at the end of the train car rattled open and Toby came ambling in. As he got closer it became clear that there was something off about him. More so than usual, even. His face was bright red and he looked freaked out and exhilarated at the same time. He stumbled down the aisle, then dropped to his knees on the seat beside me, facing Jay and Clarissa. He didn't say anything at first, just shook his head back and forth like he couldn't quite believe what was happening. The three of us looked at one another. It was Clarissa who decided to dive in.

"Uh . . . everything okay there, Toby?"

No response. My turn.

"Did you make it to the roof of the train?" I asked. "Or get hit on the head or something?"

Toby fixed his gaze on the brown vinyl seatback in front of him, studying it intently, like he'd never seen anything like it before. He took it in both hands and squeezed.

"*This,*" he said emphatically to the cushion before grabbing my shoulder and squeezing that too. "And this?" He held both hands out in front of him like he was cradling the air in his palms. "And this. I love *all* of this because . . ." He struggled for words to describe the enormity of his feelings. "Because you *have* to. You *have* to love all of it, all of the time, because it might not, it might not *be there* tomorrow. The air? And the seat? And Lucy? It all might be gone just like . . ." He lifted his open hand and blew across it like he was blowing off a leaf. "Like that."

He swallowed hard and winced.

"Does anybody have any water?"

Clarissa went into her bag and handed him a bottle of water. Toby drained half of it in one long gulp, then let out a long "aaaaahhhh" before holding the bottle out to her. She took it but he didn't let go; in fact he drew her closer.

"You're *so* pretty," he gushed. "Like a pony in a cartoon."

Her eyes sparkled with joy. "*Thank you.*"

Toby huffed in three quick, deep breaths like he was about to dive underwater for a long swim. He held it in until his eyes went red, then let it out in a rush. He laughed like a little kid.

Right, I thought. *Of course.*

"So, uh, what exactly did you take there, Toby?"

He dug around in his pocket, then held out his open palm. In it there was a small pile of dried mushrooms.

"Don't worry," he said. "I brought doses for everyone."

"Uh, thanks, Toby," Jay said. "But I don't think any of us are going to want to—"

Clarissa snatched the mushrooms out of Toby's hand. Before anyone could say a word, she shoved them in her mouth and started to chew. Her face contorted like she was working on a wad of hot garbage. I stepped back, sure she was going to retch, but then she yanked the bottle of water out of Toby's hand and upended it, forcing the shrooms down her throat. We all stared at her in complete silence until Toby put his hand on her shoulder.

"Cartoon Pony," he said. "That was *all* the doses."

ACT TWO: PRAYER FOR A DYING WORLD

The shrooms didn't seem to kick in until we stepped off the bus that ran from the train station to the concert venue, a repurposed warehouse on the west side of Harlow.

"They're all so *beautiful,*" Clarissa breathed.

While it was true that the Snuggle Dungeon fans lined up at the door veered toward the fabulous, it was *also* true that Ms. Perin was very much a resident of Psychedelic Land at that point. She probably would have said the same thing about a bunch of people waiting in line at the post office.

"Look at that *lady!*" Toby exclaimed, pointing without a shred of shame at an astoundingly tall woman who was decked out head to toe in neon-green velvet.

Clarissa took Toby's hand and started running. "We have to go talk to her! We have to tell her who we *are!*"

They raced out ahead of us. We tried to call them back, but it was no use. They weren't operating on our plane of existence.

"So, is it safe to say this is *not* what you imagined a date with Clarissa Perin would be like when you were in middle school?"

Jay didn't even look at me; he kept walking, head down, hands stuffed in his pockets.

"She definitely likes you," I said. "She gets this wide-eyed, apple-cheeked kind of thing going when she looks at you. It makes her look a little bit like a demented Barbie doll, but still. And I have to admit, pounding that triple dose of shrooms was impressive. Even if she didn't know she was doing it."

Still nothing. Not even a glare.

"Oh, come on, Jay! You're the one who invited Toby Wolfowitz. It's like inviting a great white shark to your pool party, then acting surprised when a few people get eaten. This could have been just you and Miss Golden Hair 2049. You'd probably be making out by now."

Jay came to a sudden halt and whirled around. "Can you please stop?"

"Stop what?"

"Pretending to be my friend."

A cheer went up around the parking lot. The door to the venue had opened and people were starting to file inside. I stood there, rocked back on my heels, like I'd been slapped. "Jay, I . . ."

"Why did you even come tonight? Why didn't you just say no?" He waited for an answer, but I didn't have one to give. "You know, I heard about your boyfriend. He bails on you right after the sixteenth, and since you don't have anything else going on, you grab the first loser you can find so you'll at least have someone to keep you company."

"No! Jay —"

"Forget it. I don't know what I was thinking with this. It was stupid."

Someone up ahead of us shouted, "Jay Karras!"

"Jaybird!"

"Jayhawk!"

Clarissa and Toby were at the very back of the line, hopping up and down on their toes and frantically waving their arms.

"We need tickets!"

Jay took out his phone and started swiping through screens. The glow lit his face in icy blues and grays.

"There's a train leaving for Bethany in twenty minutes," he said. "If you go now, you can make it."

I started to say something, but before I could get a word out, he'd turned away from me and was moving toward the line. When he got there, Clarissa threw her arms around him with a squeal. Jay showed the tickets to the man at the door and the three of them disappeared inside. After that, the parking lot was empty. I could hear the faint buzz of the streetlights and the distant sounds of cars way out on the highway. I kicked at a crumbling piece of asphalt at my feet. Behind me, brakes screeched as a city bus came to a halt at the corner, on its way to the train station. There was a hiss and the double doors flew open. The inside was all lit up, bright as day, but it was empty except for the driver.

"Hey, kid!"

I turned. It was the doorman, a hulking dude with a shaved head, dressed all in black.

"You coming?"

"What?"

I could see him roll his eyes from all the way across the lot. "That group had four tickets. Are you their fourth or what? I'm not standing out here all night."

———

The venue was small and dark, no seats, just a stage. It was too crowded to find Jay or the others, so I headed upstairs to a catwalk-type balcony. I found an open spot by the railing and claimed it. The stage was empty except for a pile of instruments on one side and a table with a laptop and microphone on the other. Down on the floor, the crowd milled around and talked. After a few minutes of searching I spotted Clarissa and Toby off on the far right-hand side near a stack of speakers, swaying to the atmospheric preshow music. Jay was nowhere to be seen, so I scanned the floor in sections. I finally found him near the edge of the stage on the far left-hand side, leaning against a steel pillar.

He didn't look like someone primed to enjoy a concert by his new favorite band. His head was down and his arms were crossed tightly over his chest. People jostled past him on their way to the bathrooms or the bar, but he hardly seemed to notice. I didn't care if he was pissed at me; I wasn't going to stand there and let this be ruined for him. I turned around, intending to go back downstairs and join him, but in the minutes since I'd found my spot, hundreds of people had crowded in behind me. I tried to push my way through, but there was barely a sliver of space between one body and the next.

"Hey, excuse me, can I please — "

A voice came over the loudspeakers. "Please welcome... Snuggle Dungeon."

The crowd threw their arms over their heads and screamed, spinning me around and sending me back toward the railing. Below, the audience surged, pressing themselves up against the stage. Even Jay got caught up in it, driven away from his pillar and out into the middle of the floor. When Snuggle Dungeon himself came out, there was even more screaming. He wasn't anything like I expected. I'd imagined a pasty white hipster with oversize glasses and stupid clothes, but he turned out to be an older Asian dude in a perfectly tailored, orange suit and tie. He barely seemed to notice the excitement of the crowd; he simply moved to the pile of instruments and equipment and selected a drum machine. The cheering abruptly cut out and the hall filled with a slow heartbeat thump. It played for a while, not loud, but insistent and deep, so it kind of worked its way into your bones. He turned to the laptop and fiddled with something as the thump continued. Then he strapped on a weathered acoustic guitar, and played a stream of bright notes over the beat that he sampled and looped. He played a small keyboard next and then an electric bass. Last, he used a small black egg to add a rhythmic shake. When he seemed satisfied, he stepped up to the microphone and sang with a voice that was deep and rich, with a faint British accent.

The first song was about love, the second was about sex, and the third was about death. For the next two hours his set continued in that exact same pattern. Love, sex, death. The songs themselves varied. Some were funny. Some were sad. Some were quiet and thoughtful, while others were like wails of horror or pain. The only thing that didn't vary was the pattern. Love sex death love sex death love sex death. After enough repetitions the order seemed to blur. Did death follow love and sex, or did death come first? Did it grow out of love and sex like a flower in a pot of soil?

While he played, I watched the crowd below me. Toby and Clarissa were still over by the speakers, blissed out. Toby had his shirt off and was wriggling to the music, utterly without rhythm. Clarissa stood a few people over from him. Her eyes were wide and bright. Her smile was enormous, like a half-moon. At one point she raised her arms over her head and waved them gently back and forth in a way that made me think of seaweed swaying in ocean tides. Jay had moved up close to the stage, and was standing straight, his head and shoulders thrown back. He looked overwhelmed with awe. There was a couple beside him, two boys with matching blond hair, who had their arms wrapped around each other and were kissing so slowly it was like their bodies had become trapped in a pocket of time moving at quarter speed. I saw couples of every kind with their arms wrapped around each other. Friends. Family. Lovers. At one point the music eased and I saw a girl with bright pink hair disengage and lay her head on her boyfriend's shoulder. They swayed gently, both of them smiling so hard they glowed, like angels in some old painting. It was the kind of joy that came from being at the perfect place at the perfect time with the perfect person and nothing could touch you. I knew the look. I knew the feeling. Even though I'd lost it, somehow in that moment even I believed in the kind of love that could go on forever.

A song ended and Snuggle Dungeon, shining with sweat, spoke into the silence with a soft voice.

"This is the last song of the night. It's called 'Prayer for a Dying World.'"

There were no loops this time. Just him and his guitar. As he played the first strains of the song, everyone around me started to move. I didn't understand until a grandmotherly woman put her hand on my shoulder and said, "This is the last song; we have to get ready for the finale."

"Get ready?"

She smiled and turned me toward the stairs. As I followed the crowd, Snuggle Dungeon's voice haunted the hall. The song was about a man standing on the shore of an enormous lake as a terrible storm starts to roll in over the water. As much as he wants to run away, to hide from the wind and the rain and the lightning, he can't seem to move. All he can do is stand and watch as a fleet of ships is broken on the rocks and all the trees and houses that surround the lake are ripped up and reduced to splinters. At first the man thinks he can't move because he's too afraid, but eventually he comes to realize that it's because he's in awe. He never knew how beautiful a terrible thing could be.

We came down the stairs from the balcony and filed onto the main floor. The people already there made room for us, shifting and adjusting until we were packed in, shoulder to shoulder. Suddenly, everyone, following some signal I never saw, sat on the floor, facing one another in small circles. The song swooped and reeled over our heads. I looked for Jay, or Toby, or Clarissa, but they were nowhere to be found.

The next thing I knew, the stage lights went out. There was a moment of complete darkness that was broken by the flickering light of candles. They were on the stage at first, but then they were passed down into the audience, moving from person to person. They kept coming until nearly everybody had one and the hall was filled with a haze of light. A candle moved into my hand. I turned to see who it had come from. It was the older woman who'd shown me the way upstairs. She smiled. In the candlelight her green eyes sparkled.

In the following verses, the song told about how the man was pulled away from the shore moments before the storm would have struck him. He found himself in the arms of a woman and a man and three small children. He fought them, but they managed to carry him off to a cave cut into the side of a mountain, where a fire was burning. It was warm there and dry. The six of them sat around the fire, shoulder to shoulder, as the storm battered the mountain above. They mourned the dying world and dreamed of the one that might come to take its place.

As the song ended, a line of people dressed simply in jeans and loose white shirts appeared in the wings. They were old and young. Men and women. They came down off the stage and moved barefoot through the hall, passing out small tin cups to everyone in the audience. When we each had one, they disappeared and returned again, this time carrying loaves of bread and earthenware jugs. The song was over by then and Mika was gone (the stage was empty; we'd never even seen him leave). There was no sound except a low shuffling and whispers of thanks as they moved through the theater, filling everyone's cups from the jugs and inviting each of us to tear off a piece of bread.

When my time came I lifted my dented cup and was surprised to see that it was Mika himself who was about to serve me. His orange suit was gone, replaced with the same jeans and white shirt as the others. He filled my cup, then turned to do the same for the woman next to me, passing her a large hunk of bread before moving on. I lifted the cup to my lips. It was wine, plummy and rich. I tipped the cup back and a gentle heat moved through me. The woman handed me some of the bread and we ate together. It was steaming hot, crisp on the outside and pillowy soft on the inside: a dream of bread. I finished the piece in my hand and someone else gave me more. For a time it was like everyone in the hall was connected by an invisible thread — eating as one, drinking as one, breathing as one, possessed of a single heartbeat — and then we were done and the main doors were thrown open. A breath of night air, cool after the heat of the packed venue, flooded the room. Mika waved to us from his place by the stage and then we all, slowly and quietly, walked outside.

I looked up as my feet hit the sidewalk. The sky was full of stars and the moon was high and bright. I was strangely numb, and there was a tingling buzz in my head and all through my chest. In the tips of my fingers. The woman I'd been sitting next to pulled me into a hug, kissing my cheek before she glided away into the parking lot and disappeared. All around me, strangers were hugging and giving each other big, dopey grins. I stood there awhile, taking it all in, and then the crowd parted and I saw Jay for the first time since the show had started. He'd gone off by himself and was looking up at the sky, his back to the brick wall of the venue. I moved away from the crowd and took a place beside him. Out in the parking lot people started saying their goodbyes and peeling off toward their cars, toward the bus stop.

"That was pretty great," I ventured.

Jay kept his eyes on the stars. I thought he wasn't going to say anything at all, that he was still pissed at me from before, but then he asked me what my favorite song was.

"The last one," I said.

He turned toward me, his shoulder up against the brick wall. "Mine's 'Marietta, Georgia, 1923.' The one about how he finds that black-and-white picture of a woman in an antique store and falls in love with her."

"I liked that one too. The way he kept seeing her everywhere he went. On the street. In bookstores. Even though she'd been dead for a hundred years."

Jay stared at the ground and we stood there awkwardly while stragglers milled around in the parking lot, hugging and laughing, not wanting the night to be over.

"I wasn't pretending to be your friend," I said.

Jay glanced up at me, then back at the ground. He nodded. A car honked, tearing our attention away from each other. A group piled into the back seat, laughing. They waved to us as they pulled away. Security started to hurry along the few clusters of people who were left. Jay said, "Guess we'd better try to find Toby and Clarissa before they get themselves in trouble."

"Yeah. I need to text my dad first. He's going to think I got kidnapped or something."

I took out my phone and froze when I saw what was there waiting for me.

"Oh, shit."

"Lucy? What's wrong?"

"Check your phone."

"What? Why? Damn it, what happened now?" Jay woke his phone's screen and read. "Oh no. No."

"Yeah."

The first text had been sent to both of us almost an hour earlier. We'd missed it, as well as the many, many texts that followed. I present the entire thread exactly as Jay and I received it.

TOBY: Jay and Lucy!
CLARISSA: Jay and Lucy !!!!!!😄!!!!!!
TOBY: This is amazing!
CLARISSA: 🎐So amazing!🎐
TOBY: But we have to go!

CLARISSA: We have a calling!

TOBY: ☀A calling from the universe!☀

CLARISSA: And you're invited!

TOBY: Come!

CLARISSA: Meet us at the front doors in 5!

TOBY: 🤖🐱👾‼👧🐾👫🐛🦋🐍🌿🍭

CLARISSA: OK you didn't come, but that's fine.

TOBY: We all have our own journeys.

CLARISSA: Our journey is currently on this bus. 🚌

TOBY: This bus is AMAZING! It's like a bullet of light shooting through the city and we're riding INSIDE it.

CLARISSA: The air is delicious in here. It tastes like cotton candy and 7-up. I can FEEL it.

TOBY: OH MY GOD LOOK! There's a guy dressed up as the statue of liberty!

CLARISSA: I love America! 🇺🇸

TOBY: We love America! ☀🇺🇸☀

CLARISSA: Toby is dancing now so if you were here you'd see Toby dancing he's a really terrible dancer but it's beautiful because the NEED to dance is always beautiful even if the dancing itself isn't.

CLARISSA: Now Toby is sitting and breathing, just breathing in and out, and I can see the air sparkling like pop rocks when it swirls around him and as he takes it in and lets it out and now everything is breathing with him

CLARISSA: the seats and the poles and the driver and the city outside, which is all colored in red and yellow and green and is so so so shiny it's hard to even look at

CLARISSA: this seat is made of like plastic or something blue plastic and if I look at it really closely I can see every individual atom like they're mountains like each one is a world of its own filled with people looking back and oh my god the universe is so incredible it makes me want to cry sometimes I wish you guys were here to see this I wish I was too

    CLARISSA: Toby says we're getting off now and we're going to go run through the woods like wild deer because we are children of god and that's what children of god do in the moonlight they run

    TOBY: Oh my god this guy is selling hot dogs!

    CLARISSA: 🌭🌭🌭🌭🌭🌭🌭🌭!!!!!!!!!!!!!!!!!!!

    TOBY: SEE YOU SOON WE WILL BUY 🌭🌭 FOR YOU TOO AND SODAS AND PEANUTS IF THEY HAVE THEM UNLESS YOU ARE ALLERGIC TO THEM IN WHICH CASE WE WON'T AND WE'LL HAVE THE MONEY FOR ICE CREAM LATER IF THE GUY IS STILL HERE WE LOVE YOU ALL AND EVERYTHING SO MUCH 🐶🐶🐶🐶🐶🐶

    CLARISSA: 🌿☀️🍃★🌭💫🍒😊😵😁😸🎃😺🤘‼️

    TOBY: Oh! Right! We're in Grant Park!

    CLARISSA: Come!

    TOBY: COME!!

    CLARISSA: COME!!! (sent with fireworks)

ACT THREE: Less of You Than There Was Before

By the time we found the right bus and got to Grant Park it was nearly midnight. Toby and Clarissa weren't answering any of our texts or phone calls, so we had no choice but to ignore the many PARK CLOSES AT DUSK signs and go in. Following the lights on our phones, we started down a narrow trail that wound through a mix of grassy fields and stands of trees. Every few minutes we called out their names.

"I swear to God, if Toby Wolfowitz gets us ax-murdered in Harlow, New York, I will haunt the *shit* out of him."

Jay stopped in the middle of the trail. "Didn't we already come this way?"

I looked around. Benches. Rocks. Trees. I threw up my hands. Jay brought up a map on his phone and studied it.

"Ah, okay. This way, maybe."

He took us down a trail that branched off from the one we were on. We passed a playground, then paused at a sign pointing toward baseball fields. I made a megaphone out of my hands and shouted.

"Toby! Clarissa!" Nothing. "Hey! Assholes!"

I checked my phone. Nothing there either. Dad had texted a couple of times so I let him know I was okay and then we moved on. The trail banked and turned. There was a trickle of water up ahead and then a small, wooden bridge appeared. The planks were a little loose. They clattered under our feet as we crossed it. On the other side, the trail ended at a line of tall, gray boulders. The map on Jay's phone showed an open field beyond them.

He craned his neck, searching. "Maybe we'll get a better view if we climb up to the top."

I took the lead and Jay followed. When we got there he sat and dangled his feet over the edge. A field stretched out ahead us, dotted with lampposts and ending in a stand of trees. Beyond that was the bright streak of the highway and a line of office buildings, like canyon walls, all lit up, but empty. A song from earlier in the night echoed in my ears, something about a haunted city sitting all alone on a desert plain.

"How'd Harlow do on that map you saw?"

"There's a big factory not far from here," Jay said. "Makes parts for military drones or something."

I imagined a flash out on the horizon and then a wave of fire rolling through Harlow, smashing windows, melting steel, turning concrete to dust and the park we were standing in to ash.

"Goodbye, Harlow, New York."

Jay selected a rock from a pile of gravel on the boulder and threw it out into the park. "Yep."

"See if you can hit that lamppost."

He tried but came up short. I stood up beside him and gave it a shot. There was a clang of metal.

"Yes! Try for the fence."

That time, he connected and I missed. We picked targets back and forth until we'd exhausted our supply of ammo. A fire engine went by out on the highway, sirens going, red lights flashing. It lit up the field below us and then passed into the distance. The park fell silent again.

"Did you really trash your Yale acceptance?"

Jay waved if off like it was no big deal. "I decided I was going to go to Yale and be a lawyer in like the seventh grade, but after the sixteenth . . . I don't know. I sat there looking at that letter, thinking I didn't even *know* the guy who thought this made any sense. I mean, corporate tax law? Seriously? That's the best I could come up with? *That* was my dream?"

I laughed. "I have to admit, as dreams go, it *is* pretty lame."

"What was yours?"

I shrugged. "I was going to travel around for a while with Luke and then . . . I don't know. I think there was a house involved, and a dog."

Saying it made my cheeks burn with embarrassment. Barely a month earlier it had made so much sense, had seemed so right, but sitting there with Jay the whole thing sounded like something a ten-year-old would have come up with. Traveling the world with my high school boyfriend, then settling down to play mom and dad to his little brother in some fantasy version of Colorado? Why didn't I just add a pony while I was at it? Or mention that I wanted to be an actress once? I struggled for something that didn't sound absurd and was surprised by what I landed on.

"Actually, I wanted to be a lawyer too when I was little. For about a minute."

Jay cocked one thick eyebrow. "Seriously?"

"Sure," I said. "What little girl doesn't want to be like her mom?"

The words jumped out before I could stop them. Ordinarily, I would have clammed up or tried to change the subject, but right then I didn't care. Maybe it was lingering good vibes from the concert. Maybe it was the easy feeling of being in that park late at night with Jay.

"You know who she is, right?"

Jay nodded.

"You never said anything."

"I guess I never thought your mom was the most interesting thing about you."

He smiled, kind and crooked. I sat back down beside him.

"Look," I said. "I'm sorry about the thing with Clarissa. Setting you guys up without telling you was shitty. I really do think she likes you though."

"I thought you said she was a demented Barbie."

"I was just being an asshole."

"Why?"

All of a sudden, I was back on the train, listening to the two of them whispering and laughing, connected by the thin line of the headphone's cord, Clarissa's hair shining in the sun streaming through the window. I said I didn't know.

"Why'd you come tonight?" he asked again, his voice soft. "You could have said no. Not shown up. Why'd you come with us?"

What could I say? From the moment he told me he'd gotten the tickets, it had never even occurred to me to say no. Not for a second. Not even after he told me Toby was going to be my date.

Jay had one last rock in his hand. He threw it into the dark. It didn't make a sound. It just disappeared.

"Have you heard from him lately?" he asked.

"Heard from who?"

"Luke."

It was strange to hear his name spoken out loud, stranger still to hear it come from Jay. It sat there between us, awkward and heavy. I shook my head.

"Do you know where he is?"

"I guess he's in Brazil somewhere, but . . . no. Not anymore. Not really."

"So you're just going to wait for him to —"

"Jay."

"Nothing makes sense to me but this, Lucy."

He'd turned away from the edge of the boulder and was facing me. The dim light from the lampposts below us turned his face into plains of shadow and silvery gray. He spoke quietly, slowly. I felt like I was back in my room again, lights out, phone pressed to my ear.

"There are things you think can't ever happen," he said. "Ever. But then they do happen, and . . ." he searched for the words. "I sat in my room after prom, still in that stupid suit, and I watched videos of all those people trying to get out of DC. And that girl — that girl in the yellow dress — I kept seeing her turning to the camera, over and over. I'd close my eyes, but she'd still be there. After that, all the plans I'd made, all the things I'd wanted . . . none of them seemed to matter. I tried to *make* things matter; I wrote bad poetry, I drew ugly pictures, but none of them did. And then I met you and—" He cut himself off, started again. "For so long it seemed liked everything was over, and then, all of a sudden, it was like something was starting."

Jay sat there, waiting, his face painted silver by the moonlight. Another rush of cars passed by at the tip of the park. In my head, I was back on a bus heading to school on a drizzly, cold morning. It was junior year. We came to a stop and the doors opened. Luke appeared in the stairwell, looking lost and anxious. I watched him come down the aisle, tentative, holding on to the backs of seats to keep from falling as the bus chugged to life. I slid toward the window to let him take a place beside me. I didn't even think about it. Why would I? How could such a tiny thing ever make a difference? Sitting there with Jay, I wondered what would have happened if I *had* thought about it, if I'd stayed where I was, if I'd kept my place and forced Luke to find another seat at the back of the bus. Of course, I knew the answer. Nothing would have happened. Nothing at all. I would have gone to school, moving silently from class to class like I did every other day, and then I would have come home to Dad and Carol and Bernie, completely unaware that there was anything missing. I would have lost the time Luke and I had together, but I would've also lost that night on Bethany Ridge when he told me he was leaving. I would have lost all the time after that too, all the days and weeks I spent watching the world falling apart for everyone else when it had already fallen apart for me.

The longer you're with someone, the more room they take up inside you. Eventually they crowd out your lungs and your heart, your liver and your kidneys. You share a spine and blood. It happens so slowly that you don't even realize it. And then one day they leave and take everything with them. How are you supposed to go on when there's so much less of you than there was before? When you've got no lungs to breathe and no heart to beat? When you want to scream but you don't have a mouth or a tongue? The only hope is to never open the door and let anyone in. It was a lesson I should have learned from Luke, one I should have learned from Mom before him, but I hadn't.

"Lucy?"

Jay reached for my hand but I moved it away. "They're here," I said.

"What? Who?"

I nodded toward the field below. Two figures were moving toward us, their cell phone flashlights sweeping back and forth.

"Toby and Clarissa," I said. "They found us."

"Luc—"

"Come on," I stepped to the edge of the boulder and started looking for a way down. "Let's go."

Jay didn't move, so I started off into the darkness on my own.

END OF PLAY.

THE CONCEPT OF NIRVANA, AS UNDERSTOOD BY TOBY WOLFOWITZ

SIXTEEN

I HUGGED MY KNEES to my chest as *The Wizard of Oz* lit up the screen at the Beth. I was in my uniform, but it was kind of a formality. The only other person there was Mr. Stahlberg, and I didn't even bother making him buy a ticket anymore.

It got to the part where the Wicked Witch of the West sends her army of blue-faced monkey things after Dorothy and her friends. "Fly! Fly! Fly!" she cackled as the music lurched. One by one the creatures hopped up onto her balcony, gibbering madly, and leapt off. Soon the sky was filled with them flying jerkily. When they swooped down out of the night and set upon Dorothy in the Haunted Forest there was a twinge of dread. It was a shadow of what I'd felt during *Cannibal Creek* or *Black Suitcase,* and it passed quickly, but it was there.

Soon, the heroes triumphed and Dorothy returned from somewhere over the rainbow to be reunited with Auntie Em and her soft focus, black-and-white farm. It had all been a dream. Bullshit music swelled. Credits rolled.

Mr. Stahlberg stretched as the house lights came up.

"Now, *that* was a movie," he yawned from the seat beside

me. "But I must say, I'm surprised you picked it, Lucy. Given that you've always been a devotee of the Grand Guignol."

I shook my box of Mike and Ikes and was disappointed to find it empty.

"Well, I was thinking about putting on *Massacre at Bikini Beach* next, if you're up for a double feature."

He checked his battered watch. "Tempting. But dinner calls. And you have a dinner to get to as well, if I remember correctly."

I looked at the time on my phone. He was right. A swampland of dread settled in my gut. Stahlberg struggled to get out of his chair. He looked thinner than he had the last time I'd seen him. More frail, too. I wondered if he'd been eating. I offered him my arm, allowing him to mask his unsteadiness in chivalry, and led him up the aisle of the empty theater. It was sad seeing the place so empty. It'd never exactly been standing room only at the Beth, but in the last few days the place had turned downright ghostly. Even my boss had bailed. He'd tossed me the keys on his way out of town, heading to some underground survivalist camp in Montana. He said he'd keep paying the bills and manage the Beth remotely — between small arms training and, I don't know, learning to drink his own urine — but I hadn't heard from him since.

"*The Wizard of Oz* always puts me in mind of God," Stahlberg said.

"Why's that?"

"Because of its creator," he said, putting on the old college-professor voice he'd learned from his late wife, Amanda. "L. Frank Baum was the mastermind behind the whole thing. Brought joy to millions upon millions of children and adults the world over.

He was a leading proponent of women being granted the right to vote."

"Sounds like a good guy."

He grunted. "He was also an outspoken cheerleader for the genocide of Native Americans. Said every last one of them should be rounded up and slaughtered so the white man could take his rightful place as ruler of the continent. He maintained that the native peoples were depraved and despicable, while we were naturally superior."

"And this makes you think about God?"

Mr. Stahlberg came to a halt at the top of the aisle to catch his breath. A small line of sweat showed at his forehead, despite the fact that I had the AC pumping. He wiped it away with the back of his hand.

"Frank Baum is a reminder that one can create a beautiful, wondrous thing that brings joy to all who see it and still be a monstrous bastard."

Usually Mr. Stahlberg waited in the lobby while I closed up, but he said he had to get moving.

"No time to waste! Big plans tonight!"

"Hitting the town?"

He laughed. "No, just dinner and a long-hoarded bottle of Bordeaux."

The bell on the door jingled as he opened it.

"Feel that air!" he exclaimed. "Like hot soup. Did you hear? There's a hurricane headed for Texas. Category seven. The first ever. They're calling it Persephone, which is a lovely name for a hurricane. It'll be one hell of a blow. I wonder if everyone will stop killing each other long enough to watch it."

"Mr. Stahlberg, why don't you wait for me? You don't look good. I want to make sure you get home okay."

His grin was weary but wide. "No, my dear. When my Amanda makes her lasagna Bolognese, you don't want to be one second late."

He stepped through the door and let it close behind him. That's when it hit me. Had he said *Amanda*?

"Wait! Mr. Stahlberg!"

I went after him, but he was already slipping into his car, which he'd parked at the curb right in front of the Beth. The engine turned over and he pulled away. I called to him, but all he did was wave over his shoulder. I stood there watching him drive off. The sky was overcast. Bruised. For a second I thought I heard a witch's cackle and the gibbering approach of thousands of lumpy, winged monsters jerking through the sky.

"Nice bow tie, Weaver."

I spun around, startled. Even when I saw who was standing there it took a second for it to sink in. The Target ensemble Jenna Pearl had been wearing the last time I'd seen her was gone, replaced by full-on outdoorsy gear. Leather hiking boots. Khaki shorts with all kinds of pockets and zippers and what I was pretty sure was a sheath for a small knife on her belt. She looked more fit too, with ridges of muscle running along her arms and calves. She'd even chopped off most of her hair. What was left was boyish and messy, and the back of her neck was covered in bristly stubble.

"Jenna. Hey. What are you doing here?"

"Killing time before I go to this thing," she said casually, like she hadn't fallen off the face of the earth after getting into that Range Rover outside the Yankee Clipper. She popped up on her toes and peeked into the theater. "Got any Buncha Crunch in there?"

"Uh, yeah, come on in while I close up."

Jenna followed me inside. I reached over the candy counter and tossed a box to her. She trailed along, munching, while I went into the back to change.

"Hey! Did you go to graduation?"

I pulled off my black bow tie and tossed it on the table. "No. You?"

"Nah." Jenna tossed some candy in the air. It landed in her mouth with a pop. "I heard they had to cancel the Bailey Center. Did it in the gym this year."

"Why?"

"Hardly anyone was going," she said. "It's like the entire senior class said fuck it all at once."

"If we were smart we would've said that a long time ago."

"Ain't that the truth."

I stuffed my uniform into my bag, then went back into the theater to make sure all the doors were locked. The place may have been on its last legs, but there was no reason to neglect it.

"So, are you and Grant still . . ."

Jenna laughed. "You didn't hear?"

"No," I said. "What?"

"He came out two weeks after prom and moved to Chicago with his boyfriend."

"No way. Really?"

"I wasn't surprised," she said. "Things didn't . . . turn out the way I thought they were going to when we got to that hotel room after prom. Anyway, I've been too busy to think about him."

"Busy with what?"

"This and that."

Theater secure, I hit the lights and we headed outside. The front gate rattled as I pulled it down. While I fumbled with the padlock Jenna scanned Main Street. It was practically deserted, nothing but a small handful of couples walking along. More than half the stores were dark. Some were boarded up. Jenna whistled, long and low.

"Man, this place is dead. What the hell happened while I was gone?"

I snapped the lock into place. "A lot of people left."

"Canada?"

"Mostly."

Jenna and I hit the sidewalk and headed north. A lot had happened since my night in Harlow. The US, along with our fascist besties in Europe, were now officially at war with both the al-Asiri and *their* new best friends, the Russians. The fighting had been fairly old-school up to that point — nothing but good old-fashioned guns and bombs — but if the al-Asiri made good on their plan to take Iran and its stockpile of nuclear weapons, which was looking more and more likely, it wasn't going to stay that way. General Barrington had all but promised that the second the al-Asiri had the bomb we were launching our missiles, which had prompted the Russians to promise that if we did they'd launch theirs at *us*. President Chin was trying put the brakes on the whole thing, calling for peace talks and cease fires, but no one was listening to him.

Anyway. Canada had stayed out of all the craziness, so people figured it'd be a safe haven when things inevitably got out of hand.

Technically, the border was closed, but it was said that enough cash could get you through. Those with a slightly lower budget headed south, into Mexico, which had its own problems for sure, but was at least out of the direct line of fire. Others, like my boss, fled to underground shelters and armed camps out west. The super-rich and obscenely powerful were all supposedly heading to New Zealand. The rest of us hunkered down and hoped for the best.

I kept expecting Jenna to stop and get in one of the vehicles parked along Main, but she hung in there, eating her candy. When she turned to look at a rare passing car I caught sight of a tattoo peeking out from under her collar. Something spiky and black. I wondered what "this and that" meant.

"Hey, do you have another one of those cloves on you?"

Jenna shook her head. "Had to give 'em up. Along with coffee and booze and soda and sugar."

"Why?"

"Don't want to be dependent on things that might not be around much longer."

I let that go. Walking with her threw me right back to middle school, before Mom, before we had cars or boyfriends or money of our own. We'd get tired of lying around her room watching movies and would end up on these epically long walks, usually late at night. No direction. No plan. Just wandering. We'd start out talking about movies or whatever play we were doing at the time, but we'd inevitably end up talking about the future, about what things would be like when we were in high school or college or when we were old and had families. We'd work through an entire lifetime in one night, then erase it all and start again the next day.

"So," Jenna said, head down, hands in her pockets. "I've been meaning to apologize."

"For what?"

She glanced over at me. "That night at the diner. Calling you a tourist."

I almost laughed. It felt like a million years ago. "Oh, right. That." I shrugged it off. "It's okay."

"No, it was a crappy thing to say. I don't know. I guess I was still kind of messed up about things back then."

"We all were. And hey, you might've been right."

We veered off Main onto Spruce. Lights were on in every third or fourth house. The rest of them were hunched up in the darkness. The soft clap of our footsteps was the only sound.

"So, I heard you were madly in love with Jay Karras."

Luckily I wasn't drinking anything, or I would have spat it out all over the street.

"Where'd you hear that?"

"I don't know," she said. "Around. Not true?"

"We were hanging out," I said, then quickly added, "Friends hanging out. Not hanging out, hanging out."

"Were? You're not anymore?"

I shook my head and a kind of gloom settled around me. Jay and I hadn't spoken since Harlow. Not even a text. I'd lost count of the times I'd picked up my phone, wanting to text him, to say hi, to hear his voice. Every time, I put it down again, telling myself it was for the best. For me. For him. We rounded a corner and my house appeared at the end of the street. I found myself slowing down so we wouldn't get there too fast.

Jenna laughed to herself. "You remember the time we made

up that dance to — oh damn, what was it? We thought we were so cool! What was that song?"

I laughed, remembering too. "'Me Boy You Girl.'"

Jenna howled. "'Me Boy You Girl'! Right! By . . ."

"Little Three."

"Little Three! Damn! I wonder what happened to them."

"I think Donny got killed in a car accident a few years ago."

"No way!"

"Benji's like a priest now or something."

"So I take it you're still in the fan club."

I pressed my first three fingers together and crossed my heart three times like we used to. "Little Three forever."

Jenna laughed. "That dance was pretty cool."

For a horrifying second I thought we were going to drop what we were doing and perform it right there on the street, Jenna beatboxing and me singing the melody like always, but her phone pinged. The screen lit up her face as she looked.

"Goddamn it."

"Everything okay?"

"Yeah," she said, tapping out a response, then slipping the phone back in her pocket. "It's the people I'm meeting. Hey! Tyler Greenbaum is finally doing his Halloween thing tomorrow night. You going?"

"Nah. Don't really feel like partying."

"It'll be fun. He was going to do it as his house, but then he found this crazy abandoned mansion way out on the west side. The owners up and bailed."

"I don't know."

"Come on, we could talk some more. Before I leave."

"Where are you going?"

Her phone pinged again. "Damn it." She backed away from me as she texted a reply. "I gotta go, but I'll tell you all about it at the party."

"Jenna—"

"Come on! It's been forever. I'll even drive! Promise me!"

I laughed as she skipped away, phone in hand. "Okay. Okay!"

"I'll swing by at nine and get you! Don't forget to wear a costume!"

When she was gone I turned toward home. All the lights were on downstairs and jazz was floating out of the kitchen window. Bernie and Dad were bustling around inside, getting ready. It was strange. It used to be that there wasn't much I looked forward to more than our family dinners, but I was dreading this one.

Probably because I knew it was going to be our last.

———

Dad made pasta. Nothing fancy. We all sat in our places around the table. Dad's jazz played lightly in the background. Forks clinked on plates. Copperfield stalked the perimeter of the table, rubbing against our legs in turn.

"This is good, Rog."

Dad smiled. "Wish I could have done something fancier."

"You could have made grilled cheese and it would have been fine," Bernie said, leaning back in her chair. "Ah, the humble grilled cheese. That monument to the ingenuity of mankind. The perfect encapsulation of humanity's—"

Dad threw a balled-up napkin at her head, and we all laughed. I swirled some pasta and sauce around on my plate. It was good, but I wasn't hungry.

I laid my fork down and pushed back from the table. "So what's Edmonton like, Bernie?"

"Haven't really been there since I was little," she said. "Dad was American, so when he and Mom split up he brought me down here."

Carol reached across the table and took Bernie's hand. "We know it's cold —"

"But not as cold as it used to be."

"But not as cold as it used to be, yes. And the people there like hockey. *And* it has a world-class theater festival."

It had been decided a few days earlier. The people who ran the home Bernie's mom lived in called and said she'd taken a turn for the worse, and it was more than they were equipped to handle. Since Bernie had been born there and had what qualified as a family emergency, she and Carol were able to get permission to cross the border. When they told Dad and me, I asked how long they planned to stay and was greeted by an awkward silence that was as clear as if they'd spoken. Bernie and Carol would raise their son or daughter in Canada. Dad said we'd visit as soon as we could. He said it casually, enthusiastically, like we'd hop on a plane, jet up there, and jet back. I knew what he was doing. He was trying to make them, to make all of us, feel better about the decision. But the world wasn't like that anymore and we all knew it.

Dad served dessert, a slightly stale grocery-store cake that he tried to touch up by drizzling it with sugar and some old brandy he had lying around. It was both tasty and potent. When we were done, Bernie stretched her arms over her head and yawned. Carol rubbed her wife's back.

"This one's been loading a truck all day," she said. "Probably better get her to bed."

"I'm fine, babe. We can hang out."

"No, I'm pretty beat too," Carol said. "And we've got a hell of a long drive tomorrow."

Dad started gathering plates and glasses. "You guys cutting straight north?"

Bernie nodded. "We were thinking of heading west first, but we decided it'd be smarter to get over the border as soon as we can."

She grabbed some dishes and headed into the kitchen with Dad to discuss driving routes. Carol covered her mouth and yawned, then let her hand drop to her belly. Her eyes were puffy and her hair looked like it hadn't been brushed, but her peaches-and-cream skin looked like it was lit from behind.

"The little peanut is a kicking machine," she said with a faint smile. "Bernie already found some good martial arts schools in Edmonton. She's pretty sure we have a prodigy on our hands."

"Maybe a second-generation marine," I said. "Are there marines in Canada?"

"If there are, the peanut will not be one of them." A shine came into her eyes as she rubbed her belly. "No guns for her. Or him. Ever."

I wondered how likely it was that the peanut would be able to live up to Carol's vow. Canada was safe for now, but it wasn't on the moon.

One night, years ago, Mom and Dad and Carol and Bernie had talked over dinner about how they were going to buy a huge house on a lake farther upstate so they could all live together.

There'd be enough room for everyone, enough so that Bernie and Carol's kids and I could come back on our breaks from college and, later, with spouses and kids of our own. The Weaver Family Commune, they'd called it. It was a joke at first, the product of too much wine and laughing, but joking led to casual searching on the Internet for houses and then, as the idea settled in, more serious searching. The four of them even started putting money away for it. They said it would be a few years, maybe five or even ten, but they'd make it happen. It was our future. All of us together. Forever.

Carol abruptly reached across the table, gripped my hand, and said, "I'm sorry, Lucy."

I shook my head. "Leaving for Canada is smart."

"Not for Canada."

"For what, then?"

Her eyes drifted toward the tablecloth. A fine pattern of blue and yellow daisies on white linen. She'd bought it for us herself last Christmas. Dishes clanked in the kitchen. Dad laughed at something Bernie said.

"You were right," she said. "What you said that night at dinner. We all knew a time like this was coming, our *parents* knew, but we didn't do much about it. We barely even tried."

"My mom did."

I hadn't planned to say it. It just popped out. Carol's blue-green eyes flared briefly, then went still. Mom was almost never mentioned in our family, especially by Carol. When reporters had surrounded the house during the trial, when they'd hassled us at the market and at work and at school, Carol had cursed her name faster than anybody.

"Your mom was . . ."

What would it be this time? A monster? A sociopath? Carol let out a long breath like she was facing a hill too steep to climb.

"The first time I met her, when Roger brought her home to meet our parents, I didn't think it would last. She was sweet but she seemed too, I don't know, insubstantial for your dad. I called her the manic pixie dream lawyer. But I got used to her. I got to know her. And then she had you and I loved her. And then . . ."

Carol brushed the flat of her hand against the tablecloth like she was smoothing out a wrinkle.

"Did you know that Hurricane William just about wiped Florida State off the map? Everybody remembers what happened to Miami, but people forget that. Half the campus. Gone. Like it was never there. No one thought it was possible."

We both went silent. In the kitchen, glasses pinged as Dad washed and Bernie dried. I moved closer to Carol, took her hand like she'd taken mine.

"Everything's going to be okay," I said. "People always think the world is about to end. Right? World War One. World War Two. Vietnam. September eleventh. Saudi Arabia. North Korea. Those were all supposed to be the end, but they weren't."

Carol dipped her head.

"And President Chin is — he's had a hard time but he's a good guy. And he's still in charge. He won't let things get out of control. Honestly, I think pretty soon everyone is going to see how crazy things have gotten. It'll be like a wake-up call. A year from now, me and Dad, we'll be visiting you and Bernie and the peanut in Canada and this will all — it'll seem like some movie we all sat through once."

Footsteps in the hallway. Dad and Bernie.

"Babe?" Bernie said. "You ready?"

Carol nodded and squeezed my hand. Her eyes were shiny. With a sad smile she said, "Yeah, I think you're right, Goose."

The four of us made a grim little procession to the front door. Hugs were given all around. Dad cried first. Then Carol. Then Bernie. Then me. We stood there silently as the clouds shifted and the stars came out. Eventually there was nothing left to say. They broke off from us, hand in hand, and followed the walk down to the driveway. There was a soft engine hum as Bernie and Carol pulled away. They waved and were gone. We stood there looking out at all the empty houses, listening to night sounds in the trees. A small breeze rattled Mr. Giolotti's wind chimes across the street.

We went back inside and shut the door.

SEVENTEEN

JENNA DID A DOUBLE-TAKE when I came out of the house the night of the party.

"Are you supposed to be . . . ?"

"Yep."

I tossed my suitcase into the back seat and got in the car. Jenna took off as I checked my look in the mirror. Pale skin. Penciled-in widow's peak. Hair pulled into a bun so tight I was pretty sure my eyes were going to pop out. The white blouse and drab gray suit I'd found in a box of Mom's old things were almost startlingly accurate. I put the mirror back up and turned to Jenna. She was in shorts and hiking boots again.

"Where the hell is *your* costume?"

"In the back. I'll put it on when we get there."

Jenna's car zoomed noiselessly onto the highway. The lines of it were sleek and razor sharp. Leather seats. Gleaming faux-wood dash. Sweet new-car smell.

"Uh, Jenna? Whose car is this?"

"You like it? My dad bought my mom and me one each. He got himself a BMW."

Jenna's dad was an economics professor at a small college. Her mom ran a bath shop on Main Street.

"So Dave Pearl won the lottery?"

Jenna laughed. "He took out loans from three different banks. It might have technically been fraud, but he'd always wanted a nice car. Thought we should have ones too, which may have had something to do with his long-standing guilt about being a raging asshole all those years."

"How is he going to pay for them?"

Jenna's car shot past a guy on a motorcycle. "Please. The world economy is a month or two from total collapse. The banks are all going to go under. Companies, too. Tons of countries. He decided it'd be better to have his money in things like cars and gold."

"Wow. So the Pearl family is really embracing the whole experience, then."

"Things were weird for a while," she said. "Lots of crying and denial. Then we all kind of, I don't know, melted into it. When I got back from training, things were more chill in my house than they've been since I was little. No more fighting. Dad cooks all the time. We play board games. Go on little road trips."

I was about to ask what training she'd gotten back from, but the car swung into a driveway and came to a stop. Jenna let out an awed *"Damn."*

She was right. The place was a straight-up mansion. A four-story sprawl of gray stone with a tree-lined lawn and a circular driveway that was choked with cars, all of them packed in tight with a Tetris-like complexity. Most of the windows and the front door were wide open, so as soon as we stepped out of Jenna's ride we were surrounded by the steady *unz-unz-unz* beat of crappy EDM that was streaming out of the house.

"Why is it that the people who throw parties and the people who have shitty taste in music are always the same people?"

"One of life's great mysteries," Jenna said.

I retrieved my suitcase and came around to the back of the car, where Jenna was pulling a set of long black robes out of the trunk. I thought she was making a return to goth Jenna, but once she put them on it all became clear. It was a nun's habit, complete with a little black-and-white snood that covered her hair and a chunky wooden crucifix. Beneath her costume the trunk was packed with what looked like camping gear. A huge pack. A tent. Great curled lengths of rope and spiky climbing gear.

"Another Pearl family hobby?"

"Not quite." Jenna slammed the trunk shut. "All right," she said. "Let's do this."

The music rose to an eardrum-assaulting thump as we approached the mansion. Inside, it was the Platonic ideal of a mid-twenty-first-century teen party. The air was thick with the smell of spilled beer, pot, and bad cologne. People were packed in tight. I counted maybe two guys who were actually wearing shirts. The rest were bare-chested in low-slung shorts with only the slightest nod to an actual costume. Camo for army man, six-shooter in a holster for cowboy, badge for cop. The girls were, predictably enough, outfitted in various iterations of sexy fill-in-the-blank. Sexy cheerleaders. Sexy nurses. Sexy librarians.

I paused by the marble staircase and shouted over the music,

"You know, I used to wonder why I didn't go to more things like this in high school."

"Yeah, we really missed out, didn't we? Ah, crap."

"What?"

Jenna reached through her nun's habit and pulled out her phone. She checked the screen and said, "I have to go talk to some people."

"Now? About what?"

"Nothing. It's just — it's a whole thing. I'll explain later, okay?"

"You're seriously leaving me? I'm only here because of you!"

"I know, I know. I'm sorry. Look, I'll just be out back. One hour, tops. Find me then, okay?"

"Jenna!"

"Have fun! Mingle!"

She called back another sorry and pushed her way through the writhing bodies, offering a solemn blessing to anyone she jostled. The music changed to something even more annoying. I looked back at the door and considered bailing, but figured I was there, I was wearing an awesome costume, I might as well make the best of it. The living room/dance floor was way too much for me to handle, so I made my way down a hall big enough to drive a bus through, pulling my suitcase behind me. Each room I came across was its own little world. I could almost hear the soothing tones of a museum docent as I walked.

On our right we can see the union of latter-day hippies and honky Rastas in Ganja World — I said hi to Wade, Lorenzo, Stank, and Cooper — *while in Dude-Bro Pavilion you can find all the drinking games and date-rapeyness the ancient world had to offer.*

Now come right this way as we move into the Hall of Drunken Groping.

I climbed another set of stairs at the end of the hallway. Every few steps there was a couple draped over each other, making out sloppily. I lifted my suitcase and picked my way around them and up to the second floor. It was quieter there, the blare of the music reduced to a vibration that buzzed up into my ankles through the hardwood. I found myself in another long hallway, lined with closed doors. Thumps and grunts and laughter came from the other side of most of them. I opened one with no sounds behind it and entered a master bedroom that was easily as big as the whole downstairs of my house. The place looked as if it had been designed for French royalty who had somehow found themselves living in exile in Bethany, New York. It was done up in lilac and ivory. There was a white iron canopy bed and a vanity with crystal bottles of makeup and perfume laid out on a silver tray. There were two walk-in closets, each one filled with clothes. Whoever had lived here really had up and bailed. I wondered if their new home was even more opulent than this, or if they'd gone another way entirely. Maybe all the time spent in this pampered cage had filled them with some kind of back-to-nature zeal and they were currently living rough in the woods, making fires with sticks and eating fish out of mountain streams.

"Hey. You mind if we . . ."

A sexy maid and her scrawny bro boyfriend were standing in the doorway, open bottles of champagne dangling from their fingers. They were looking past me at the gigantic bed.

"Oh," I said. "Sure. Sorry."

I started out past them, but sexy maid stopped me. "You could join us if you want."

The dude grinned so wide it was a wonder his jaw didn't snap. He clearly could not believe his luck. Neither could I, really.

"I'm good," I said. "Thanks."

The door shut behind me and I continued my wander, the suitcase's wheels making a pleasant little *click-clack* behind me as they hit the seams in the hardwood floors. The house seemed like it went on forever. Room after room. An entire upstairs kitchen. A gym. At the far end of the hall there was another open door. Through it I could see shelves stacked with books and glass cases full of taxidermy.

The room turned out to be a kind of library-museum hybrid. Alongside the books and stuffed forest creatures there were glass cases full of old jewelry, rocks in a multitude of colors, and shards of vases. In one corner there was a stand of headdresses, masks, and spears. I lifted the lid off one of the cases and took out a yellowy slab of rock with what looked like black scribbles all over it. At first I thought it was some kind of hieroglyph, but when I turned the rock over I saw that the black marks went straight through it to the other side.

My phone buzzed in the pocket of my suit. I pulled it out, thinking maybe it was Jenna calling to tell me she was ready to be a decent friend again, but it was some number I didn't recognize. I cut it off three rings in and put the phone away. Footsteps behind me. More young lovers, no doubt. I turned to leave, but froze when I saw who was standing in the doorway. It was Jay.

He was wearing a little paper cap and blue hospital scrubs that were too big for him. His dad's, I guessed. A mask and stethoscope hung around his neck. I expected him to beat a hasty retreat at the sight of me, but he was as frozen as I was, until he noticed the rock I had in my hand anyway.

"Whoa. I've never seen one in that good shape before. You mind if I . . ."

"Oh. Yeah. Sure."

I handed the rock over and Jay held it up into the light to study it.

"What is it?" I asked.

"Graphic granite," he said. "It's an alkali feldspar matrix with bits of quartz in it. The quartz is what makes it look like it has writing on it."

"There's more."

Jay followed me back to the case.

"Nice," he said, lifting out pieces and examining each one. "Tourmaline. Vanadinite. Limonite. That's a seriously huge garnet."

"Yours for the taking."

He picked up a sea-green stone that had been polished smooth and turned it over in his hands, then put it back and took another. When he finished looking at the rocks, we both stood there while the music thumped downstairs. Another couple peeked inside and moved on. I picked at the hem of my too-tight jacket.

"My costume. It's from —"

"*Black Suitcase*," he said. "I know. You're Esperanza."

"You *watched* it? But you're a coward."

"Oh, don't get me wrong, I whimpered like a two-year-old

through most of it. Oh man, when she walks up that mountain road at the end, all by herself? And there are all those noises out in the dark? And then she goes inside the cave?"

"And her twin is in there, only it's not *really* her twin."

Jay shivered visibly. "And the trees? I can't even look at trees anymore."

"God, you *are* a coward!"

Jay laughed. "What's really cool though is it's not like something you're watching. It's not like a story. It's more like —"

"— an experience."

"Right! Exactly. It's like this thing that's *happening* to you and all you can do is surrender to it." He crossed his arms and leaned against the case, smiling a little. "I think you've got it all wrong though."

"Got what wrong?"

"What it's about," he said. "Esperanza isn't in hell."

"So where is she?"

"*Nowhere*. She imagined the whole thing. In reality, she never even left the park bench."

"WHAT! No way. I'm totally calling bullshit."

"I'm serious," he said. "If you look at the story like it's a —"

"Jay?"

We turned toward the door. Clarissa was dressed as a superhero. Not a sexy superhero. Just a superhero. Red bodysuit. Flowing black cape. A small mask that covered her eyes. Her hair was down, hanging over her shoulders in golden waves. Her eyes lit up and she bolted into the room to give me a hug.

"Lucy Weaver! How's it going?"

"Uh, great," I said. "I'm . . . great."

She retreated, then wrapped her arm around Jay's waist, pulling him in tight. His hand disappeared and reappeared on her shoulder, hanging there in a way that seemed almost, but not totally, natural.

"Wendy's on her way," she said, looking up at him. "Do you want to hang out here awhile longer and then we'll all go over to King's?"

"Yeah," Jay said. "Sure."

"Oh! Lucy, you should come with us," she said. "It's kind of dorky, but we're all going to drink beer and watch dumb movies."

A devilish part of me almost accepted the invitation so I could witness the sheer, hilarious awkwardness of the whole thing, but then I saw the look of abject horror on Jay's face and couldn't go through with it. "Thanks," I said. "But I'm going to hang out here for a while. My friend is around somewhere."

Clarissa's phone dinged. "Oh! Wendy's here. You ready, Dr. Karras?"

Jay said he was and then they said goodbye and swept toward the door. Clarissa stopped abruptly like she had forgotten something and came running back into the room. To my surprise she threw her arms around me again and whispered in my ear.

"Thanks so much for making this happen. You're a lifesaver!"

Before I could say anything she gave me a squeeze and then dashed into the hallway, her black cape fluttering behind her. I moved to the doorway. Jay looked back over Clarissa's shoulder. I waved and he waved back. I watched the two of them until they made it to the end of the hallway and disappeared down the stairs, hand in hand.

—

The mansion's backyard was maybe half the size of your average state park. There was an Olympic-size pool with a towering diving board, rows of lounge chairs, and pieces of Roman-inspired statuary in white marble. Alongside that there were two hot tubs, each one full of barely dressed kids, their bodies stretched out in the warm water, drinking cheap beer from crystal goblets. Beyond the light of the pool area there were regulation tennis and basketball courts. Four boys were running up and down one of them with a basketball, mindlessly drunk, taking impossible shots and laughing when they missed.

I left my suitcase by the door and grabbed a beer from a nearby cooler. I drained it fast, then grabbed another as I scanned the yard for Jenna. She was nowhere to be found. I texted her but got no response. Further out in the yard I caught sight of firelight coming through a stand of trees. It was a warm night so a bonfire was kind of ridiculous, but I guess if you give a bunch of drunk people enough space and things to burn, you're going to get a fire. Seeing no other option, I crossed the lawn, soft as deep-pile carpet, and headed into the woods. As I made my way through the trees the firelight grew brighter. Twenty or thirty people were gathered around it.

"Hey! Weaver! Over here!"

Jenna rushed toward me from the far side of the fire. She had gotten rid of most of her nun's habit, leaving her in shorts, a T-shirt, and the black-and-white snood. It was quite a look.

"Come on," she said. "I want you to meet some people."

Jenna dragged me toward where a group of ten or so was sitting in a rough circle. They looked older than us, college-age, some even older, and they were all wearing the same kind of outdoorsy gear that Jenna was. Hiking boots. Shorts. Trim haircuts. They were seated boy-girl, boy-girl. Everyone was talking quietly to one another. No one was drinking or smoking. They didn't even look particularly relaxed. They sat there, legs crossed, straight-backed and alert, like they might have to spring into action at any second. But to do what?

"Piers! This is the friend I was telling you about, Lucy Weaver."

One of the men jumped up from the circle and stuck out his hand. "Lucy. Great to meet you. Piers Carroll."

Piers was tall and muscular with a head of thick blond curls. He had the white teeth and solid handshake of a politician. We all sat down by the fire. I wanted to ask Jenna what she'd been telling this guy about me, and why, but she jumped up and ran over to say hi to someone across the circle. My phone rang again. I checked it, but it was that same number I didn't recognize. Some determined telemarketer, no doubt. I put the phone away and glanced over my shoulder toward the mansion, wondering if there was someone I could catch a ride home with.

"Leave something back there?"

Piers was leaning forward, elbows on his knees, smiling. I noticed dark shapes in the gloom behind him. The bonfire flared, and I saw the domes of tents. I cracked the beer I'd taken earlier.

"You all been living out here or something?"

Piers followed my eyes to the mass of equipment. "Not for much longer. Once a few more of our people join us we'll be heading out."

"Where to?"

"Mary and Satoshi are heading west, toward Missouri," Piers

said, pointing around the circle. "Dave and Lisa are going to Canada if they can get in. Marcus and Noor are headed south, toward Georgia. The rest are fanning out around the country."

I sighed. Looked like I was having a conversation with this guy whether I liked it or not. "And why exactly will they be doing this, Piers?"

Instead of answering, he looked over my head in the direction of the mansion. "All that back there. The party. The music. The drinking. You like it?"

I took a sip of my beer. "I guess the drinking doesn't bother me so much."

Piers forced a tight smile. "Seriously."

"Seriously? I guess it's not really my thing."

His eyes lit up like I'd fallen into a cunningly laid trap. "Yes! Mine either. It's seems so desperate, doesn't it? Searching for happiness, for meaning, in substances, in sex, when the world is crumbling around us. It's a waste of time. Sad, really."

The fire crackled and flared as someone threw on another log. Piers smiled, showing off those huge white teeth.

"I'm sorry. You asked a simple question. Why are we doing what we're doing? We're doing it because we're Wagnerites."

The way he said it made me think he expected me to know what that meant. I'd never heard of them.

"And that's . . . what? Some kind of cult?"

He laughed. "No. Not at all. Back in the early twenties a professor at Yale, Heinrich Wagner, was looking at the climate-change data and saw, before almost anyone else, that we'd waited far too long and done far too little. We were on the verge of a global catastrophe, one so great that the very continuation of the species was uncertain. But what to do?"

He ticked three points off on his long fingers.

"Scatter, survive, rebuild. Wagner's idea was that if small groups of skilled individuals dispersed over a wide enough area, you'd increase the chances that some of them would survive the cataclysm and rebuild society. But Wagner took this one step further. He saw that the coming disaster — however horrific, however painful — was also an opportunity."

"An opportunity for what?"

He leaned in even closer. Ribbons of firelight danced across his dark eyes.

"Lucy, if you could go back in time — back to when you were five or six, say — and start your life again, knowing what you know now, would you take that opportunity? If you could re-chart the course of your life, fix mistakes, take opportunities you passed up, wouldn't you *have* to? Well, *that's* the opportunity being handed to us right now. The cataclysm that Wagner predicted is our chance to go back to the beginning, knowing all we know now, and restart civilization from scratch. We'll be able to make new choices, create new institutions. We'll be able to single-handedly redefine what society is for the next millennium."

I counted twenty people around the fire. A few more out in the woods. "And these people are going to do all of that."

Piers threw his head back and laughed again, a little too dramatically. "No! Of course not! We're only one of forty cells in North America. There are others on every continent. Each cell member is a trained survivalist as well as being schooled in a discipline that post-civilization societies will need. Engineers. Farmers. Doctors. Your friend Jenna's our microbiologist."

Stupid as it was, that was the first moment I put it together that Jenna was actually *with* Piers and his friends. It didn't seem possible. She was too smart. They were too nuts. But there was no way around it. There she was, sitting in their circle, talking with another girl who was dressed just like her — minus the snood, of course.

"She only finished her survival training last week," Piers continued. "But she's already one of our finest. Truly dedicated. She and Diego are heading out on assignment to Iowa. There's still room left, you know."

"Room for what?"

He said nothing, just kept smiling, like he could will the answer straight into my head, which I guess he did. I was a goddamn sucker. The victim of a con. Is *this* why Jenna had shown up at the Beth? Not to reignite our friendship, but to get me to join her little cult? I stood up and tossed my empty beer can onto the ground.

"Thanks, but I think I'll pass."

I walked off, away from the fire and back toward the mansion, trying to figure out who might be able to give me a ride home. Was Jay still there? No, too awkward. One of the Hacky Sack dudes?

"Weaver! Lucy! Wait!"

Jenna ran up beside me.

"I'm going home."

"Slow down," she said, hustling to keep up with me. "Please. Look, I'm supposed to partner with Diego, but Piers said I could partner with *you* instead. Think about it. Me and you, together, just like when we were kids."

"Pass."

"Lucy!"

"I'm not a *survivalist*, Jenna. I can barely climb a flight of stairs without getting winded. Besides, I don't think you and I can be much help repopulating the earth."

"That doesn't matter. Piers has a totally different job in mind for you. For us. We'd be going out and recruiting new teams. We'd travel all over the world. But it has to be you and me."

"Why?"

When Jenna didn't respond, I stopped walking. She was standing behind me, blank-faced. An actress who'd run out of lines.

"Jenna, why does it have to be you and me?"

Still nothing. I was about to say to hell with it and walk away, but something she'd said had sunk a hook into me. A special job. Just for us. Recruiting. *Why would they want me to be a—?* Everything clicked into place at once. I stormed off through the woods, toward the mansion.

"Lucy, wait!"

"Leave me alone, Jenna!"

"People will listen to you! They'll understand. Your mom—"

"Don't talk to me about my mother."

Jenna yanked me back by my arm. "People didn't understand what she did back then. They will now. I do. Piers does. She's a hero to all of us. An *inspiration*. She saw what was coming and she *did* something about it."

"Jenna—"

"What have *you* done, Lucy? Anything? You spent four years

of high school floating around, not doing shit that was worth anything to anybody, and you were planning on doing the exact same
after graduation. You have a chance now to do something that
matters. That means something."

We were close enough to the mansion to hear the throb of the
music. Spotlights flared in time with the beat, throwing colored
beams out into the woods. Camouflage patterns of light and dark
danced across Jenna's face, making it seem to shift and move. I
wrenched my arm out of her hand.

"Fuck you, Jenna."

She called after me but I didn't turn around, didn't stop moving. Soon the woods broke and the mansion appeared at the end
of the lawn. The music was deafening, an electronic hammer
pounding at my ears. Someone had focused one of the floodlights
on the gray stone face of the house. Others had moved in front of it
and were throwing giant shadows against the walls. They reached
their arms up toward the roof and mimed pulling it down. Each
try was timed to a wave of screams, then laughter, then screams
again.

—

The road that led away from the mansion was long and winding,
turning through towering woods and silent neighborhoods full of
dark-eyed houses. There was no sidewalk, only a broken, weedy
shoulder. My stupid suitcase caught on every crack and seam,
tumbling over, refusing to move. I yanked at it so hard, crying
and cussing, that I was pretty sure the muscles in my shoulder
were about to shred. Most of the streetlights were out. The mansion was long gone behind me.

After I left Jenna, I'd gone back into the party and shared

the better part of a bottle of vodka with some kid in a werewolf mask whose name I didn't know. At first the liquor was warm and sweet, but it grew fangs quickly, gnawing at my stomach, at my brain. Eventually the werewolf grabbed my ass. His eyes were bloodshot beneath his mask. Unsteady. I punched him in the chest as hard as I could, then went stumbling out of the house and into the dark.

Another crack caught my suitcase. I pulled hard and there was the sound of plastic breaking. One of the wheels had snapped in two.

"Fuck fuck fuck fuck fuck!"

I tried to pull the thing on one wheel, but it was practically impossible. The suitcase teetered and twisted and dropped on the side of the road. I went to pick it up again and that was when my stomach decided to rebel. I hit my knees, doubled over, and puked into the weeds. When my stomach stopped convulsing I stayed where I was, too wiped out to move. My head was buzzing and spinning. There was a whirlpool in my gut. Mom's suit was damp with sweat and flecked with bits of vomit. I peeled off the jacket and undid the scarf. The gravelly road was hard, so I sat on the suitcase. I dropped my head in my hands and shut my eyes.

I was with Mom the day Hurricane William hit Florida. It was a Saturday. We were sitting in the waiting room at the mechanic's counting the seconds until our car was fixed. I was reading and Mom was fiddling with her phone. There was a TV playing in the background, but it was on a news station so I wasn't paying any attention to it. Someone's name was called over the loudspeaker. People moved in and out. I flipped through my book, bored and anxious, wondering how much longer it would be before we could leave. I was thinking about making another visit to the table of free cookies when the feel of the room suddenly changed. It was like the air had gotten heavier. I looked up and everyone in the place, fifteen or twenty people, was staring at the TV, utterly silent. I didn't get it. All I saw was a man standing in the rain with a microphone. Palm trees were bent nearly in half behind him and waves crashed. It was a hurricane. We'd seen hurricanes before. Dozens of them.

An old man by the door shook his head and said, "Category six. The third this season. Unbelievable."

"The keys are already gone," someone else said. "Miami is half drowned."

"State'll never survive. Not after last year."

A man by the door dialed his phone. When someone answered, he said, "Are you seeing this? Are you?"

An older woman let her gossip magazine sag in her hands. "Those poor people," she said.

The woman next to her closed her eyes. "Those poor people."

I tugged at Mom's sleeve, but it was like I wasn't even there. Her eyes were locked on the screen and her face was drained of color, like someone who'd been shaken awake from a nightmare. We didn't talk on the ride home and, after dinner, Mom and Dad sent me to bed early and stayed up to watch the news. Reporters' voices filtered up through the floorboards. I caught bits and pieces as I lay there, unable to sleep. The southern half of the state was practically underwater, and the north wasn't faring much better. Constant rain had caused floods that swamped buildings and ripped houses from their foundations. High winds tore palm trees from their roots, sending them hurtling through the air like javelins while cars and trucks tumbled end over end through parking lots and down city streets. Highways turned into canals. Monster waves ripped coastlines apart.

At one point the governor came on and said, through tears, that he didn't believe there was any way his state could survive. He was right. Thousands died over the next few days, but it was nothing compared to what came later. People began running out of food and water, and every safety net that had been put in place to help people like them collapsed under the weight of so much need. As local governments went bankrupt one by one, the state turned to the federal government for help. But after years of wildfires and mudslides in California, and the droughts in the southwest, and competing hurricanes in Louisiana and Texas, the feds threw up their hands. The governor announced that there was nothing left to do but call it quits. The state government disbanded. The people fled. Some towns were absorbed into Georgia and Alabama, but Florida was no more. Fifty states became forty-nine.

I lay there listening all through the night and then, not long before dawn, the news reports mixed with another completely unfamiliar sound—Mom and Dad, shouting. I crept out of bed and found a spot halfway down the staircase where I could see them but they couldn't see me. Dad was on the couch, slumped over with his head in his hands. Mom was pacing back and forth in front of him, talking fast, slashing at the air with her hands.

". . . and the thing is, it doesn't even matter. This storm? It doesn't fucking matter. None of them do!"

"Laila."

"Systems matter. Governments matter. The planet is a closed loop. Yes? More heat in the loop means more disasters—more floods, more droughts, more heat waves, more wildfires. People lose their homes. Their jobs. There's not enough food. Not enough water. They try to flee, but there's nowhere to go. No one wants them. It all puts pressure on *systems*. Too much pressure and they break. Governments fail. Countries collapse."

Mom dropped onto the coffee table in front of Dad. The bones of her face seemed to strain against her skin.

"Laila, please."

"Governments folded all over the Middle East and North Africa, and who swooped in to take advantage? The al-Asiri. A few million refugees flooded Europe and everyone started voting for the second coming of Adolf Hitler. And then Russia —"

"Okay, I get it."

"And we think we're safe!" She threw back her head and laughed. It was a horrible, wrenching *HA!* "We've convinced ourselves that the world is ending for *those* people, not for us. Never for us! All we have to do is close our borders and pretend nothing's happening. But I swear to you Roger, it's coming for us too. All it's gonna take is a spark, just one single spark, and the whole goddamn world is going to lose its mind. We're going to end up cutting each other's throats over a glass of water and we will fucking *deserve* it. Because no one is listening! No one even FUCKING CARES!"

"Keep your voice down! Lucy is right upstairs!"

"Good!" Mom howled. "Lucy needs to hear this! She needs to know what's coming!"

A car horn sounded, shocking me out of the memory. The world wavered, then came into focus. A pickup truck was idling beside me. There was an electric whir as its window lowered.

"Lucy Weaver! Need a lift?"

I looked up and saw a bald head, a beaming smile, and electric blue eyes.

——

Toby gulped at a pint of whiskey as he steered us through town. The last thing I needed was more to drink, but when he handed over the bottle I tossed some back. It tasted like a mixture of licorice and battery acid. I liked the way it burned.

"You're not a Teenage Mutant Ninja Turtle," I said, my voice coming out all slow and sludgy.

He laughed. "Right. That. No, we never got a fourth. Besides, there was a change of plans. A big change!"

He took a turn too fast, sending us skidding off onto the shoulder with a spray of gravel before swerving back onto the road.

"You don't have autonomous on this thing?"

Instead of answering he took another swallow of booze. "Man! I can't believe I saw you! Tonight of all nights. I mean, I go out on a whiskey run and you're right there on the side of the road? That's supposed to be a coincidence? It's fate. It's *convergence*. Multiple roads coming together at the same time."

I didn't know what he was talking about and didn't really care. Ever since I'd gotten in the truck, he'd been referring to something that was going to happen that night. (Or maybe something that had already happened? It was all a little vague.) He seemed excited about it, but I hadn't asked him what it was and I hadn't checked my phone either. I was sick of knowing things.

I rested my head against the cool glass of the passenger side window. "So. Who do you think should be in charge when it's all over?"

"What do you mean?" Toby asked. "Like what country?"

I shook my head, which was a mistake since it set off a wave of spins.

"No, no, no. They'll all be gone. Wiped out. So what takes over? I mean, okay, listen. First there were these single-celled amoeba thingies. Right? And for a while they were tops, but then some of them turned into fish and the fish took over. And then the fish crawled up out of the water and turned into dinosaurs and that was it for the fish. Tyrannosaurus was in charge. Of course, he didn't know he was called Tyrannosaurus. He probably thought he was, like, Tim or something."

Toby laughed and took the bottle from me. "Tim the Tyrannosaur."

"But then that asteroid came and wiped out Tim and all his friends, which gave these tiny little mammal thingies a shot. And then eventually they turned into apes and the apes turned into us, and so I'm wondering who do you think should take over once *we're* gone."

Toby drifted into the oncoming lane, then back again. He drank and handed me the bottle. A dreamy grin spread across his face.

"Nothing," he said.

I tipped the bottle back and hissed at the burn. A car's horn blared as it went by us. Toby jerked the truck to the right and laughed. I did too. Whiskey was sloshing inside me. My limbs were like putty. *Nothing.* I imagined an immense darkness drawing over the whole earth like a blanket. Not a gray room, a black one. No sound. No movement. No heat or cold. In that moment I was sure I'd never imagined anything sweeter, or more beautiful.

"Nothing," I said, loving the feel of the word on my tongue. "Absolutely nothing."

We passed through Bethany and out again. If Toby had a destination, it wasn't my house. Not that I cared. I could go anywhere. After all, I had my black suitcase. I watched the landscape pass. Houses. Shops. Trees. I lowered the window. The air was scented with far-off traces of smoke. There was something closer, too, something that smelled sharp and chemical.

"Toby? Can I ask you something?"

He let his arm fall out the window, his hand undulating like a wave in the breeze. "Sure."

"Why do you always smell like gasoline?"

He didn't take his eyes off the road. His hand dipped into and out of the wind. After a moment he turned to me and he smiled and said, "Funny you should ask."

—

He parked the truck on a back road. There were no streetlights, so when his headlights went out it was fully dark. There was a click, and then a flashlight beam lanced through the windshield.

"Come on. We have to walk a bit. I'm so glad I found you. You *have* to see this."

He pushed his door open. I got out too and staggered around to the back of the truck.

"See what? Where are we going?"

"This way."

The flashlight cast a cone of brightness into a stand of trees by the side of the road. The way was uneven, choked with brambles and old leaves and cracked ground. Luckily, I'd skipped Esperanza Belén's heels and opted for flats instead. Still, with all the booze sloshing around in my stomach and clouding my head it was a miracle I didn't fall and break something. Ahead of me Toby was whistling a merry tune and practically skipping. Water was rushing somewhere nearby. I could still hear the thump-thump-thump of the party music in my head. See the shifting lights and the bonfire and Jenna. After a while the trees ended and we were out in an open field.

"Toby? Where are we going? I don't —"

"Almost there," he called back. "Not long now. Stay close. Light's going out."

The flashlight beam disappeared. All I had left to follow were Toby's footsteps and his whistling. I kept close. Only a step or two behind. He stopped short and I nearly ran into him. There was a squeak as a door opened, and then we were inside. Not a house. Someplace bigger. Wide open. Tile floors. Dim safety lights up above. Glowing exit signs. There was a smell I recognized. I'd been in this place before. When my eyes finally adjusted I looked around and saw banks of lockers and classroom doors. School. We were at school.

"Why are we here?"

"It's a surprise."

His whistling got faster. More disjointed. I started to smell gas. It got stronger with every step, combining with the alcohol, making my head feel like it was full of helium. I stopped and puked in a corner. I called out for him, but he didn't answer. Then a brighter light appeared at the end of a long hallway. When I stopped heaving and was able to walk again I moved toward it, staggering along. As the light got brighter and brighter, I found myself in the cafeteria. Toby had toppled all the tables and pushed them to the center of the room, along with dozens of chairs, heaps of papers, and a library's worth of books. Beside him were two large metal cans. He picked them up and splashed their contents onto the pile. Gasoline. A small lake of it sat on the floor, shimmering in the light. The smell was overwhelming. More than a smell, a physical thing, a humid fog, pouring into my mouth and up my nose, pushing out the air.

"Toby, what are you . . ."

My vision blurred and dimmed. My knees weakened. Toby came toward me, smiling. That was the last thing I saw before everything went black.

—

I woke up on the soccer field. My head was pounding. The stink of vomit was all around me. I groaned as I pushed myself upright.

"Feeling better?"

Toby was beside me. When I didn't say anything he laughed and pulled something out of his pocket. A small, shiny stone. No, not a stone. A box. There was a metallic ping as he flicked it with his thumb. A cover fell back on a hinge. It was a lighter. He turned the wheel and a flame appeared, lighting his face in flickering orange

"I love school," he said, almost tenderly. "Ever since I was little. The way it smells. You know? That school smell? And the teachers? It's like they've got all the secrets of the universe and they're just handing them to you."

"So why —?"

"Do you know what a sand mandala is? I saw one in a museum once when I was a kid. These Tibetan monks get down on their hands and knees and they use colored sand to create a huge painting on the floor. Five feet square. Incredibly intricate. It takes them weeks. The one I saw was so beautiful, I cried. I didn't understand how something like that could even be possible. But that wasn't even the most incredible part. Do you know what the most incredible part was?"

I shook my head. Toby snapped the lighter shut again, dropping us into darkness.

"The most incredible part was, as soon as they were done, the monks swept up all the sand and tossed it in the nearest river. Can you believe that? I saw them do it. This astounding thing, this thing they sweated over, that they broke their backs over. Gone. I was so mad I grabbed one of the monks by his robes and I said, 'Why? Why would you destroy something so beautiful?' And do you know what he said?"

Toby leaned in close like he was imparting a great secret.

"He said the only reason they made the mandala in the first place was so they *could* destroy it. You see? People are unhappy because they get attached to things and they don't want them to change. But the nature of the universe *is* change. Destroying the mandala was about acknowledging that. It was about letting go. Even of the things you love the most. Once you do that, you can reach nirvana."

Toby produced a clear glass bottle from the darkness beside him. It had something sloshing around inside of it. I thought it was a beer at first, but then he pulled a white rag out of his back pocket and stuffed it down through the neck until the fabric met the liquid. The odor of gas filtered out into the air around us. Toby said, "Did you know that the word *nirvana* literally means 'blown out' or 'extinguished,' like a candle? Or like a fire that's gone out because all the fuel has been burned up. It's peace. Perfect peace."

He put the lighter into my hand. The metal was warm and smooth. The ping when I flipped the cover off was bell-like. Toby tipped the bottle and its rag wick toward me. I was shocked by how much I wanted to light it, how much I wanted to take the bottle in my hand and throw it as hard as I could. The muscles in my arm hummed just like they had the day Toby and I smashed those panes of glass in the courtyard behind Jimmy's. But this would be better. A thousand times better. There'd be the crash of the bottle shattering and then the whoosh of flames as they raced toward the river of gas inside the school. In my head I watched the fire flood the halls and classrooms, burning desks and chairs and old posters. It would take the library and the gym and the cafeteria. Finally, it would invade the auditorium, consuming its papier-mâché trees and pipe cleaner flowers; its cheap, bullshit magic. It wouldn't be long before there'd be the gunshot bang of timbers exploding, then bricks crumbling, and then the final sigh as it all collapsed into a heap of ashes. Just thinking about it set off a gnawing hunger deep inside of me and I thought, *Is this what my mother felt?*

She'd disappeared a little over a month after our camping trip. The next time I saw her she was on the news, head shaved, eyes like shards of flint. Even after Jessica Ramos read out Mom's name in that flat, news anchor voice of hers, I could hardly believe it was real. Then she listed the charges. Nine bombs in five states. Power plants. Office parks. Government buildings. At first it seemed like she was trying to avoid hurting anyone — setting off the explosions late at night, calling in warnings — but by the end she either got careless or she simply stopped caring.

Frank Lennon. Marsha Baer. Martin Rodriquez. Jenny Rodriquez. Al Jacobs. Greg Toland.

By the end of that summer I'd memorized those six names, repeating them over and over before bed, like little prayers, so I'd never forget. Al was a grandfather. Marsha had recently given birth to twins, Carrie and Cristina. Martin was getting ready to go to college on a baseball scholarship. He wasn't even supposed to be in the building that day, but his mom, Jenny, had left her lunch at home and he was dropping it off on the way to his job at a local burger place.

I used to tell myself that my mother left us because she wanted people to listen, because she wanted to make things better. But sitting there with Toby — the school out ahead of us and the lighter in my hand — I thought maybe she felt the same hunger I did. The hunger to break. The hunger to burn. The hunger to wipe it all away and walk in the ashes. Maybe, in the end, it had consumed her too.

I thumbed the lighter's cover shut with a snap, then collapsed over my crossed legs, spent, hanging my head. Toby eased the lighter out of my hand. He sat back with a sigh. The wind blew through the trees behind us. He raked the wheel and another flame appeared. When he touched it to the rag the fabric smoldered, then burned.

"Nirvana," he breathed, and then he stood up and heaved the bottle into the darkness. The sound of the glass shattering when it hit was just as beautiful as I thought it would be.

EIGHTEEN

MINUTES LATER, the first sirens came wailing down the road. I tried to get Toby to run, but he just tossed me the flashlight and the keys to his truck. Said he had to see nirvana for himself. I took one last look at the flames, then fled through the woods.

My head was still full of booze and gas fumes so it took every ounce of concentration I had to keep Toby's manual-only truck on the road. On top of that, emergency vehicles were zipping by, lights flashing. I needed to get off the road, but no destination seemed right until a sign for Bethany Ridge appeared in my headlights. Bingo! Tires squealed as I threw the wheel to the left. The narrow mountain road twisted up and up. My stomach churned. Finally, I swung into a spot in the empty visitor center lot and cut the engine.

I released my death grip on the steering wheel and collapsed into the seat, panting. Sirens passed by down below, but they were faint whines, barely making it up through the trees. The inside of the truck reeked, a sour mix of booze, puke, and smoke. I sniffed my jacket. It was me. My clothes. My hair. My skin. Disgusting. I threw open the door, hoping for a little fresh air, and went sprawling onto the ground in a heap. The night sky swirled. I shut my eyes, hoping to make it go still, but that only made things worse. Waiting in the darkness were flashes of the last few hours. The chaos of the house party. Piers Carroll's blond curls and huge teeth gleaming in the firelight. Jay and Clarissa. Jenna — fucking Jenna — and Toby. I wrestled off my jacket, Mom's jacket, and threw it across the lot. How did I still not get it after all this time? No one was who you thought they were. No one.

An electric trill cut through the mountaintop quiet. *Dad*, I thought, and took out my phone. He'd texted a few times, asking me to come home. I started to text him back, but was distracted by notifications of three missed calls from the same unknown number that had been trying me earlier that night. The final time they'd called, they left a voice message. A long one. Curious, I hit play. There was static at first, a hissing crackle, and then there was a sharp click and a voice. It was distant-sounding and hollow, but it was unmistakably him.

It was Luke.

"Aw, man," he said. "I can't believe I missed you. Not sure when I'm going to get another chance. I'm on a borrowed land-line. Don't know how long I'll be able to —"

His voice dissolved into scratches and fuzz. A fist closed around my heart and didn't let go until it came back again mid-sentence.

"— wanted to call earlier, I tried to, but service has been" — *screech* — "Pastor Todd got arrested in Sao Paulo. We were in Colombia for a while. Then Peru. We're in Argentina now. Near the beach. I think . . ."

More static. Luke was still there, though. I could hear his steady breathing beneath the hiss.

"I know it sounds crazy," he said. "But I think it's been good. What we needed, maybe. The four of us do a lot of hiking and looking at the ocean. We fish. We play games. We talk a lot. Not like Mom and Dad and kids, like people, you know? Carter is handling things pretty well. Even picking up some Spanish."

In the background there was a high-pitched shout of "Hi Lucy!" that made me feel like someone had punched the air out of my lungs. Luke chuckled in my ear, then turned away from the phone. "Wait for me outside, buddy, okay?"

There was a pause. A door shut. When Luke came back, his voice was low and serious.

"Lucy, we saw the news. We know what's happened. What's about to happen, I guess. I never thought things would go this far or —"

He was lost in another electric squelch. What was he talking about? What news? By the time his voice came back, he'd moved on.

"— going to be fine. I know you are. Whatever happens." Someone called his name in the background. Maybe his mom. "Damn it. I thought I'd have more time. I thought you'd pick up. I don't think we're going to stay in Argentina much longer. People say New Zealand might be safer. Or maybe —" More voices behind him, shouting in Spanish. "Okay. I have to go." There was a final pause and then he said, simply, "Love you, Luce. I hope you —"

The line went dead. I brought up the number he called from and frantically mashed keys, trying to get him back, but all I got was a long, flat tone. After my fourth try I dropped the phone onto the gravel. My head fell against the truck and my eyes shut. The world lurched backward until I was lying in bed with Luke's arms around me, the after-school sunshine coming through my window turning our skin gold. In front of us there were maps, and a box of colored markers, and an open notebook full of clean, empty pages, waiting to be filled. The memory of that moment, of the two of us piecing together our future out of rest stops and road signs, stung so badly that I tried to replace it with other ones. Luke telling me he was leaving and then walking away for the last time. Me, staring at my phone in the dark, desperate for some word from him, and the furious, broken feeling when there was nothing, day after day. I wanted to hate him — it would have been so much easier to hate him — but no matter how hard I tried to dredge up those feelings, they wouldn't come. Instead, I kept hearing his faraway voice on the other end of the line — *Love you, Luce* — and imagining him and his mom and dad and Carter hiking and fishing and talking to each other, not like parents and kids, but like people. *I know it sounds crazy. But I think it's been good. What we needed, maybe.* He sounded happy. At peace, even. How could you want anything different for someone you love?

Another wave of sirens passed the base of Bethany Ridge, more of them this time, louder. Luke's voice came back again. *We saw the news. We know what's happened.*

My phone was still on the ground beside me. The rectangle of the screen gleamed in the moonlight, like a black door. A small wind, smelling of grass and honeysuckle and distant smoke, blew across the top of the ridge. Above me, the sky was vast and speckled with stars, cold, but so beautiful it hurt to look at it. I could feel Dad out there in the night, waiting for me to come home. I could feel Carol and Bernie too, and Jay, and Mom, and Luke. We were like points of light spread out all over the world, distant but connected. I reached for the phone. It was cool in my hand, and hard. I took a deep breath and I opened the door.

NOTHING LEFT TO BURN

NINETEEN

I FOUGHT MY WAY DOWN Main Street, bent nearly in half against the blizzard. The wind shrieked, burning my cheeks and slipping through every tiny gap in my coat, around the buttons and up my sleeves. I ducked into a doorway to escape it. The storm had rolled in out of nowhere that morning and buried Bethany calf deep in snow the color of old wool. I tried to catch my breath and stamp some warmth into my feet, which had gone from stinging to numb. *Stupid.* Ten seconds is all it would have taken to go down to the basement and get my snow boots before I left, but I'd been in too much of a hurry to bother. That, and part of my brain was still screaming that it was early October and this storm couldn't possibly be happening.

I leaned out of the doorway, arm up like a shield to keep the hurtling sleet out of my eyes. There was a low, brick building on the next corner. Snow was flying into it through a shattered window and collecting on a line of bookcases. Bethany Books. That meant the cross street up ahead was Willow, which ran straight downhill to the neighborhoods on Bethany's east side. I was heading in the right direction, anyway. The wind shifted, hitting me full-on. Needles of ice filled my ears. It hurt to breathe. I looked back the way I'd come. How long had it been since I'd left the house? Thirty minutes? Forty? Whichever it was, it was too damn long to turn back. I had to get moving. I pulled my coat tight around me and set off down Willow Street. I wanted to run, but a voice in my head whispered, *Careful, Lucy. Twist your ankle and they'll be digging your body out of the ice come Spring. If there even is a spring.*

We hadn't been prepared for the snow. When the electrical grid crashed it took with it everything we relied on for information—the Internet, mobile phone networks, newsfeeds. One of the last things I knew for sure—learned as I stood on Bethany Ridge, phone in hand, head reeling from smoke and booze—was that the al-Asiri had finally crossed that bright red line and taken Iran and its nuclear weapons. When President Chin tried to stop Barrington from living up to his promise to unleash holy hell, the general had him arrested. Congress was dissolved a day later. The Supreme Court the day after that. Once all of that was out of the way, the missiles started to fly. I remembered sitting in the living room with Dad just before we lost the newsfeeds, watching General Barrington, eyes bloodshot and uniform askew, assuring us all that we were finally on the path to peace. I wondered if Toby was sitting in a jail cell somewhere thinking, like me, that what we were really on was the path to nirvana.

I stumbled in a deep drift. My left knee struck something hard and the pain threw me onto my side. I tried to get up, but I was so tired and so cold. All I wanted to do was close my eyes. Just for a second. The storm swirled around me. My hand went numb. Then my side. I thought about home, about the urgency that had sent me out into the storm, but it all seemed so far away.

After the blackout, we didn't know much of anything. How many missiles had been launched. What was gone and what remained. Who had won and who had lost. There were other questions too, dozens of them, but the truth was none of them really mattered. As far as I could tell, only two things did. One: Roughly forty-eight hours after it all started, the sky had gone dark with soot, enough to block out the sun and turn early fall into the dead of winter. And two: We were on our own.

I rolled over. Something was sticking up out of the snow by my hip, a flash of neon green. I reached for it. A skateboard. Written on the bottom of it in thick black marker were the words *Do Not Touch. Property of Wendall Karras.*

In the near distance, partially obscured by the snow, was a familiar three-story house. Smoke was rising out of the chimney. Dim lantern light flickered inside. I'd done it. I was there. I got to my feet and staggered up the driveway to the front door. It took everything in me to raise my fist and knock. Boom. Boom. Boom. No answer. What if they weren't home? What if I'd come all this way for nothing? What would we do then?

The door flew open. A woman with long black hair appeared before me. A name came to me. Halla. Jay's aunt. My knees buckled and I fell into her arms.

"Please help me," I said. "It's my dad. I think he's dying."

—

After a nearly hourlong trek through the storm, Halla and I were back at my house. I stood by the fireplace with Oscar and Johnny — two stray dogs Dad had brought home a couple of weeks earlier — while she knelt by the couch, pressing a stethoscope to Dad's chest. He'd been unconscious when I left and had only woken up briefly when we'd arrived. He'd groaned weakly, barely aware of our presence, before passing out again. Even in the warm light of the fire, his skin looked gray. His blue pajamas were damp with sweat. My stomach twisted into knots looking at him.

"We thought it was the flu," I said. "But then the fever got worse. The coughing too. This morning, there was blood. I knew Jay's dad was a doctor, so I made a run for it. I didn't know what else to do."

"You did the right thing."

She traded the stethoscope for a thermometer and slipped it between Dad's cracked lips. Jay and his parents were at the hospital when I got there, so she'd grabbed a doctor's bag, put Marla in charge of the other kids, and headed out with me into the storm.

"I thought you owned a gallery or something."

"Not a whole lot of use for an art gallery these days," she said. "The hospital is short-staffed, so Fred — that's Jay's dad — taught me and Jay and his mom some basics so we could help out."

She removed the thermometer and held it into the light.

"How bad is it?"

"Hundred and five," she said. "It probably *was* the flu, but that can turn into pneumonia. I think that's what happened."

"Is he going to be okay?"

"He needs antibiotics." Halla turned toward the living room window. Sleet and snow, blown nearly horizontal by the wind, pelted the glass. "I'll go to the hospital first thing in the morning and talk Fred out of some."

I snatched my coat off Dad's chair and headed for the door. "I'll go now."

"Lucy."

"Just tell me who to talk to. I can get there before dark."

"And how will you get back?"

I stopped where I was, coat in hand. Jay's house was two or three miles away. The hospital was ten, at least. It was why I hadn't tried to go there in the first place. Halla was right. In the dark, with the storm blowing harder than ever, I'd never make it back home. Dad shifted in his sleep and coughed.

"So what do we do?"

Halla considered a moment. "You have any tea?"

"Tea?"

"You know, the hot beverage? Enjoyed around the world for its restorative properties?"

"Uh . . . yeah. I think so."

"Great. I saw you guys had a camp stove in the kitchen. I'll make us a cup."

"But Dad—"

"Needs his rest," she said. "When he wakes up again we'll get some water and aspirin into him. Nothing else we can do until tomorrow. Come on. Pretend-doctor's orders."

Halla turned and went into the kitchen. I added another log to the fire, then squeezed Dad's hand and tucked the blanket more tightly around him.

"Be right back," I whispered.

I followed Halla. Even something as simple as making tea had turned into a huge production. Used to be, all I did was pop a mug in the microwave and voilà. Now I had to make sure there was enough fuel in the camp stove, get it lit, then fill a kettle with bottles of water from the pallet by the back door. The pallets of water — along with the firewood, fuel for the stove, and any food we hadn't stockpiled ourselves — came from disaster relief supplies dropped off by the National Guard which, as far as we could tell, was the only part of the government that was still working. I'd found the portable stove in the attic, deep in a box of some of Mom's old camping equipment.

While we were waiting for the water to boil, Johnny and Oscar came trotting into the kitchen, their claws making little *tick-tack-tick* sounds on the tile floor. Halla bent down to scratch at Oscar's ears, which made Johnny instantly jealous. They jockeyed for attention.

"Where'd you get these two?"

"Dad found them wandering around somewhere," I said. "The black lab is Johnny Cash. Oscar's the grouchy mutt. Copperfield is around here somewhere too. That's the cat."

"How do you feed them? The Guard doesn't give out dog food, does it?"

"Dad cleared out every pet store he could find before he got sick. Half the basement is filled with bags of kibble."

Having gotten their fill of attention, Johnny and Oscar trotted off to the living room where they settled down in front of the fireplace. The water boiled. Halla filled two big mugs and we sat down at the table. The steam rising from the rim chased away the last of the chill. I lifted it and drank. It was extra sweet and almost too hot to drink, just the way I liked it.

"See?" Halla said. "Restorative properties."

I managed a brief smile.

"You two been getting by okay until this?"

"Good as anyone," I said. "You?"

"The younger kids don't really get what's happening. They keep asking when they can go to school again. Can you believe that? Years of tantrums every weekday morning, and now they want to go back. *And* I have to keep trying to explain why they can't go play in the snow."

"You think it's radioactive?"

It was something we'd been worrying about ever since the snow started falling and we'd seen its weird gray color. Halla's brow furrowed as she looked out the window.

"Some of that soot up there must be, right? And if the snow is mixing with it, then . . ." she shook her head. "Can't be too careful, I guess."

"Maybe if it keeps falling it'll clear up the sky a bit," I said. "Dad said it was that way with the rain that fell. Remember? That black rain? Maybe we'll see the sun a little sooner."

The corner of Halla's lip curled in a kind of smile. "Everything's maybe now."

We traded rumors back and forth for a while — an outbreak of cholera in the next town over, the US government re-forming in Philadelphia, al-Asiri soldiers marching into Baltimore — and then Halla got up and poured the last of the tea. Her spoon clinked against the side of our mugs as she stirred in a bit of sugar. It was quiet after that, nothing but the sound of the wind and the fire crackling in the other room. It was strange having someone else in the house. Ever since the war started it had pretty much been me and Dad, shuffling between a few dark and chilly rooms, making small meals and playing board games to pass the time. It was good to be reminded that we weren't the only two people left alive.

"How's Jay?"

I was surprised when the words came out — I hadn't planned on asking — but once I did, I realized that the question had been queued up in my brain ever since I'd set foot in the Karras's house. Being there had thrown me back to that morning, the chaos of Jay's family, and then later, the two of us down in his basement on that couch, watching horror movies in the dark. The quiver in my stomach afterward.

Halla didn't answer right away, and when I looked up from my mug I found her watching me. Her eyes were a lot like Jay's, large and brown and warm, but sharp, too. I wondered how much he had told her about us.

"He's good," she said finally. "Fred thinks he'll make a great doctor one day. If that's what he wants to do. It's been a little hard for him with Clarissa gone, though."

The words hung there. I swirled the dregs of tea in the bottom of my cup.

"What happened to Clarissa?"

"Her family left town a couple weeks ago," she said. "Heading for one of those survivalist places people say are out west, I think. You know, I'm sure Jay'd love to see you. Maybe you could —"

"I've got a lot to do here," I said quickly.

"Yeah, but —"

"Goose!"

It was Dad, calling from the living room. I jumped out of my chair and ran to find him sitting up on the couch. Johnny and Oscar were huddled around him, shuffling and whining with concern. I pushed them out of the way and sat by his side. I could feel fever pulsing off him.

"Hey. How are you feeling?"

"I'm fine," he said, wincing as he forced the words out. "Better. I think I needed to —"

The last word was strangled when he threw himself forward and slapped his palm over his mouth. The cough came out in a series of hacking spasms. His eyes squeezed shut at the effort and his face went an awful scarlet. I slid around behind him and gently stroked his back.

"It's okay. You're going to be okay. Halla!"

She rushed into the room. When the coughs finally subsided, she brought a bottle of water to his lips.

"Here. Drink this. Slowly."

"Who —"

"Just do it."

Dad took the bottle and tipped it back. He stopped to cough three times along the way, but managed to get half of it down. I held on tight to his arm to let him know I was there. Halla took a small bottle out of the bag she'd brought with her.

"Here. These will help with the fever."

She dropped four white pills into his hand. Dad tossed them into his mouth and chased them with more water. When he was done I eased him back onto the pillows. There was another fit of coughing, and then he settled, exhausted. His breathing was an ugly rasp. Halla reached out with a dishtowel she'd brought from the kitchen and gently mopped the sweat from his forehead and cheeks.

Dad opened his eyes, puzzled. "Who are you?"

Halla smiled. "Your guardian angel."

—

"That's it!" Dad crowed. "You're out, Goose. Bankrupt."

"Oh, come *on!*"

It was maybe a week later. Halla, Dad, and I were spread out by the fireplace playing a cutthroat game of Monopoly. I was down to a hundred dollars in the bank and had just landed on his hotel for the third time. I looked to Halla for help out of my predicament, but she was cold as ice. Ever since that first night, whenever she wasn't helping out at the hospital or at home, she'd come by to check on Dad's progress. In that time, they had clearly formed a team against me. They tried to act like they hadn't, but I could see right through them. Dad reached for the last of my cash. "Sorry, daughter of mine. Rules are rules. All of your sweet, sweet cash belongs to me now!"

"I walked through a *blizzard* for you! A possibly *radioactive* blizzard. I saved your *life!* And this is how you repay me?"

He flicked a Monopoly dollar into my lap. "Don't spend it all in one place."

"Ugh! You're the worst."

I stomped off toward the kitchen.

"Where are you going?" Dad called after me.

"It's pill time!" I said. "See? I'm *still* saving your dumb life."

I grabbed his antibiotics off the counter, then filled a glass from a bottle of water. The pallet the Guard had brought us on their last visit was getting low. I packed away a twinge of panic before it could get out of hand. They'd be back. There'd be more. I returned to the living room and held the medicine out to Dad.

"Seriously," he said. "I'm fine."

Halla and I both answered him at once. "No, you're not!"

"Honestly, Roger," she added. "Have you *never* heard that

once you start a course of antibiotics you have to take the whole thing?"

"She's right, Dad. Ten-year-olds know this."

"I'm just saying, maybe someone who needs them more than I do can take them. It's not like they're making more at the moment."

I forced the pills into his hand. "Swallow."

He turned to Halla, but she didn't give an inch. He rolled his eyes and did as he was told. Dad and Halla may have formed a team against me when it came to Monopoly, but she and I had formed a team against him when it came to virtually everything else.

Dad yawned and stretched. "Okay, Halla, you ready for me to humiliate you like I did my daughter?"

"Rain check," she said. "I told Jay I'd meet him at the hospital to help out."

"Maybe you should take Lucy with you."

That got my attention. "What? Why?"

"You've gotta be sick of being cooped up in here," he said. "Don't you want to see somebody other than us for a change?"

They sat there, staring at me, waiting for an answer. It wasn't the first time one of them had tried to angle me into a position where I'd see Jay. Apparently they had formed a team against me in *that* department as well. I reached for my coat.

"Maybe another time," I said. "We're running low on firewood."

"We're fine on firewood."

"Always good to have extra," I said. I headed for the back door. "See ya later, Halla."

Johnny and Oscar shot past me when I opened it, bounding off into the dirty snow. After the storm had passed, the temperature rebounded a little — still frigid for October, but enough that the world was starting to emerge. You almost could have mistaken it for any other time the town was coming out of a blizzard, if it wasn't for the fact that the snow was the color of ash and the grimy swirl of the sky kept us in perpetual twilight. It was quiet too. No snow blowers. No plows. No planes flying overhead. Nothing but the wind and the trickle of slowly melting ice.

I went down the stairs, pulled the tarp off our wood pile, and grabbed the ax. What we got from the Guard still had to be chopped into logs small enough to fit in the fireplace. It had been Dad's job until he got sick, then I took over. Never in a million years would I have imagined myself playing lumberjack with an old ax I'd found in the shed, but there I was. To tell the truth, I didn't actually mind so much. I got into the rhythm of the whole thing — sending the ax in an arc over my head, the *ka-chunk* as the log splintered, seeing the wood pile rise. I didn't even mind when the muscles in my arms started to shred or the freezing air bit into my lungs. The pain pushed everything else out of my head. The fear that the snow might come again, or that we might run out of food or water, or that some horrible thing we couldn't even imagine was about to hit us. It also kept me from thinking about all the people who weren't there. My mother. Luke. Carol and Bernie and my little cousin whose name I didn't even know. Left to its own devices, my brain wrestled with itself in an endless, obsessive back and forth. Maybe they were safe and warm. Maybe they were scared and lost and halfway to starving. Maybe they were already gone and I didn't even know it, might *never* know it.

And then there was Jay. Ever since the day I'd brought Halla home, my thoughts went back to him again and again. Mostly it was just these little scraps of memories. I'd be building a fire or cleaning the house and I'd suddenly see him standing in his driveway with Wendall asleep in his arms; or the desperate, hopeful look he'd had on his face when he'd handed over that notebook full of god-awful poetry. Sometimes, lying in bed at night, I'd imagine his voice in my ear. He'd whisper about the bits and pieces of his day. How his brothers and sisters were doing. What it was like to work in the hospital with his dad. Sometimes I'd even talk back, letting out every bit of the hopelessness and fear I'd spent the whole day holding inside so Dad wouldn't see.

I split the last of the wood with a grunt and then stacked the logs until the pile rose higher than my waist. Seeing it all sitting there and feeling that hum in my muscles made something inside me settle. Johnny barked, then came racing toward me through the snow with Oscar in hot pursuit. The black Lab's eyes were fiery with excitement. He had something in his mouth. It wasn't until he got closer that I saw it was a squirrel. A big one.

"Ew," I said, stomach churning, when he dropped it at my feet. "But good job, I guess. You have proved yourself to be an adequate hunter."

I gathered an armful of wood and started back up the steps. Johnny took his prey in his teeth and followed.

"No way, pal. Uh-uh. You're eating that thing out here. And share it with your brother."

I set the logs down inside the door, got my coat off, and started opening cans for Dad's lunch. I left the kitchen to ask if he wanted a cup of tea too, but stopped shy of the doorway to the living room. Halla hadn't left yet. She was sitting on the couch alongside Dad, her legs drawn up beneath her, our big blue flannel blanket covering them both. She was speaking too low for me to hear the words, but whatever she was saying, Dad seemed utterly engrossed by it. When he finally said something, Halla tossed back her head and laughed, her dark hair swinging like a fan.

"God," she said with mock exasperation. "You are *such* a dork."

"I know. I can't help it. I'm cursed."

She smiled. They were quiet then, looking at each other. Halla had a good face for firelight. It was strong and angular, a little like Jay's, actually. The glow of the flames softened the lines around her eyes. Dad looked better than he had in weeks. Bright-eyed, his cheeks flushed with pink. He rested his hand lightly on her leg. After a moment, she covered it with her own. They sat that way for some time, not saying a word. I felt a different kind of ache, this one deep in my chest. I faded back into the kitchen and pulled my coat on again. I thought maybe it was a good time to take a walk.

TWENTY

OVER THE NEXT few days, whenever Halla would visit I'd hang out long enough to be polite and then I'd say I had to go check on Mr. Stahlberg or see a friend from school.

The checking on Mr. Stahlberg part was true—I went by a couple times a week to make sure he was okay and had enough supplies—but mostly I wandered around. By then nearly all of the snow had melted, trickling away in dark, sooty streams and exposing weedy grass and mud. Many of the people who'd stuck it out in Bethany through the early weeks of the war were gone—chasing the ever-present rumors about places with more resources—so I rarely saw anyone else, just empty houses, abandoned shops, and shuttered churches. Once, I stumbled across a family of red foxes that had come down from the hills around Bethany Ridge to root through the dumpsters on Main Street. They eyeballed me as I passed, then quickly went back to their business, unconcerned, the fur on their puffy, rust-colored tails ruffling in the wind. There was something strangely peaceful about it all. The perpetual dusk. The overwhelming quiet. It was like the whole town, the whole world maybe, was at rest.

One day I'd had enough of walking and decided to kill some time in what was left of Bethany Books. The door was locked, but all I had to do was step through the broken window. Most everything had been ruined when the snow blew in, but a few of the more unpopular sections in back had been spared the worst of it. Auto repair manuals. Parenting guides. A shelf of plays. I knelt and riffled through the thin volumes. *Angels in America. Eurydice. Buried Child. Blood Wedding. Marisol.* I'd read all of them of course, and was about to move on, when I came to one I didn't recognize, a thick paperback with the title *Out Brief Candle: William Shakespeare at the End of the World* stamped on the cover. I pulled it out and thumbed through the pages. It was a collection of Shakespeare's plays along with production notes and photos from performances done in places that had since been torn apart by war and disaster. *Romeo and Juliet* in Lagos, Nigeria. *King Lear* in Mexico City. *Titus Andronicus* in Rome. Toward the end of the book I found a picture of a large-bellied man wearing fierce makeup and some kind of scaly fish costume. It was frightening and ridiculous and beautiful, all at the same time. The photo was from a production of *The Tempest* that had been done on a small island in Southeast Asia one year before it slipped beneath the seas and disappeared forever.

I flipped from production to production, from play to play. In each one, groups of actors had come together, often under threat of arrest or persecution, to perform plays written hundreds of years in the past. When asked why they decided to do *King Lear,* the director of the Mexico City production, Juan Rivera, said, "Many of us had not eaten properly in days. There was never enough water. The city was going mad. For us, performing *Lear* was a way to hold on. To life. To beauty. To each other. But per-haps most of all, performing *Lear* was a way for us to scream."

The muscles in my legs and back began to ache. I stood and turned toward the broken window. The sun had dropped low behind the clouds. How long had I been kneeling on that cold floor? However long, it was past time to go. I stepped back out through the window frame and pulled on my gloves. The con-crete sidewalk at my feet was starting to crumble, so much so that the street sign on the corner had keeled over. It squeaked as I pushed it back up. White letters on a green background spelled out WILLOW STREET.

I looked down the hill that led to the east side of Bethany. The trees lining Willow rustled in the wind, dropping their few remaining leaves into the mud by the side of the road. It was hard to believe that it had been barely two weeks since I'd taken that same road, head down against a blizzard, sneakers filling with snow. Now the street was clear — rutted with potholes, but clear. In the distance, I could make out the turnoff into Jay's subdivi-sion. Before I'd left, Halla had not-so-subtly mentioned that he'd stayed home from the hospital that day so he could look after his brothers and sisters. In a flash I saw myself standing on their front porch. I'd knock and Jay would open the door, chaos raging in the entryway behind him. In my head, he looked exactly like he did that day at Shangri-La: smiling, his mop of black hair messy, his cheeks pink from excitement, his hand reaching out to me, filled with what I thought was blood, but that turned out to be jewels.

Hey! Look at what I found!

My pulse quickened, painfully. The sun had dropped farther toward the horizon, draining away a little more of what passed for daylight. It wouldn't be long until it was dark. I reminded myself that the Guard was supposed to have made a delivery that day. There'd be wood to chop and piles of supplies to haul in and put away. I tucked *Out Brief Candle* into my coat pocket, then turned my back on Willow Street.

—

I was halfway home when I heard a jumble of raised voices the next street over. Curious, I followed the sound until I found forty or fifty people gathered at the front steps of the old courthouse. They were all jockeying for position around the front door, shouting and pushing. Someone ran past me to join them.

"Hey! What's going on?"

A girl I didn't know spun around. "You didn't hear?"

"Hear what?"

"They caught 'em! Can you believe it?"

"Caught who?"

"The people who bombed DC!"

The girl turned again and sprinted off. There was no way I could've heard her right. The people responsible for the sixteenth had been caught in Bethany, New York? It didn't make any sense. I followed her to the back of the crowd but the wall of people blocked our view.

"Dammit!" she said. "I can't see anything. Come on!"

I trailed her as she threw herself against the mob, ignoring the shouts and curses that rained down on us as we shoved our way through. She called back over her shoulder, "A few days ago these men showed up in town, ex-FBI they said. They'd been investigating this group since before the war started and had heard some of them might be hiding nearby. My dad took them out to the

abandoned mansions on the west side and that's where they found
them."

"Who are they? al-Asiri? Russians?"

"Americans."

"*What?*"

The girl forced an opening in the crowd and we tumbled
out of it at the top of the stairs leading to the door of the courthouse.

"Look!" she shouted. "There they are!"

Four men — two beer-bellied guys in flannel and two hard-
looking military types — appeared on the sidewalk that led from
the parking lot to the building. Two lead the way and two brought
up the rear, and they all either carried rifles or had guns strapped
to their sides. Between them, three prisoners shuffled along, their
wrists and ankles bound with rope. Their clothes were torn and
bruises covered their faces. Great blotches of purple and black.
One had his arm in a sling while another was bleeding from a
gash on his cheek. As soon as the crowd saw them, they went wild,
cursing and shouting, their faces contorted with rage. After all
that had happened, after a goddamn *world war*, could I really be
looking at the people responsible?

I leaned into the girl's ear so she could hear me over the noise.
"How do they know they did it?"

She pointed to the tallest of the three. "Their leader actually
confessed."

I looked at the gash on the man's cheek and the purple and
black bruise that had sealed his right eye shut. *Yeah,* I thought. *I
bet he did.*

"What are they going to do with them?"

"A few of their friends got away," the girl said. "As soon as they find them there's going to be a trial. I'm guessing I know how *that's* going to turn out." She turned away from me and I watched while one of the guards hunted through his pockets, searching, I guessed, for a set of keys that would get them into the courthouse. The prisoners huddled together with their heads down, cringing when someone in the crowd threw a clod of chill-hardened mud at them. My eye kept going to the man with the swollen eye and bloody cheek, the one who was supposedly the leader. He was thin but sturdy-looking. His hair was matted with dirt and dried blood, but clean, I guessed it would have been blond. A memory stirred. I looked from him to one of the others. He was short with a shaved head. Black tattoos peeked out from beneath his collar. Diego. His name was Diego. And the blond man with the swollen eye; I knew him too. We'd sat together at a bonfire once. Even though it felt like a million years ago, I could still see him as he was then, with his golden hair and his toothy smile, lit by the flames. A name dropped into my head. Piers. Piers Carroll. My heart sank and I thought, *But if they're here, where's Jenna?*

—

I couldn't sleep that night. When I got home from the courthouse, I'd learned that the Guard hadn't shown up, which meant there was nothing for me to do. No wood to chop. No supplies to haul. Nothing to clear my head. After a distracted game of one-on-one Monopoly with Dad, I went to bed. I lay there for hours, wide-awake and staring out the window but seeing Piers and his friends, bloody and bruised, and hearing that screaming mob. Finally, I couldn't stand it anymore, so I stepped into my boots and crept downstairs and out the back. There was still a sheet of ice covering half the porch. There was plenty of room to get around it and to the woodpile, but that wasn't the point. The point was that I needed something to do. I made my way down the steps and across the yard to the shed. I'd seen a metal scraper in with Dad's painting things and thought it would probably do the trick. I'd have to take it slow and be quiet so I didn't wake him, but I bet I could get all the ice off the porch and be back in bed before dawn.

When I got to the shed, the door was open. The pink combination lock was undone and hanging from its clasp. I'd been in there the other day, and was sure I'd locked it behind me. And Dad was even more fanatical than I was about keeping the place secure.

I turned to scan the driveway and the trees surrounding the shed, then looked back at the house, where Dad lay sleeping. No lights. No movement. Nothing. I gently pushed the door open. There was a rusty squeal, extra loud in all that silence. I paused, then stepped inside, enveloped by the smell of old paint and sawdust. It was too dark to see, but I knew there was a workbench beside me. I felt around on it until I touched a flashlight. I picked it up and flicked it on. Its thin beam filled the space. Nothing but shelves stocked with paint cans and rusty tools. Metal hooks secured a couple of dusty mountain bikes to the ceiling.

There was a rustling sound. I followed it to some bags of mulch in the back. I could hear someone breathing behind them, even though they were trying not to make a sound.

"It's okay, Jenna. No one else is here. You can come out."

Another rustle, a breath, and then she stood up from behind the stack of bags and cringed against the glare of the flashlight. Despite the cold, all she had on was a thin T-shirt and a mud-stained pair of jeans. There was a bruise on her jaw and dozens of tiny scratches all up and down her arms.

"Come on," I said. "We'd better get you inside."

———

"How'd you get these?" I asked.

Jenna and I were sitting cross-legged on the floor at the foot of my bed. Somehow, I'd managed to get us upstairs without any of the animals freaking out and waking Dad. I'd taken the first-aid kit out from under the bathroom sink, and was cleaning the cuts on Jenna's arms with cotton balls soaked in disinfectant.

"Had to jump in some bushes," she said. "Unfortunately, they were thorn bushes."

I looked at her forearm in the light of the oil lamp I kept on my nightstand. I'd wiped away the dirt and the dried blood, leaving a spray of ruby-colored slashes. I got some Band-aids out of the kit and covered the worst of them.

"Figured they'd look for me at my mom and dad's," she said. "I would've headed for the mountains, but I had to leave so fast I didn't have time to grab any equipment, not even any decent clothes. Then I saw your place . . ."

"It's fine."

"How'd you know it was me? In the shed."

"You're the only person but me and Dad who knows the combination."

Jenna smiled. "When I saw that lock I thought, *There's no way they haven't changed the combination since middle school,* but then I gave it a shot anyway, and there it was. Nine, fourteen, twenty-four, Benji Clark's birthday. Little Three forever."

She crossed her heart three times, then waited for me to do

the same. I dropped the Band-Aid wrappers into the wastebasket, then closed the first-aid kit.

"I think those should be okay now."

She pulled down the sleeve of the sweatshirt I'd given her. "Thanks."

On our way upstairs I'd emptied some canned beans into a bowl. Jenna picked at them, wincing as she chewed and sometimes reaching up to cradle the bruise on her jaw. It was a nasty one, red and purple with traces of yellow at the borders. It reminded me of the times the two of us would cram ourselves into her upstairs bathroom after school, theater class makeup kits teetering on the edge of the sink, painting our faces so we looked like zombies.

"They got Piers to confess," I said. "Of course, with the way they'd beaten him he probably would've said just about anything. Maybe once some time passes people will realize that. They'll see how crazy this whole thing is."

Jenna nodded vaguely, then hugged herself tightly with her scraped-up arms. "It's cold in here."

I handed her a blanket off my bed. She draped it over her shoulders and peered out the window like she was searching for something.

"Jenna?"

Her eyes went glossy. A tear fell down her cheek and over the bruise on her jaw. She scraped it away with the heel of her hand. Something icy filled my stomach. "Jenna?"

Her eyes didn't move from the window. "After the Halloween party, when we all saw what was happening, Piers was so excited that he let it slip."

"Let what slip?"

"He said they'd gotten tired of waiting for the world to fall apart on its own so they'd decided to give it a little nudge. That's what he called it, a little nudge. He was laughing, saying he couldn't believe it worked as well as it did."

She drew the blanket more tightly around herself.

"None us knew about it when we joined. It was a separate part of the group that did it. They built the bomb and smuggled it into DC."

Neither of us moved. The icy feeling in my stomach spread out, filling my chest, numbing me to my fingertips. It was really true. It hadn't been the al-Asiri or the Russians or the fascists. It had been them. *Us.* After everything that had happened in the past few months, I would've thought I'd be immune to new and awful things, but I wasn't. I saw Piers smiling at me in the light of that campfire and felt sick. Had he smiled as he watched the destruction in DC? While Dad and Carol and Bernie and I sat slumped in our chairs, overcome with horror, had he been laughing? I wanted to break something. I wanted to scream. I wanted to wrap my hands around his throat and squeeze, but he wasn't there, so I said, as acidly as I could, "You know what they'll do when they find you."

Jenna nodded. Her lips pressed together, trembling. Her eyes gleamed and she clamped her hands down over them. It was like she was trying to hold something back that was too big for her body to contain. Without thinking, I reached out for her. The moment I touched her, she folded, turning as she did, so she could bury her face in my shoulder. I stiffened at first — how could she have joined those people? How could she have stayed with them after she learned what they did? — but I didn't have it in me to push her away. I wanted to, but I couldn't. My arms went around her as the tears came in waves, reddening her face, bending her in half. When she finally got it all out she took a long, stuttering breath and leaned against me, exhausted.

Around us, the house settled, the timbers in the attic making a faint ticking sound.

"Do you remember Kenny Whitney?" She asked it in a small, dreamy voice. "He was that kid with the freckles. In Mrs. Hannigan's class. The one with the lisp."

The lisp made it come back. Kenny was a skinny, redheaded kid we'd known in middle school. He was small for his age and wore the same pair of royal blue corduroys to school every single day. By the end of the year there were gaping holes in both knees. He'd fallen hopelessly in love with Jenna when he was in the sixth grade and we were in seventh. One day he passed her a note, asking if she wanted to be his girlfriend. There were boxes she could check if the answer was yes, no, or maybe.

"I don't know why, but a few weeks ago he popped into my head and wouldn't leave. It doesn't make any sense. All this going on, and I'm thinking about Kenny Whitney." She shook her head. "I told the whole damn school he wrote that note. Showed it to anyone who asked. I was so fucking mean to him and I didn't even know why. It never occurred to me not to be." Jenna sighed. "I keep wondering what happened to him. If he's okay. I hope he is."

"Do you remember Larissa Peterson?"

"God, yes. She was awful."

"And Mrs. Castro?"

"She was the best," Jenna said. "She used to hide those candies in her desk. The butterscotch ones. Used to give me one every day after lunch."

We talked about nothing for a while after that. Plays we'd done. Movies we'd watched. Boys we'd had crushes on. The time when we'd broken our arms within two weeks of each other —her playing rugby, me falling out of a tree. We slid from one topic to another without a pause, just like we had during our old sleepovers when the two of us would stay up until dawn, devouring endless bowls of popcorn and whispering secrets in the dark.

"I should have been there," Jenna said after having fallen quiet for some time. "When everything happened with your mom."

I gently stroked her arm. "You were busy being a genius."

"I didn't know what to say. Then it seemed too late to say anything at all."

"There wasn't anything you could've said."

"I should have tried. I shouldn't have just . . . disappeared."

"I shouldn't have let you."

Jenna turned to look at me. Her eyes were red and swollen, surrounded by deep shadows.

"Do you hate her for all the things she did?"

I'd lost count of how many times I'd been asked that question, and how many different answers I'd come up with. Most times, I'd divided my mother in two and said that I loved one and hated the other. That had satisfied the therapists they made me see all through my freshman year, but I knew it was bullshit. An easy out. There weren't two Laila Weavers, one good and one bad. There was only one.

I took Jenna's hand and held it as tightly as I could. I said, "I try to, sometimes. But I can't."

TWENTY-ONE

A WEEK LATER I was sitting on my bed staring out the window at the twilight when Halla came in and took a place beside me. She had a mug in each hand. She offered me one, but I shook my head, so she set it on the windowsill. Steam billowed over the rim and fogged the glass.

I hadn't seen Jenna since she'd slipped out our back door a few minutes before dawn that day, carrying my old school backpack full of food and bottles of water. I told her she didn't have to, that we'd hide her up in the attic or down in the basement, but she insisted that it was too dangerous. If someone discovered her, we'd be in as much trouble as she was. She said she'd find a way to escape capture. When I asked her how, she leaned in close and whispered, "Don't you remember? I'm a *genius*."

Since then, Piers Carroll and the other men I'd seen at the courthouse had been quickly tried and even more quickly hanged. They'd done it at a hastily assembled gallows in a small park across the street from Bethany Square, where people used to sip espressos and check their email on the café's free Wi-Fi. I liked to think the fact that I hadn't heard anything more about Jenna meant she'd gotten away, but it could've been that they'd caught her somewhere else. Either way, I'd never know.

Halla took a sip of her tea. "How was your walk? You were out a long time."

I shrugged. I thought maybe if I kept my mouth shut she might get the hint and leave, but she was persistent.

"Where did you go?"

"Around."

"Don't you get cold?"

I'd started going for walks even when Halla wasn't visiting Dad, sometimes more than once a day. I'd make up an excuse and then I'd set out for hours at a time, along the streets or out in the woods near the ridge. I walked until my calves ached, until my stomach groaned. By the time I got back, my body would be like a fist clenched too long and starting to cramp. My head would be like a box of air. I'd stumble up to my room, close the door so Oscar and Johnny wouldn't follow me inside, and pass out until morning.

"Mina and Fred are having a dinner tomorrow night," Halla went on. "They want you and your dad to come. One of Fred's patients is a farmer. Gave him half a lamb for setting his broken leg. It'll be quite the farewell-to-Bethany feast."

"You two go."

"It's gonna be fun."

I stared at the road outside and the trees, the way light was falling around them. I fantasized about being out there, walking until the rhythm of my feet on the road erased everything else, every thought, every feeling. Maybe after Dad went to bed . . .

"Your dad and I don't want to rush you, but it's probably time to start thinking about what you want to take and what you want to leave behind."

"Halla."

"If you need help packing, we can —"

"I don't want to talk about this."

"At some point you have to."

"We have supplies saved up," I said. "Food. Water. Firewood."

"It's not enough."

Halla waited for some kind of response. When she didn't get one, she set her mug on the windowsill next to mine.

"Canada's out unfortunately," she said. "Apparently their military has the border closed up tight and isn't letting anybody through, even if you have family there. The only choice is south. As far as we can get."

I squeezed my eyed shut. How could they not see how insane this was? "But it could be worse there than it is here."

"It could be."

"And if it's better, *everybody* will be trying to get in. The last thing they'll want is more mouths to feed."

Halla let out a pent-up breath.

"The Guard's missed two drop-offs in a row now and no one's heard a word from them. That last snowstorm was brutal. What's it going to be like when winter hits for real?"

"Maybe the sky will clear up."

"Even if it does, we can't survive a winter without power, or supplies, or food. We just can't. We'll go south until the weather breaks. When it does we'll come back and try the border again. Maybe things will have calmed down by then. If we can make it across, we'll go to Edmonton and find your aunts."

I didn't look at her, didn't say anything. The last thing I wanted right then was someone telling me that everything was going to be all right. I stared out the window, hoping she'd get the hint and go away. There was a clicking sound on the floor behind us. Oscar came in, tail wagging, and plopped down in front of Halla. She slid off the bed to join him on the floor. He leaned into her chest as she rubbed his ears and his back.

"I was seven when we left home. Mina was eight. The al-Asiri had taken Cairo a week earlier and our family was in hiding. Mama and Baba were university professors, art and literature, but they'd been posting resistance videos against the empire ever since they had taken over Yemen. Called them a gang of criminals taking advantage of people who were scared and desperate. When the al-Asiri shut down the Internet, Mama and Baba printed leaflets and handed them out on the streets." Oscar turned over so Halla could rub his belly.

"One day we saw three men in black with their faces covered coming down the street, banging on doors, trying to find our apartment. Baba grabbed Mina and me and took us to our neighbors, the Bisharas. He kissed us and told us he loved us and that he and Mama would be back soon. But one night passed. And then another. On the third night, Mrs. Bishara came to our room and told us that they'd been taken. It had happened to enough people by then that we knew what it meant. If you were taken, you didn't come back. The Bisharas made arrangements with a smuggler who said he could get us into Libya and then to a boat that would take us to Italy. We made it all the way to the border before we were stopped. The smuggler tried to pay off the guards, but they wouldn't take the money. They shot him and Mr. and Mrs.

Bishara, who were riding with him in the cab of the truck. Mina and I were hiding in the back under some tarps and managed to slip away."

Halla turned and pulled her hair aside, exposing a jagged scar that started behind her ear and ran down her neck, disappearing beneath the collar of her shirt.

"We had to duck through coils of razor wire to get across the border. It was pitch-black. Mina almost lost an eye. I got this. We escaped, but ended up alone in the desert with nothing but a little food and water in our bookbags. It was almost a week before we came across another group of refugees."

Oscar had fallen asleep. Halla stood, retrieved her mug from the windowsill, and held it in her hands.

"I wanted to give up every day," she said. "All I could do was think about Baba and Mama and our little apartment. My books. The vendors on the street downstairs. The smell of Mama's molokhia. Mina had some paper and a few colored pencils in her bag. She was always a better artist than me. She drew pictures of silly, made-up animals — cat lizards, lion camels, an elephant with a trunk made out of fire — and put made-up facts about them on the back, like trading cards. 'The fire-nosed elephant is universally feared for his incredible exploding boogers.' She said she'd draw me a new one every single day, and that we just had to keep going. So we did. Eventually, we made it here. I would have died if it wasn't for Mina. I think she probably would've died without me, too."

Halla got up and moved toward the door. It had gotten dark outside, enough that I could see her reflection in the window as she turned back and leaned against the doorway.

"We're having dinner soon," she said. "Your dad got ahold of some eggs. After that we're going to play Monopoly."

She called to Oscar and the dog got up and trotted out behind her. The stairs creaked. There were hushed voices and then the sound of a log falling on the fire. My face hung in the window, ghostly in the empty room.

———

The next morning, I snuck out of the house as the sun was starting to rise. After the war, dawn was a strange thing. There wasn't a hard line between night and day, no dramatic layers of gold and orange on the horizon, only a gradual brightening.

I buttoned my coat to my neck and hunched my shoulders against a razor sharp wind. It didn't seem possible, but Bethany was even more quiet than before. It used to be that I'd at least hear birds singing or squirrels chattering up in the trees, but that day there was nothing. It was like being on the surface of the moon. I wondered if everyone who'd remained, every person and every animal, had the same idea as Dad and Halla. Get out while you can. Get out before more snows come.

I cut through abandoned neighborhoods and across roads until I came to a stretch of woods. The ground was covered in piles of fallen leaves and dead branches. I forced my way through, holding on to tree trunks for support. I jumped a narrow stream and then, soon after that, the woods broke. I stepped onto a scrubby hill and looked across the soccer field at Bethany High.

I hadn't been back since the night of the fire. I'd considered it, but had always turned away at the last minute, afraid of the memories it might dredge up. The place had fared better than I would have thought. The basic structure was still there — the roof and walls were blackened, but mostly intact — except for the north side where the old engineering shop had been. There, the ceiling had collapsed entirely, leaving a messy square of ash and scorched machines. The desk where I'd sat had been burned to cinders.

I descended the hill and crossed the field. The back door was still there, but the collapse near the shop had opened up an entire wall, so I stepped through that and into the school. I figured that the fact that the place was still standing despite the damage probably meant the whole thing wasn't going to come crashing down on my head. Inside, everything was burned: the walls, the lockers, even the tile floors. Glass from broken windows lay in piles. In classrooms, the plastic tables and chairs had melted into strangely colored, toadstool-shaped lumps. Their metal frameworks remained, like skeletons.

I made my way down the hall toward the lunchroom. The pile of tables and chairs Toby used to start the fire had turned into a twisted, ashy heap. It had burned hot enough to make a hole in the ceiling, so it was only a little bit dimmer inside than outside. I wandered around in the destruction, rubble crunching under my feet, trying to decide where to go next. The library? The science labs? I came around a blackened pillar and found the doors to the auditorium standing open. I passed through them and stood at the back.

The seats had all turned to sludge and the strip of carpet that ran down the aisle had melted, then hardened into a black slick. Walking down it was like trying to balance on asphalt that had been coated in ice. I kept to the edges and took it slow. When I got to the orchestra pit, I peeked down into a jumble of music stands and toppled chairs. A violin case sat near the back wall, untouched. I left the pit and made my way up the steps at the edge of the stage.

The crew had never gotten around to striking the set for *A Midsummer Night's Dream,* so it had burned along with everything else. A forest fire raging within a school. The trees were gone and so were the painted flats that had shown the sky and the sun. The platforms that had been used to create hillsides were more or less unharmed, but they were bare of the grassy fabric that had covered them. I went to the edge of the stage and knelt by the flower beds. The metal stalks were there, but the flowers had burned, and the resin that had been used to make them sparkle had dripped into hard dollops on the floor. The fairies had disappeared and the elves, too.

The first show Jenna and I ever did together was some silly pageant about environmentalism that Mr. Cronin had put together with Mr. Rickert, the science teacher. I'd been cast in the role of Tree but was incredibly jealous of Jenna because she'd landed Cloud #1, which meant she got to wear a white bodysuit covered in cotton balls and stand at the top of a ladder that had been painted sky blue. The second the show was over, our parents rushed the stage and threw us bouquets of roses wrapped in cellophane, shouting "Bravo! Bravo!" We blushed and curtsied like stars. The next day some kid in our gym class came up to me and said that the show was stupid, so Jenna punched him in the eye.

I laughed at the memory, but the laugh quickly turned into this choking sound and then into tears. They hit the stage and mixed with the ashes. My throat ached. My chest heaved. In my head was everything and everyone that had disappeared. A whole world. Gone. And it wasn't even over. Every time you think you're safe, every time you think you have nothing left to lose, you find out you're wrong. There's always more.

Finally, the tears subsided. I wiped my cheeks with my sleeve and then I left the stage and walked back up the aisle. On my way out, I closed the door behind me.

Halfway to the engineering shop I stopped at the sound of something moving in the kitchen area behind the lunchroom. Rattling pots and pans. Probably some animals looking for food, I thought, and kept walking. But when I passed the door I saw someone standing on one of the steel food prep tables, reaching into a high cabinet. When he heard me, he stopped what he was doing and turned around.

"Oh," I said, surprised to see the smallest member of the Hacky Sackers. "Hey, Stank."

It took a second, but recognition finally dawned on him. "Lucy Weaver. What's up?"

I leaned against the metal doorframe. "Nothing much. What are you doing?"

He turned back to the cabinet he'd been rooting around in. "Looking for this bag of En Fuego Cheesy Curls that Svetlana said she left here before the fire. We're heading west with some of her friends tomorrow and I wanted to take it with us."

"Any luck?"

"Nah. It's all right. If the universe wants you to have En Fuego Cheesy Curls, it provides En Fuego Cheesy Curls."

"You have a lot of faith in the universe, Stank."

He hopped down off the table. "Well, the universe, it's just . . . it's everywhere. You know? Anyway. What are *you* doing here?"

"Looking around, I guess."

"Communing with the sprits."

"Yeah," I said. "Maybe."

He pulled a multicolored Hacky Sack out of his pocket and held it up. "Wanna play a round?"

"Thanks, but I better get going."

Stank and I left the kitchen and started back down the hall. He kicked at some piles of ash, marveling at the destruction.

"Man, someone actually went and burned down the school. I mean, we've all thought about it, I know I did, but to actually light the match? Damn! Who do you think would do something like that, Weaver?"

"Toby Wolfowitz."

"No way. Seriously?"

I nodded. We stepped through the broken wall and onto the grass. I looked out across the soccer field at the hill where I'd left Toby the night of the fire. I wondered what had happened to him. Had he been arrested? Thrown in jail? And if so, what had the jailers done when everything fell apart and they couldn't care for the prisoners anymore? Set them free? Let them rot? My thoughts drifted from Toby to Mom. What had her jailers done? Where was she?

"Why'd he do it?"

"What?" I said, distracted. "Oh. Well, he said a lot of stuff, but it basically came down to 'Tibetan Buddhism made me do it.'"

Stank chewed on that for a second, then shook his head. "I don't know, Weaver. I'm not, like, a scholar of the eastern mysteries or anything, but I think it's possible that dude's interpretation of Tibetan Buddhism is wack."

"Well said, Stank."

We came to the hill at the edge of the field. The trees were bare enough that I could see a bit of the road heading north. Stank held up the sack again, a crocheted ball of black, yellow, and red.

"You sure you don't want to partake? The other dudes are all gone and I haven't played in forever."

"What about Svetlana?"

Stank laughed. "Aw, man, my lady is a lot of things, but a Hacky Sacker she is not."

I checked out the road again. It was a straight shot from the school all the way to the next town. About six miles total. Most of it uphill.

"Well . . . how do you do it?"

Stank took my arm and led me onto the field. "It's easy. All you have to do is keep the sack in the air using anything but your hands. Feet. Legs. Head. Chest. They're all fair game."

"How do you win?"

"By creating a shared space of peaceful cooperation and respect for all living things."

"What if I drop the ball?"

"You pick it up and start again. Here!"

Stank kicked the sack toward me with the side of his foot. Instinct sent me jumping backwards, but somehow I thought to lift my knee at just the right time to send it flying back to him.

"Nice one! Now try this."

Dead grass crunched under our feet as Stank and I moved across the field, doing everything we could to keep that little ball in the air. We played for an hour or so and then he said he had to get going. Svetlana was waiting. I wished him luck out west. He told me to follow the quiet voice of my heart in all things, and then he headed for the road on the other side of the bus loop, eventually disappearing in the gray distance.

Once he was gone there wasn't the slightest hint of sound. No wind. No birds in the trees or squirrels rustling through the woods. No planes. Not even the trickle of melting snow. I could stay there for years, I thought, decades maybe, and nothing would change. Maybe the weeds would grow a little bit taller, or the school walls would crumble a bit more, but that was it. Everything that had ever happened in that place, everything that ever *would* happen, had run its course. It was finished. Complete.

I found a spot at the top of the hill and stared at the ashes.

TWENTY-TWO

THE MORNING WE were going to leave Bethany, Dad got me up early. He moved through the dark house, his breath filling the hallways with clouds of white as he packed small, last-minute things. Extra socks and candles. A pile of family pictures. I sat on my bed in the gloom, staring at the backpack he'd brought down from the attic for me. It was one of Mom's old ones. I'd tried to fill it a half-dozen times, but always ended up with a messy pile of clothes and an empty pack. When Dad was finished, he offered to make me breakfast, but I told him I wasn't hungry. When he pushed I said I had to go to Mr. Stahlberg's to see if he needed any help.

The sun rose as I walked through Bethany. It was a cold, gray morning, just like all the other cold, gray mornings, but the town didn't have the abandoned feel it usually did. Most of the other families that had stuck it out were getting ready to leave too. Bags were being packed and dragged out onto lawns. I imagined that by the next day, the whole town would feel like that field around Bethany High, empty and still, like the surface of the moon.

I took a left at the end of Water Street. Mr. Stahlberg's house was a nice old place, two floors with a big porch and a single castle-like turret on one side. The yard was bare in patches, over-grown in others. Some windows were broken and repaired, by me, with cardboard and duct tape. I climbed the porch steps and knocked on the door. No answer. I lifted the welcome mat and took the key he always left for me. The doorknob turned with a squeak. The inside of the house was dim and cold and filled with a faint smell of mildew that I hadn't noticed the last time I was there. I called for Mr. Stahlberg but got no answer.

The first floor was full of overflowing bookcases and tables packed with framed pictures of him and Amanda. Art crowded the walls. Handmade afghans warmed the backs of couches.

The stairs complained as I went up. The first bedroom I came to was empty and so was the bathroom. Clean towels hung on silver bars. The mirror above the sink gleamed in the light coming in from a small, frosted window. There was one more room at the end of the hall. Mr. Stahlberg's. The smell of mildew became stronger the closer I got.

"Mr. Stahlberg?"

The door was open a crack. I pushed it and stepped inside. It was a large but spare-looking bedroom, with cream-colored walls and a four-poster bed covered in sheets the color of tangerines. Mr. Stahlberg was lying beneath them, his hair a messy white halo against the deep orange of the pillows.

". . . Mr. Stahlberg?"

His eyes fluttered open. When he saw it was me, he waved me over.

"Lucy. Come. Sit."

His voice was frail. There was a wheeze as his chest rose and fell.

"We have to go," I said. "It's time."

He ignored me, patting the bedspread by his hip. I came into the room and sat beside him.

"Have you packed? I can get your things for you if you —"

"Did I ever tell you that I was the one who decorated this house?"

"We should really —"

"Everyone thought it was Amanda, but the truth was, she had awful taste. The worst. If it had been up to her we would have gone to that Swedish place and filled our home with pressboard monstrosities and the kind of art you find in cheap motels." He chuckled to himself, then coughed into his fist. "I always loved old things. Things that were made with care. Beautiful things."

He let out a long breath and scanned the pressed-tin ceiling.

"I met Amanda in college, at a frat party of all places. I didn't want to go. I hated that sort of thing, but my friend was in love with the fraternity's president and he made me come with him for moral support. The party was in this old mansion way up in the hills. It reeked of pot smoke and old beer. The music was awful. I told my friend I'd stay for twenty minutes, max, and then I went into the kitchen to get a glass of wine, and there she was, wearing a dress the color of daffodils, her hair hanging down over her shoulders. She had a tumbler of whiskey in her hand and was talking to someone about Victor Hugo and laughing. It was spring. The air coming through the open window beside her smelled like lavender. She looked like she'd been carved from a block of sunlight."

He shut his eyes tight, like he was trying to fix the memory in place, to make sure it never escaped.

"There are days when I remember that she's gone and there are days that I don't. The days I don't are better. On those days, she's always just about to walk through the front door. She'll drop her things on the chair in the hall and flop down beside me on the couch with this beautiful sigh, so full of relief. I'll pour her a glass of wine. We'll talk and laugh. Amanda told the worst jokes, but she had the most amazing laugh."

I started to say something, but he laid his hand over mine before I could open my mouth. His eyes were open, bright and clear.

"This is my home, Lucy. I don't want another one."

He squeezed my hand and smiled.

"You should go. Amanda will be here soon. I want to be ready for her."

—

By the time I got back, a crowd had gathered on the street outside our house. Some were our neighbors — Mr. Giolotti, the Walkers — and some I didn't know at all. Everyone was dressed in bulky layers, long coats over multiple shirts and sweaters, like they were wearing every bit of clothing they owned. Everything else was packed into overnight bags, backpacks, and rolling suitcases. A few rusty shopping carts sat by our driveway, filled with bottles of water and extra food. I searched around for Dad and found him standing on the Ivanchuk's front porch with Copperfield in his arms. Mrs. Ivanchuk and her son had decided to stay behind and had agreed to look after the cat for us.

My backpack was leaning against the curb next to Dad's. They were stuffed near to bursting, with rolled-up blankets and tents strapped to their sides. A misty shower began to fall, glazing the vacant houses and leafless trees. I put up the hood on my jacket, listening to the patter of the rain against vinyl.

I looked past our packs at our house. Mom had been pregnant with me when they'd found it. Dad said they knew it was the one before they'd even finished parking the car. It never made much sense to me before. It was small and plain, like all the others on our street. But right then I thought maybe I could see why. It was a sunny yellow, summer bright, even in the gray drizzle. Set into patches of mulch on either side of the front steps were beds of wildflowers and two fir trees whose tops brushed the rain gutters. It was strange how vividly I remembered the day Mom planted them. I was in the living room watching cartoons and listening to the chatter of voices and laughter as Carol and Bernie helped Dad get ready for the cookout we were having later that night. While they worked, I climbed onto the couch and watched Mom through the front window. She was kneeling in the dirt, her round face bright with sweat and sunburn, her knobby knees covered in mulch. She dug two holes, then guided the saplings in before gently covering the roots with dark soil and watering them. After dinner that night, as we picked at the remains of the barbecue, she said that by the time I graduated from college the trees would be taller than the house. I laughed — the moment seemed impossibly far away — but Mom swore it was true. She said we'd have a party out in the front yard to celebrate and everyone would be invited. She said she could see it all so clearly, it was like it had already happened.

Another wave of people came down Spruce Street and joined the others. The noise was overwhelming, dozens of voices and squeaking carts. I stomped inside the house and slammed the door behind me. My heart was pounding. I shut my eyes and breathed, my back pressed against the door like I was prepared for an invasion. When my heartbeat calmed I looked around. We were taking so little with us that the place was nearly unchanged. A few pictures left on the walls. Neat stacks of books and magazines on the coffee table. I crept up the stairs to my room. It was the same there. Bed made. Shades drawn. The bulk of my clothes still on their hangers. I knelt by the open closet door. My prom dress lay on the carpet, a rumpled heap next to my shoes and my box of keepsakes, which held Mom's letters, Luke's old sunglasses, and three small garnets.

My hand shook as I lifted the stones out of the box and let them roll around in my palm. I could almost feel the sun on my skin and hear the crash of the river in Shangri-La. Tree branches, heavy with waxy leaves, brushed our shoulders as we walked back to the car. Jay's hip had bumped mine as he dropped the garnets into my hand. "Your share of the buried treasure," he'd said in a weird pirate voice that made me laugh. The sky had been so blue, the memory of it made me ache.

"Lucy!"

It was Dad, calling me from outside. The thought of leaving set off a familiar jolt of horror, but it wasn't that trembling-in-your-seat-with-a-box-of-Mike-and-Ikes, movie theater horror. It was the real thing. The same horror I thought Mr. Stahlberg might have been feeling. The horror of being forced to step out of one world—where there were things you could count on, that you could be sure of—and into another where there was no way to know what you might lose, or what you might become.

Dad called again, louder this time, more urgent.

I turned my hand over, letting the garnets tumble back into the box, and then I drifted out of my room. I forced my legs to move, one step at a time, down the dim hallway. As I approached Dad's office door I noticed that it was slightly open. Through the crack I caught an unexpected flash of color, ocean blue. Curious, I opened the door. When I saw what was inside, my breath caught. The walls, nearly every inch of them, were covered in paintings. Dad's desk was too, along with his chair and the windowsill and the gray metal file cabinet by the door. Some were done on paper, some on stretched canvas, some on scraps of wood or bits of broken glass. There were portraits — of me, of Mom, of Halla, of the dogs and Copperfield — along with still lifes and landscapes. Huge art books sat open on the floor. I recognized them from the boxes in the attic. They were Dad's old textbooks from college. All those times he'd been locked away in his office, this was what he'd been doing. *This.*

A group of paintings by the window, maybe fifteen of them, were more abstract than the others. A series in red. A series in green. One in orange and one in blue. The way the paint was put down was rough, almost like he had done it with his fingers. In many of them, ghostly, ash-gray figures lurked in the background. I took one down and held it up in the watery light coming through the window. A block of muddy, swirling green hung over a block of brushed gold. A storm over a field of wheat. I'd seen pictures of some of the work Dad had done when he was an art student, but it was nothing like this. These paintings sliced right through the dullness in my head. They were frightening and beautiful, almost impossible to look away from.

"I think that one's my favorite."

I turned around, startled. Dad was near the top of the stairs, pack on his shoulders, his scruffy hair wet from the rain.

"The others are just ripping off one artist or another," he said. "Art school nonsense."

"Why didn't you tell me? Why didn't you show me?"

He stepped into the office and leaned against the wall. "Back when I was in school I used to run to show people the things I made. Before the paint was dry usually. These weren't about that."

"What were they about?"

He took the painting from my hands and held it out in front of him. He loved it. I could tell because he looked at it the same way he looked at Halla. The way he looked at me.

"Getting back something I lost, I guess."

"We can't leave them here," I said. "We have to take them. They can go in one of the carts or —"

Dad moved past me and carefully re-hung the painting alongside the others. He stood there with his back to me, surrounded by a universe of color, looking from one to the next like he was surveying a roomful of friends. The mist outside turned to a steady rain, tapping against the roof and the windows. Dad turned around again.

"Come on," he said. "We'd better get moving."

He slipped past me and started down the stairs, then stopped when he realized I wasn't following him.

"Lucy? We have to go. Everyone's waiting."

Silence filled the landing. I stared at the scuffed wood floor.

"Lucy."

"Mr. Stahlberg is staying. So are Mrs. Ivanchuk and her son.

If the Guard doesn't come back, we'll figure out some other way to get by, or we'll . . ."

He came back up the steps and reached for my arm. I pulled away and we stood there for some time, neither one of us looking at the other.

"I used to pretend that none of it ever happened," he said. "Everything with your mother. I'd lie in bed after you went to sleep and imagine that it was all a mistake and she was home and we were together, the three of us. I made myself sick. Could barely get out of bed in the morning because I knew that as soon as I did I'd be back in the real world. Know what pulled me out of it?"

I shook my head.

"Packing your lunch." I looked up at him. He shrugged. "Not exactly Nobel Prize material, but your mom always used to do it and then she was gone and . . . I told myself that it was something you needed, and it was something I could do, so I made myself get out of bed and do it. Cut the sandwich into triangles and the carrots into sticks. Throw in one of those little packets of hot sauce you used to put on everything. It was like climbing up out of a well. But after a while, there I was. There *we* were."

Two figures appeared in the doorway downstairs. Halla and Oscar. Halla didn't say anything; she just gave Dad a nod. He nodded back and she went out into the rain again.

"Come on, Goose," he said quietly, gently. "Let's go."

He held out his hand. I took it and let him lead me down to the front walk. By then, there were maybe fifty people milling about in the rain. Everyone was getting ready to go, checking their gear, hoisting backpacks onto their shoulders. Dad jogged ahead to talk to Halla and some of the others. My pack was still sitting by the curb. I started toward it but stopped when the crowd shifted, revealing the whole Karras family. Wendall. Marla. Eric. Parviz. A small throng of kids whose names I'd never learned. Their parents.

Jay.

He was in a black rain jacket with a big pack on his shoulders and a shopping cart loaded with gear in front of him. He took off his glasses and polished them on a bit of flannel shirt that poked out from beneath his jacket. Just seeing him again was a shock. He was thinner than he'd been that night at the party and the dark shadows around his eyes had returned. His hair was a shaggy mess, heavy with rainwater, and he'd grown a thin beard. He finished cleaning his glasses and put them back on. In the instant before they were covered in rain again, our eyes met. I drew in a sharp breath and held it. It felt like my lungs were going to burst. Neither of us moved.

Dad's voice cut through the rain. "Okay everybody, let's go!"

The crowd surged forward and carried Jay's family with it. He took hold of his cart and moved away to join them. Thunder rumbled and the rain picked up, turning the air between us a smoky gray. I got my pack onto my shoulders, but I couldn't seem to make my legs work. My feet were rooted in place, sunk in concrete. The group passed Elder Lane and then Oak. The wheels on Jay's cart squeaked as he moved farther and farther away. Dad called my name. I yelled into the storm, "Jay!"

He stopped at the sound of my voice and turned around. Before I knew it, I was tearing across our lawn and into the street. I stopped right in front of him. Rain was beading on his glasses and coursing over his dark brows and down the crooked track of his nose. For a second, there was no storm, there was no crowd, there was no street. It was like we'd slipped away to some other place. How was that possible? How could one person's face, nothing but a collection of curves and angles and patches of dark and light, reach inside of you and make everything go still all at once?

"Jay? Lucy?"

It was Halla, a block away, but sounding a hundred times more distant. Jay nodded to her. The rest of the crowd was making the turn toward Main Street. Jay started to move. Before he could, I took hold of his wrist just above the spot where his heartbeat pulsed. I drew my fingers down the back of his hand and turned it over. His skin was more calloused than it had been, but there was still that hairline scar at the base of his thumb. I traced it with a fingertip. There were so many things I wanted to say — explanations I wanted to give, apologies I had to make — that I didn't know where to start, so I curled my hand around his and I said, "Think it would be okay if I walked with you for a while?"

My heart stopped beating the second the words came out of my mouth. It didn't start again until I looked up and saw Jay's face brighten with a smile.

The only thing left to do was leave.

TOMORROW, AND TOMORROW, AND TOMORROW . . .

TWENTY-THREE

JUST OFF SHORE, a trio of rowboats fought against the waves, trying to make their way out to deeper water. It was hard not to root for them. They were raggedy things, with peeling paint, manned by an unlikely mix of former stockbrokers, grade school teachers, and tech entrepreneurs. I was sure that at least one of them would turn back, or possibly sink, but the crews bashed at the foam with their oars and shouted encouragement to each other until they broke through. High-fives were exchanged and then they settled in and cast homemade nets onto the water.

Above them, a streak of ashy clouds drifted off and the late afternoon sun came out, bright and hot. The water sparkled. I opened a paperback copy of *The Stand* I'd found in the ruins of a nearby Goodwill. I was at the part where the musician guy has to walk through the Lincoln Tunnel to escape a plague-ridden Manhattan when the reeds on the bluff behind me rustled. Johnny and Oscar came exploding through them, tongues lolling out the sides of their mouths. They shot past me and dove headlong into the waves, barking and chomping at the foam.

"Stupid dogs must be half fish."

Marla Karras had followed Johnny and Oscar out of the

reeds and was standing there with her black hair whipping in the breeze, one hand shading her eyes.

I nodded out toward the boats. "If they're not careful, they're going to end up in one of Mr. Noguera's seafood stews."

Marla dropped onto the sand beside me and hunched over her bent knees. She'd had like eight growth spurts since we'd left Bethany and was nearly as tall as I was, with muscly legs and powerful shoulders. Her face had changed too. The lines of her jaw and her cheekbones had sharpened and become more prominent. Her eyes were big and dark — pretty, but kind of distracted, like she was always half lost in some deeply engrossing internal drama. In short, she was fourteen. I marked my spot in the book and tossed it onto the sand.

"You bail on school?"

Marla shrugged off the question; didn't even look at me. It wasn't like her. Ever since a former high school principal we'd hooked up with in Illinois had started up a school, Marla had been the star pupil. She was even teaching math classes for the younger kids. That's when I put it all together. The lack of eye contact. The way she was trying to fold her body into a fortress. There was only one explanation.

"What did Max do now?"

She rolled her eyes, "*Nothing.*"

I gave her a deeply skeptical look.

"I mean, fine, he's being a total immature *boy,* but it's like, what else is new? You know? I told him, you can hang out with me or you can hang out with Angie Rothstein, but you can't do both."

"You said that to him?"

"Hell yes, I said that to him! And honestly, I don't even *care* which one of us he chooses. I don't! I just want him to grow a damn backbone and actually *do* the choosing. God! It's all so frustrating. And stupid. Sooo stupid." She kicked at the sand. "And on top of *that* the whole camp's whipping themselves into a frenzy over this stupid party tonight. 'Should it be down on the beach or should it be at camp?' 'What should the band play?'"

"There's a band now?"

She let out a growl of frustration. "It's like they think this is New Year's Eve and St. Patrick's Day all rolled into one. My dad is convinced he's mastered the art of making palm wine with this new batch of his. Have you tried it yet?"

I shook my head. Marla stuck a finger in her mouth and mimed a gag.

"He gave you some?"

"Pssh. Like a thimbleful. And the whole time he's acting like it's this big secret, like a bunch of cops are lying in wait to arrest us for underage drinking. Ugh! He was so pumped, I couldn't bring myself to tell him it tasted like warm donkey spit."

Spent by her tirade, Marla flopped onto her back. I knew where she was coming from. Not so much about Max (he seemed like kind of a tool to me), but about the party. People *had* lost their minds over it. It was why I'd fled to the beach in the first place. I'd spent all morning trying to figure a way out of going to it, some kind of excuse, but nothing I came up with had seemed even remotely plausible. What could I say? I had theater tickets? Another party to go to? It was one of the pitfalls of living in a post-apocalyptic world that no one ever told you about: lying your way out of social engagements was virtually impossible.

A cheer rose up out on the water. The crews had pulled in

their nets and, even from a distance, I could see the silvery avalanche of fish falling from them into the boats. There was another round of high-fives, and they tossed the nets out again.

I reached for my book but before I could get back into it, three figures appeared down the shore. A girl and two boys. The boys looked to be about nine or ten. The girl was my age, maybe a little younger. She led them to a spot just beyond the reach of the waves and they sat down. The boys' heads had been shaved, due to lice, probably, but the girl's hair was long and dirty, tangled into a knot of dreads at the back. They were all barefoot, and their clothes weren't much more than rags. One of the boys dug in the sand while the other lay on his side and slept. The girl stared at the ocean. I nudged Marla, who'd been watching them too. She shook her head.

"Poor kids."

The trio had shown up a couple weeks earlier and staked out a spot a mile or so from our camp. They'd been invited to join us more than once, but the girl always refused, usually with a growl. The last time somebody tried — bearing gifts of food and an invitation to enroll in our makeshift school — she pulled a razor from her boot to make absolutely sure we got the point.

I wished it was shocking, but it wasn't. Since leaving Bethany, we'd seen their kind more times than we could count. Bone-thin adults who shuffled along and mumbled to themselves. Kids who whipsawed between grief and rage and a blankness that was somehow even more terrifying. God only knew what had happened to them along the way, but whatever it was, it wouldn't let them go. I imagined it unspooling behind their eyes in a never-ending loop. People had taken to calling them zombies. It was cruel, but what else could you call someone who wasn't dead, but who wasn't alive, either?

Marla stood up and brushed the sand off her legs. "We should leave them alone."

I agreed and reached for my shoes.

"I was going to visit Mom and Wendall," she said. "You wanna come? Jay said he'd meet us there."

"Jay's back already?"

She nodded. Jay and Parviz had been gone for the last few days, part of a crew that was searching for medical supplies in neighboring towns. They weren't supposed to be back until the end of the week. Marla called for Oscar and Johnny and started off. The dogs jumped up and sprinted past me. I followed, passing closer to the girl and the two boys. The one I'd thought was sleeping had opened his eyes. They were the pale blue of faded denim, but there was no light in them, no movement. They were wide and utterly blank, fixed on nothing — not the sand or the waves or the sun, not even the big slobbery dogs that had run by only a few feet from him. He was deep in the gray room. I knew the look like I knew my own reflection.

There was a rustle of movement. The girl had noticed me lingering. She scowled, her hand hovering at the top of her boot. I held up my hands in surrender, then hurried to join Marla.

We took Shore Road north. It was a cracked and sun-faded highway that ran alongside blocks of shops and hotels, all of them long-abandoned and crumbling. We navigated around overgrown weeds and piles of debris — broken glass, windblown garbage, wrecked cars that had bird's nests in their open cabs and bright green lizards sunning themselves on their hoods. At one point, we came across an old sign bent nearly in half. Images of sun and waves peeked through dried mud, along with the words WELCOME TO WHEELER COVE! HOME OF THE MOST BEAUTIFUL BEACHES IN FLORIDA!

We'd never meant to end up in Florida. Not long after leaving Bethany, we'd decided to head for New Mexico — chasing warm weather and rumors of a functioning government — but we kept hitting one obstruction after another. Impassable roads. Armed locals insisting there wasn't enough food or water to go around. Blooms of radiation that set off the Geiger counter we'd taken from an army-navy store in New Jersey. Each obstruction changed our path until it became more or less aimless. Along the way our group splintered, merged with others, splintered again. We spent time in West Virginia and Kentucky. In Tennessee and Arkansas. We'd manage to stay a few weeks, sometimes even a month, but sooner or later we were always pushed out and hurried along. The closest we ever got to New Mexico was the Texas/Louisiana border, where we were met by a group of heavily armed shit weasels who gave us no choice but to head east. Mississippi didn't want us, and neither did Alabama or Georgia. And then one day, we came to a faded highway sign that was dotted with bullet holes. WELCOME TO THE SUNSHINE STATE!

Once we'd crossed the border, we breathed easy for the first time in months. No one stopped us. No one turned us away. It was far from ideal — the land was swampy, the weather was punishingly humid, and hurricane season loomed in the future, huge and inevitable. But since no one else wanted anything to do with the place, it was home.

When Marla and I left Shore Road and turned inland, the

dogs raced on ahead of us to camp. Alone, we made our way through the old touristy areas to a park that had gone wild with prehistoric-looking ferns and enough flowers to make the air thick with perfume. We jumped over a stream, then made our way through the dense foliage to a small clearing. There, thirty-nine grave markers were laid out in neat rows. They'd been cobbled together out of scrap wood and cinderblock and salvaged bricks.

Marla and I stepped in between the graves, careful not to disturb anything, until we arrived at two markers, one made of cinderblock and the other of piles of ocean-smoothed stones. Only the first one was big enough for markings. Using a hammer and a rusty screwdriver, Jay's father had carved the words, *In loving memory of Amina al-Masri Karras and one of her eight children, Wendall.*

Marla wrapped her arms around herself and lowered her head. After a few moments of silence, the bushes shifted and Jay came through them. He fell in beside me without a word. Our hands found each other and intertwined.

Amina and Wendall weren't actually buried beneath their markers. Like many in that graveyard, they'd been buried where they'd died before we'd been forced to move on again. Amina and Wendall's bodies, along with five others, were in a field somewhere in West Virginia, marked by quickly assembled piles of stone. Something in the water had killed them. Not even Dr. Karras knew what it was. We all got sick, the whole party — we'd even joked about our bad luck as we raced back and forth to the latrines we'd dug out in the woods. Most of us got better in a few days. The ones who didn't grew paler and burned with a fever that wouldn't quit no matter what we did. We'd lost other people along the way, dozens. But nothing was quite like losing Amina and Wendall. It turned everyone in our group inside out. It darkened the skies for months.

After our moment of silence, we knelt by the graves and Jay passed out some seashells, which we arranged on the sand beside others we'd left during earlier visits. There were piles of them, spirals and scalloped fans, alongside bits of colored glass worn smooth by the ocean and an assortment of rocks Jay and I had found: sandstone, limestone, quartz, glittery pyrite.

When we were done Marla said she was meeting some friends before the party and took off, leaving me and Jay alone. We left the park and headed back along the beach to camp. The sun had fallen some by then, turning the sky a deep orange. Palm trees waved. We walked in silence for a while, both of us locked up in the memories of those awful days and weeks, as we always were after a visit to the cemetery. We were nearly home when the shadow lifted a little and Jay said, "So I delivered a baby yesterday."

My head whipped around, but he kept a perfectly straight face, refusing to give anything away.

"Wait. Seriously?"

"Two of them, actually," he said. "Twins! We came across this woman and her husband while we were out looking for supplies. The woman, Janice, was pregnant and went into labor the day we got there. The husband panicked. So did I, but then Parviz reminded me that Dad had gone over what to do back in Ohio. Remember? The Polish lady at that refugee camp? Anyway, we figured, what choice did we have, right? So we went step by step."

"How was it?"

"Without a doubt, the most terrifying thing I've ever been a part of. There was all this screaming and blood. The lady punched Parviz."

"No way."

"Oh yeah. He was up there coaching her, right? Breathe, push, you're doing great, all that. And I guess she got sick of it because she hauled off and decked him. Bam! I don't know how she managed it with everything else that was going on, but I'm telling you, he went *down*."

"Is everybody okay? The family, I mean. I'm pretty sure Parviz was asking for it."

"I think so. We brought them back with us so Dad could check on them."

By the time we reached the section of beach that ran along our campsite, the fishing boats were returning. Their crews leaped into the shallows and dragged the boats high up onto the shore, where others waited to help bring in the day's catch. Jay and I waved, then left the beach and moved through a line of palm trees. On the other side was Jackson Green, a deserted campground where we'd pitched our tents when we'd arrived in Florida, three months earlier to the day. It was a temporary thing. That was the idea, at least. Hurricane season would start in a few months and by then we planned on being deeper inland and farther north. An architect who'd joined us in Maryland had found a tract of abandoned houses she said were still structurally sound, despite being infested with mold and several invasive species of flora and fauna. She had crews working day and night to clean them out and make repairs so they'd be ready in time.

As we approached the campsite it became clear that the party was already well underway. We heard the music first, a jumble of drums and accordion and what I thought was probably a trombone. The voices came next. A little over a hundred people were talking all at once. There was singing, too. Loads of singing. The camp, a maze of closely packed tents and a few semi-permanent structures made out of scrap, was lit by a bonfire and strings of Christmas lights that ran from tent to tent and looped over tree branches and coiled around their trunks. Weeks earlier, Dad and a few of his friends had dragged a large solar generator back from the one home store in the area that hadn't been completely looted. With the sky clearing, they were able to coax enough juice out of it to power the lights and a bank of freezers that they used to preserve the freshly caught fish. According to my dad, the next thing on the agenda was to find a few cars and trucks worth salvaging, and a radio they could use to try to contact others like us. *Who knows,* he said one night, *maybe by the time we're in those houses we'll be knee deep in Internet, air-conditioning, and movie marathons again.*

The lights cast a warm glow over the crowd and the band. The air smelled like woodsmoke and baking bread and roasting fish. Jay's dad was off in one corner, already theatrically tipsy, pushing cups of his homemade donkey spit into the hands of anyone who came within five feet of him — adults, kids, he didn't seem to care.

Jay said, "Oh, this is definitely going to get out of hand."

"Wanna steal one of those rowboats and flee?"

"To where?"

"I dunno. Outer Mongolia?"

"Come on," he said. "We deserve this. We've been living in one place for three whole months!"

"A place smarter people than us abandoned nearly a decade ago."

"True! But still worth celebrating. How about we —"

"*Goooooooooose!*"

Dad exploded out of the crowd, a cup of wine in each hand. He was dressed in a beach party ensemble: a Hawaiian shirt (salvaged from a nearby house that was slightly less mold-damaged than the rest) and a kilt made out of palm fronds.

"Wow. That is *quite* an outfit, Dad."

He paused to model for us, sporting a grin so bright it nearly drowned out the bonfire. "Halla says it really shows off my calves."

"It does indeed."

He pushed the cups of wine into our hands and commanded us both to drink. I did as I was told and nearly gagged. Donkey spit was accurate. Dad chuckled and patted my back as I coughed.

"Yeah, kind of stings, doesn't it? Don't worry, that stops as soon as you lose feeling in your face."

"Good to know."

Halla emerged from the crowd, decked out in her own improvised party wear — a palm-frond skirt paired with a festive but uncomfortable-looking bikini top woven out of vines and decorated with flowers. Her face was aglow with firelight. Dad kissed her on the cheek and pulled her close. I flashed back to a day in Georgia. We were all huddled beneath a highway overpass as rain fell in sheets on either side of it. Dad and Halla said their vows before a former justice of the peace who'd joined our group only days earlier. After the ceremony, the rain had stopped, and we'd had a picnic in the middle of an orchard that was overrun with wildflowers.

"Okay!" Dad announced. "Here's the agenda. First, we drink some more of this poison, then we eat, then we dance. After that there may be some vomiting, possibly a lot, but let's try not to focus on that right now. Sound good?"

Jay chugged his cup of donkey spit, threw it to the ground and let out an uncharacteristically lusty "WOO HOOOOO!", then danced away with Halla.

Another cup of wine had appeared in Dad's hand as if by magic. He poured half into my cup. He was right; it wasn't so bad once your face went numb. We stood on the sidelines, watching the dancers turn in circles around the bonfire, throwing up their hands, singing, laughing. Soon, Halla and Jay were joined by Dr. Karras and then Parviz (who was sporting a massive black eye) and Eric and Cindy and Ralph and Paolo and Gloria. Marla danced nearby with a kid named Adam Pomeroy, much to the dismay of Max, who stood glowering in a corner with his friends. Even Johnny and Oscar got into the act, shuffling back and forth among the dancers, begging food right out of people's hands.

The musicians started up another song, all drums and accordion. Dad put his arm around me and drew me close. "We made it, Goose," he said, voice cracking, his eyes shining in the electric lights. "All that's left now is . . . life."

—

I made it through two of Dad's agenda items — the drinking and the eating — before slipping out of the party and down to the beach. It was three or four o'clock in the morning, but the festivities were still going. The music had slowed, turning sweetly faint, and firelight shimmered through the palm trees, making shifting patterns on the sand. Every now and then someone would come down to walk along the shore or wade in the water, but mostly I was on my own, watching the waves roll in and out. The fishing boats I'd seen earlier were nearby. In the moonlight their hulls looked skeletal, like the ribs of beached whales. I wondered if I was strong enough to get one out past the breakers on my own and into the deep water. I could almost feel the muscles in my arms and back straining as I worked the oars, heaving myself farther and farther away until the coastline dwindled, then faded completely, until there was nothing around me but black water and an empty sky.

"Thought I might find you here."

I looked over my shoulder and caught Jay coming through the palms, grinning like a goof, his stride all wobbly from his father's wine. He flopped onto the sand beside me.

"Our dads are spectacularly wasted," he said. "When I left they were dancing with each other, since no one else could keep up. Good for them, right?"

I nodded. A big wave crashed onto the shore, sending up a plume of spray. I eyed the rowboats again. Jay bumped my shoulder with his.

"You okay?"

I said I was fine, which got me a steady stare. The thing about being on the road with somebody for nearly two years was that you couldn't get anything past them.

"Just thinking about something my dad said."

"What did he say?"

Jay waited, patient as ever. He'd kept the beard. It was deep black and thicker now, a good match for his hair, which was nearly down to his shoulders, curling at the ends. His glasses were bent in places and patched with tape but still whole, perched high on his nose. He'd changed so much since the night I'd seen him at prom, bent over his phone, his face gray with fear. And it wasn't just physical, it was this aura of seriousness, or of purpose, I guess, that he carried around with him everywhere he went. Not that he'd gone humorless on me; far from it. It was more like he'd come into focus, or like all the inessential bits of him had been burned away. He still collected rocks and did intermittently successful card tricks, and, even though he vehemently denied it, I knew he still wrote the occasional shitty poem. But it was all for fun. Jay knew who he was now.

I'd asked him once if he liked being a doctor, and he'd said he liked being useful. He liked helping people. It was a good answer, one that made me wonder when the last time was that I'd been useful, the last time I'd helped someone.

Jay slipped his arm through mine, locking us together. For a moment, the world fell away. The beach. The ocean. The fishing boats. The party behind us. There was only the darkness and our two voices.

He said, "This isn't forever, you know. Next spring we'll try for Canada."

I nodded. Dad had said the same thing. I hoped it was true. I wanted to see Bernie and Carol again and meet my cousin, but if there was one thing I knew, it was that you didn't have any say over who becomes your future and who becomes your past.

"I missed you when I was gone," Jay said, his voice quiet.

"I missed you too."

I turned my head. His breath was warm on my cheek and soft. I leaned forward and my lips found his.

—

Jay and I had danced around each other for months after leaving Bethany, drawing close only to pull away again, afraid to build something that we knew could break so easily. And then one night, we were camped in a field somewhere in Virginia. It was late. Everyone was asleep, exhausted from a long day of traveling. A strange ringing sound drew me out of my tent and into the moonlight. I thought maybe I'd imagined it, but then I heard it again, coming from a cornfield on the other side of the highway. It was faint, jangling and bright, like Christmas sleigh bells. I put on my boots and made my way through the brush to the edge of the road. Jay was already there. I asked him what was going on and he shook his head.

Light flashed through the cornstalks, and then two men appeared, carrying lanterns on long wooden poles. They were dressed like monks, in leather sandals and burlap robes tied at the waist with lengths of rope. Their heads were shaved clean and they had long, flowing beards.

We'd only been on the road for a few months at that point, but I already knew that the safest thing to do when we came across someone from outside of our party was to run. I grabbed Jay's hand and turned to go, but he didn't move, not an inch. The men didn't slow or acknowledge us. They simply came up out of the cornfield and cut diagonally across the roadway and away from our camp. As soon as they'd made it to the other side, two more appeared that were just like them, except on the poles they carried, silver stars glinted. They followed the same path as the others, heads down, moving slowly and steadily. There were two more after them, carrying moons of gold, and then another two, holding large totems in the shape of sparrows, carved out of what looked like marble.

Then, all at once, dozens of them emerged from the corn, maybe hundreds, gliding silently, like mist. Once the procession had passed, the bells chimed again, and two final figures emerged from the corn — a woman in deep scarlet robes and a towering, riderless horse that was so white its coat was like a bowl of fresh milk. The woman held a lantern in one hand and a large book in the other. They crossed the road and then they were gone too, vanished. After that everything was quiet, like nothing had happened, like it had all been a dream.

Jay and I didn't say anything. We floated back to camp. My heart was thrumming and every cell in my body, every nerve, was vibrating like a plucked string. The backs of our hands brushed against each other as we walked. My skin tingled. When we reached our tents we snapped together like a pair of magnets. His arms circled my body and mine circled his. The instant our lips touched there was this overwhelming sense of release, like when you hold your breath for so long that you feel like your lungs are going to burst, and then you let it go all at once. It occurred to me that maybe the world was like a lump of raw clay in our hands, just beginning to take shape. I wondered if we would recognize it when it was done. If we would recognize ourselves.

—

Back on the beach, Jay and I drew apart. I lay my head on his shoulder. Behind us, the music grew louder again. A handful of couples raced by us, kicking up sand and stripping off their clothes as they ran. They splashed into the surf, laughing. I looked past them at the dark water.

I said, "We could still lose everything."

Jay rested his head against mine. I thought he was going to tell me that I was wrong, that everything was going to be okay, that things would go back to normal soon, but instead he laced our fingers together and said, "Yeah. We could."

The waves came in and out. The swimmers gathered their clothes and returned to the party, leaving the beach to us. Eventually the sun appeared on the horizon. It was a sliver at first, a thin line of gold, barely visible, but it slowly grew until it took over the sky.

—

A little over a week later I was on the beach again, skin baking in the sun, a book in my hand. The three zombie kids were sitting barely four feet from me in a tight triangle, staring out at the waves. I'd come to the beach every single day since the party, and every day I'd sat slightly closer to them. In the beginning the girl had glared at me, but I guess she'd finally decided that I wasn't a threat because she hadn't so much as looked my way in three days. I lay my book onto the sand and called to the dogs. They ran to me, slobber flying. When they got to within a few feet, they stopped and shook, throwing up halos of saltwater and sand.

"Are those your dogs?"

It was the boy closest to me. He was wearing filthy corduroys that had been roughly cut into shorts and an orange T-shirt that was stained with sweat. His eyes were bright as he watched the dogs pant.

"Yep," I said. "The black lab is Johnny Cash. Oscar's the other one. They walked all the way here from New York. Can you believe that?"

"You're from New York?"

The girl turned and gave him a sharp look. "Alex," she snapped.

"But Stacey—"

"Mind your own business."

"It's okay," I said. "I don't mind. Yeah, we're from New York. Me. My dad. His wife, Halla, and her whole family. Some of them are about your age. My name's Lucy."

"Alex," he said quietly, then nodded toward the other boy. "That's my brother. Jason. He doesn't say much."

Jason was huddled in close to Stacey, looking at the water with that same hollow expression, like he wasn't really seeing it at all. I leaned in as close to Alex as I dared and whispered, "And she's your big sister, I guess?"

"Stacey's not our sister," Alex whispered back. "She *found* us."

Their situation started to come into focus. Whoever had been responsible for caring for the two boys must have been lost—maybe whoever had cared for Stacey had been lost, too—and the three of them had banded together. It wasn't all that unusual. Everywhere we went, strangers were transforming into families. Once the shift was complete, they were just as solid as ones that had formed naturally. Maybe more so. Stacey might not have been born their big sister, but that's what she was now.

Contact achieved, I nodded, picked up the book, and went back to reading. An hour or so passed. Above us, seagulls wheeled and cawed, looking for food.

"What are you reading?"

Alex had moved slightly closer. His eyes were glued to the

pages as they turned. Behind him, Stacey was lying on her side with her back to us, Jason next to her.

"A play," I said.

"What play?"

"You wouldn't like it."

"How do *you* know?" he asked, indignant.

"Because," I said. "It's very, very scary."

Alex's eyes widened. "What's it about?"

"You sure you want to know?"

He nodded solemnly.

"It's about a Scottish general way back in medieval times," I said in a hushed voice, like it was a secret. "Late one night after a huge battle, he meets three witches in the forest and they tell him he's destined to be king."

Alex was still listening. I inched closer.

"The general and his wife invite the king to stay the night at their castle. But while the king is sleeping, the general sneaks into his bedroom with a dagger and murders him."

"That does sound scary," Alex said, hesitant but intrigued.

I bent over my copy of *Out Brief Candle*. I didn't even remember packing it, could hardly believe it when I'd found the book sitting at the bottom of my pack. The cover was gone and it was water-damaged, but it was still readable. In our time on the road I must have touched it a dozen times without realizing what it was and had never given it a second's thought.

"Oh, it doesn't stop there," I said. "Driven mad by their desire to rule, the general and his wife murder everyone who gets in their way. Men, women, children. The rivers of Scotland run red with blood. Eventually they're overwhelmed by guilt. He's haunted by the ghosts of the people they've killed, and his wife goes mad, sleepwalking around the castle at night, imagining that her hands are covered in blood she can never wash off."

"*Out, damned spot . . .*"

It was Stacey. She'd sat up and was watching us. Her eyes were sharp, but her hands were empty.

"*Macbeth*," she muttered. "I read it in school."

I nodded, then glanced over at Jason. He was sitting up too. He kept his eyes on the sand, but he was listening. It felt like the universe was balanced on the head of a pin. I took a breath and continued.

"In the end, there's a huge battle — swords clanging, body parts flying everywhere. Another soldier hacks off Macbeth's — the general's — head and rolls it right down the middle of the throne room like a gore-streaked bowling ball." All eyes were on me then, even Jason's. "The last thing we see are the three witches gathered around their bubbling cauldron, laughing maniacally, surrounded by the bloody ghosts of the damned Macbeths."

I slammed the book shut, hard enough to give them all a start, even Stacey. I'd made up that last part, but it seemed to work. Alex sure thought so.

"That sounds *awesome*," he said.

"Oh, it is," I replied, then abruptly stood and tucked *Out Brief Candle* under my arm. "Anyway! Auditions are this Friday."

Stacey looked confused. "Auditions?"

"Yep." I pointed to a horseshoe-shaped notch in a nearby dune. "That's gonna be the stage over there. We'll start the show at dusk so it's completely dark by the end. We'll light it with torches.

I'll need at least twenty actors . . . thirty to do it right." I considered Jason, guessing he might not be ready for that quite yet. "Plus I need people to make costumes and props — knives, swords, armor, the witch's cauldron, that kind of thing. Oh! And we're going to need to figure out how to make fake blood. A *ton* of it. Like, gallons. Seriously, the first three rows of the audience are going to be drenched in the stuff by the time we're done."

Movement down the beach caught my eye. Dad and Halla were walking toward us hand in hand. Marla and Parviz were there too along with the rest of the Karras/al-Masri clan. Jay was bringing up the rear, his dark hair flying, his hands slipped easily into the pockets of his ragged shorts. He saw me and smiled. I smiled back.

I laid my copy of *Out Brief Candle* in front of Jason, open to a page showing a mad-eyed King Macbeth in a production done in Serbia soon after it had fallen into civil war. He was dressed in battered, rusty armor and held a sword that was covered in gore. Jason's eyes brightened and focused. He pulled the book to him and turned the pages, studying the pictures, pausing to read snatches of Shakespeare's poetry.

I said I hoped I'd see all three of them on Friday, and then I ran across the beach and joined my family.

ACKNOWLEDGMENTS

Like most writers, I didn't come anywhere near writing this book alone. For vital feedback and unerring guidance every step of the way, thanks to agent-extraordinaire Sara Crowe and super-editor Lynne Polvino. Thanks also to Rebecca Friedman for early and much-needed feedback on the book, as well as being the most awesome and supportive partner a guy could hope for.

Thanks to my pal and perpetual science advisor Dr. Kenneth Fortino for answering all of my climate change–related questions.

For schooling me on rocks and minerals, thanks to the Mid-Hudson Valley Gem and Mineral Society for introducing me to Carolyn Renard and Steve Kelland.

An extra special thank-you to all of the kind folks who agreed to answer my numerous questions about Egypt and the Middle East. Thanks to Angie Kamel, Fouad Ghorra, Farah Ibrahim, and Yara Al-Shudifat. Thanks also to Kerri Harris, librarian at Hillwood Middle in Fort Worth, Texas, for kindly arranging my chat with Farah and Yara.

Lastly, I think we all know that it's been an extremely challenging and dispiriting last few years, in our world and in our country. The best way I found to stay healthy and motivated through all of it was to do what I could to help other people. That's how I came to be a crisis counselor at an amazing organization called Crisis Text Line. If you ever feel sad, overwhelmed, stressed-out, or like it's all just too much, you can always reach out to a trained counselor at CTL. Simply text "Home" to 741741. It's free, anonymous, and confidential. Counselors are available 24/7/365. And if you'd like to learn how to help others in crisis, we're always looking for volunteers! Just apply at crisistextline.org.